STACY M. JONES

Fear City

For Mike...who gave me the idea

Acknowledgement

Thank you to the investigators I've had the pleasure of working with through the years and the knowledge and expertise shared with me. Special thanks to 17 Studio Book Design for bringing my stories to life with amazing covers. Thank you to Dj Hendrickson for your insightful editing and Liza Wood for proofreading and revisions. Thank you to my early readers for their feedback and readers who love this series.

A special thanks to Troy Innovation Garage for the comfortable (and fun) work environment over the summer. I spent the summer living and working in my hometown of Troy, NY and grabbed a desk at Troy Innovation Garage's co-working location. It was a unique and wonderful experience writing outside of my quiet office of solitude. I was worried that I might not get as much done, but it turned out I wrote almost double what I normally write each week. The staff there is such a delight and I wish all of them the very best. Thank you and don't look at your Google history! Authors search weird things….all for the novel, I promise! LOL

CHAPTER 1

My hands shook as I read the note over and over again, the meaning harder to digest than understand. I had taken a photo of the note before my husband, Det. Luke Morgan, left with it and Cat O'Conner, a local crime podcaster. She had come to our house late in the evening and delivered the note that had been left at her studio.

Our friends, Cooper Deagnan and Adele Baker, had been here listening to an episode of Cat's podcast, *Rock City Killers*, that featured Luke and one of his cases. The merriment of the occasion had been silenced by the note. If we had any thought it might have been a sick joke, those hopes were quickly dashed when Luke called the police station and found out there had been a shooting – which is what the note indicated would happen.

All we knew was that two people had been shot by what appeared to be a sniper and one of them had died. As head of the homicide division, Luke would be needed at the scene. He left immediately with Cat. Cooper and Adele followed, wanting to get back downtown to their loft, not far from where the shooting happened.

I had offered to let them spend the night to avoid the onslaught of police and onlookers, but Adele was defending a three-time repeat burglar in court the next morning and still had to prepare. She also was worried about accessing her law office, which wasn't even a full block away from the shooting.

That left me alone to read and reread the note.

The summer of 1977 in New York City has gone down in infamy. Record heat. A blackout. Murder. Tomorrow night, I will continue what he started. No one is safe. I own this city. Fear me.

The note had been dated yesterday, which made sense why the shooting happened tonight. It appeared the sniper followed through with his plan.

It had taken me by surprise that I had been the only one who knew the reference in the note. Although we were living in Little Rock, Arkansas, I was born and raised in Troy, New York, about two and a half hours north of New York City. I didn't think there was a New Yorker around who hadn't at least heard of the Son of Sam murders.

While the note referenced the summer of 1977, David Berkowitz's reign of terror in New York City had started before that. On Christmas Eve 1975, he severely injured a fifteen-year-old girl with a hunting knife and stabbed another woman who had never been identified. He had also started hundreds of fires across the boroughs of the city. A diary indicated he had started more than fourteen hundred fires – he was never caught for those.

The crimes he is most infamous for, and the ones this sniper was referencing, started on July 29, 1976, when he shot two young women in the Pelham Bay neighborhood of the Bronx, in the early morning hours as they sat in a car talking after a night out. He fired three shots and walked away. One of the women died while the other survived. Over the next year, more shootings of a similar style followed in Queens, but he also killed in the Bronx and Brooklyn.

Berkowitz targeted mostly young attractive women with long brown hair. His victims ranged in age from fifteen to twenty. It caused such panic that many women cut and dyed their hair. Beauty supply stores couldn't keep wigs in stock because they were selling so fast.

It wasn't until May 1977 that he left a letter with two bodies. In the letter addressed to New York Police Department Captain Joseph Borrelli, he called himself the Son of Sam for the first time and taunted the police for not catching him yet. He promised there'd be more shootings.

Another letter, also sent in May, this time to Jimmy Breslin of the *Daily News*, offered more of the same rambling. The letters were given to several psychiatrists and, by the end of May, police released a psychological profile, describing the killer as neurotic, possibly suffering from paranoid schizophrenia.

Tiplines were flooded but there was another shooting at the end of June. Then on July 13, New York City was plunged into darkness. For twenty-five hours, the city was without power. It led to widespread looting and fires in the streets. No one forgot there was also a serial killer on the loose. It was chaos.

The first big break in the case came when police were able to match the bullets from the crime scenes across jurisdictions. During the year that Berkowitz evaded the police, he didn't just send letters to the police and a journalist, he also sent threatening letters to his neighbors, which would be his undoing. They turned him into the police as a potential suspect. He was arrested outside of his home in Yonkers and quickly confessed to his crimes.

After his arrest, Berkowitz claimed to hear voices and claimed that demons and a black Labrador retriever owned by his neighbor Sam Carr had ordered him to commit the killings. It's where Berkowitz had garnered his now infamous moniker – Son of Sam. Today, he sits in the Sullivan County Correctional Facility. His psychiatric condition has been hotly debated. Later, Berkowitz admitted the dog and demon story was a hoax.

Now it seemed someone wanted to finish what he started.

Except, it wasn't the 1970s and Little Rock was hardly New York City. We were, however, in the middle of record heat. A hot July turned into a sweltering August. A heat dome, as the weather man called it, sat over us and wasn't moving anytime soon. But of all the places in the country to carry out such an act, why Little Rock? As far as I knew it didn't have a connection to the Son of Sam cases.

I typed a few search terms into my phone, trying to connect the Son of Sam cases and Berkowitz to Little Rock and came up short. It wasn't even a significant anniversary of the crimes – forty-six years ago he was captured. Anyone around then and paying attention to the crimes would be well into their sixties by now. None of it made a lot of sense to me.

My cellphone rang, flashing Cooper's face on my screen.

"Have you heard anything yet?" he asked when I answered.

"Nothing from Luke. The news isn't reporting much either." I turned the television back on to see if there were any updates. The same reporter as before stood in front of the crime scene tape not far from the scene. "They aren't saying anything about the victims yet. I'm sure they need to notify the family first before any details are released."

"I heard the dead girl was twenty, Riley," Cooper said with emphasis. "I've been reading up on the Son of Sam cases and his victims were young too."

"I know that, but why Little Rock? There is no connection between those cases and here." I plopped down in my favorite chair and kicked my feet up on the ottoman. I wasn't going to head upstairs to our bedroom until Luke was home – if he got home that night at all. "What do you think?"

Cooper had been a detective for the Little Rock Police Department and then started his own private investigation business. When I moved back to Little Rock several years ago, we partnered and grew the business together. While I knew more about serial killers than any healthy person should, Cooper excelled at surveillance. We had equal strengths in investigating and witness interviews. It had been a rock-solid partnership. Cooper was also Luke's long-time best friend since college, so he was more like family at this point.

"I don't know what to think. Not yet, anyway. We were able to get into our loft. They have several streets blocked off including the block where Adele's office is located. She's going to see if she can get into her office in the morning before court."

I knew Adele had wanted to get home for logistical reasons. Cooper wanted to get down there to hear the gossip on the street. "What are people saying unofficially?"

"That they were walking up Scott Street from the River Market District and were shot right there on the corner of Scott and 2nd Street. They were waiting for the light to change. One minute they were standing there and the next they were shot. The girl died from a clean shot to the head. At least she didn't suffer."

That didn't match up to the Son of Sam shootings either. "Was anyone else hurt?"

Cooper yelled something to Adele then got back on the phone. "Her friend was shot in the thigh, but she's expected to make a full recovery."

While I knew the Son of Sam cases, I didn't know the details of each murder. I typed in a search for a timeline of the murders and pulled up the information. I read it off to Cooper. "One woman was killed while her friend was shot in the thigh during the first shooting. Maybe he's targeting the victim type and method of homicide. It's certainly not going to be the same type of weapon."

Cooper agreed with that reasoning. He also had some of his own analysis to offer. "The note was short and coherent. I looked up Berkowitz's notes and his were long and rambling. They didn't make a whole lot of sense. They made him seem like he had a psychiatric condition. This killer was bold and daring. He sent the note before the shooting too. Cat said she doesn't check her mail often or we might have found it sooner."

"Found it but wouldn't have been able to do anything about it," I countered. I wasn't sure if it was better to have the note before or after the fact. The police would have been scrambling for twenty-four hours and not have been able to stop him. I told Cooper as much.

Cooper agreed. "You know Luke is going to convince himself he should have been able to stop him though."

I knew that was true. Luke was harder on himself than anyone. He expected to have superhuman qualities and when he didn't live up to it, he chastised himself for not doing better. It was nonsense as Luke was the best detective in Little Rock, possibly rivaling the best detectives in the country. I was about to ask Cooper what he knew about the victim when Luke appeared on the news standing at a podium alongside other law enforcement. "Turn on channel five. Luke is about to make a statement."

I turned up the volume in time to hear him say the victim was twenty-year-old Gemma Cullen. Luke looked right at the camera as he spoke. "Gemma and a friend were walking down Scott Street away from the River Market and approached the light on 2nd Street. They waited until it was safe to cross when one shot rang out and struck Gemma in the head killing her instantly. Her friend, whose name we are not releasing, was shot in the thigh before she could even react to what happened to her friend. She is currently in the hospital and is expected to make a full recovery."

When asked about any potential suspects, Luke explained, "We do not have a suspect yet. We believe we have found the location where he shot from, but we are not releasing that information to the public yet. We are following up on several leads."

Luke allowed a few questions, most of which he wouldn't answer including the type of weapon and the ammunition used. When reporters continued to shout questions at him, he assured the crowd he'd be making another statement when he could share more information.

He closed the press conference with a warning. "We do not believe this is going to be an isolated incident. We have reason to believe the shooter had no association with these victims and that he may look to repeat his crimes. We are asking all residents to be on guard and please report any suspicious activity."

Reporters erupted with even more questions Luke refused to answer. I couldn't believe he had released that information. Normally, Luke would be far more cautious about issuing a warning like that.

After facing a barrage of questions he wouldn't answer, Luke stepped back from the podium as they continued to shout at him. He gave the camera one last look and walked away turning his back on them.

"He shared more than I thought he would have," Cooper said as I muted the television. "I didn't think he'd be releasing the victim's name yet. That warning, Riley. The city is going to be on edge."

"As they should be. He must have been able to identify her and notify the victim's family." I checked my watch and realized a few hours had passed since we were first notified. "Do you want to meet in the morning?" I didn't know if we'd be able to help, but if this was the start, there was a lot of ground to cover – possibly more than the Little Rock Police Department could handle.

Cooper agreed we should meet at his loft at nine and decide from there what to do.

I ended the call with him and stared at the television, letting the fear sink in. Cities had seen sniper cases like this before. There had been one not long ago in the D.C. metro area. It upended normal life for those residents for three weeks. I could only hope that this case wrapped up that quickly and would not go on for more than a year like the Son of Sam.

CHAPTER 2

Luke cursed a blue streak as he pulled open the door to the police station and turned to his old partner, Bill Tyler, who would soon be Captain Bill Tyler and officially his boss. Captain Kurt Meadows was on the brink of retirement and had already found his successor. Tyler had been approved to take the job and now only needed to be sworn in. He was, for the most part, starting to take over Captain Meadow's job duties, leaving Luke without a partner.

This case would be the ultimate test for Captain Tyler. Luke didn't envy him, but if anyone was up for the job, it was him. He had already approved Luke to release a warning to the public but not the note. It was the right decision to make given the situation.

They climbed the stairs to the detective's bullpen and went right into the conference room. They hadn't released any information to the public about the type of weapon used or the ammunition because they didn't know. The crime scene techs were still scouring the area for evidence and the autopsy wouldn't be done until the next morning. The medical examiner, Ed Purvis, had promised Luke he would prioritize the case.

Gemma had been identified from her wallet and her friend provided confirmation. Gemma's parents, Grady and Rose Cullen, had been easy to track down but delivering the news to her family hadn't been easy. Grady Cullen was a big-shot defense attorney in the city and was well known across not just the state but the delta.

As Luke pulled out a chair in the conference room and sat, he slid the note encased in the evidence bag across the table to Tyler and explained his interview with Cat. "She assumed this was delivered yesterday. Cat said she doesn't check the mail often but was waiting for something from one of her advertisers and checked tonight. It was already too late. She was only four doors away from the shooting. Once she realized what was going on, she left through the back of the building to the alley and came to me immediately. She heard before I did."

"They were going to notify you, Luke," Tyler said with his eyes raised. "They were waiting to see what they had first."

Luke had meant nothing by the remark. He waved off Tyler's reassurance. "I wasn't worried about that. I was only saying Cat is at the epicenter of this."

Tyler lowered his eyes back to the note and read it. He looked up at Luke in a question then back to the note again. "I don't understand, Luke. He's going to replicate crimes from 1977. If I'm catching his meaning, this crime doesn't resemble those very closely."

Luke was going to need to read up on the Son of Sam case. He had heard of it but hadn't known any of the details until Riley mentioned it. Even now, he was hazy on some of it. "We don't know anything yet. His plan doesn't make a whole lot of sense to me. He's not replicating the type of weapon used that's for sure. He'd never get a shot off like that with a .44 caliber."

Tyler tossed the evidence bag down on the table. "You said on the news you knew where he shot from. Is that true?"

Luke shook his head. "There are only a few places where he could have taken the shot from, but I wanted the killer to believe we already knew. I have officers staked out at all the possible locations in case he's considering going back. I have crime scene techs already searching those areas."

Tyler agreed that was a good idea. "What about Cat O'Conner? What do we know about her?"

Most of what Luke knew about Cat he had learned from Cooper. "She went to college for journalism and was a freelancer. She's originally from Chicago and ended up following a boyfriend to Little Rock. They broke up and she stayed. Cooper said she always had an interest in true crime and started the podcast while she was bored and looking for something to do after the breakup. It took off faster than she planned. It's been rapidly growing over the last year. Her following is huge."

"How huge?" Tyler asked.

"I didn't ask her specifically, but she signed a deal with one of the big platforms. I don't remember the name but Cooper said Cat got a two-million-dollar payout. I assume her listeners must be global and in the millions. Captain Meadows cleared her before I did the podcast. We know she's legit."

"I wasn't concerned about that," he said with a smirk.

"What are you saying then?"

"Is there any chance she cooked up this whole thing for ratings? It would give her an even bigger platform if she's at the epicenter of a serial sniper case."

Luke sank back in the chair. That hadn't occurred to him at all. "I can't rule it out. Cat seemed genuinely freaked out when she showed up at my house. She was panicked and willingly sat down with me for an interview. Is there a reason you suspect her?"

Tyler weighed his words carefully, which was something he never did with Luke when they were partners. When he seemed hesitant to talk, Luke encouraged him. "I know your job role has changed, but you can still speak your mind with me. Whatever you speculate isn't going past these four walls. You don't need to play the politics of the position with me."

Tyler chuckled. "It's going to take some getting used to. Captain Meadows cautioned me on broad speculation with the detectives. He said don't send them running down rabbit holes." Luke said he understood and Tyler relaxed his shoulders. "We don't know Cat. She grows a crime podcast overnight and recently gets this big global deal. I'm sure there is pressure on her to produce and live up to the millions she was paid out. That's all I'm saying."

The theory wasn't the wildest Luke had ever heard. "She did conveniently open the note a day late and then bring it to me instead of going to the cops on the street or even calling 911."

"That's what I'm talking about, Luke. Look, for all we know, it happened as she said. I barely open my mail, so that doesn't strike me as odd. She knew you were a homicide detective. Maybe she looked for you on the street and didn't see you. It's possible she wanted to bring it to you directly and didn't trust anyone else." Tyler threw his hands up as if to say he didn't know what he didn't know. "Anything is possible. I don't think we should rule her out so quickly is all I'm saying."

"I can get on board with that. We aren't going to know much of anything until we get the autopsy and ballistics back." Luke looked at the wall clock. It was nearing one in the morning. "What can we get done tonight?"

"Nothing," Tyler said with a shake of his head. "Go home to bed and come back fresh in the morning. I'm sure Riley is waiting up for you."

Luke stood from the table, but when Tyler made no move to do the same, he asked, "You leaving too?"

"I will soon. There's a few things I need to go over." As Luke headed for the door, Tyler called him back. "What do we want to do about a partner for you?"

Luke leaned against the doorjamb. "Do I need one right now?"

"Captain Meadows told me to not let you get comfortable without one. I think he's worried about you. We've been partners for a long time. He said you might be lonely."

Luke had been partners with Tyler for as long as he'd been a detective. He probably would be a bit lonely but he also might settle into working alone a little too easily. "I think Captain Meadows is more worried I might like being without a partner too much."

Tyler laughed. "He said that too. It's up to you, Luke. If you need someone right away, I can move people around."

"I'm good for now. We can sort it out after you settle in," Luke said and then headed for the door. He'd take Tyler's advice and head home but there was something he wanted to do first.

Luke texted Cat on his walk over toward her studio. She had told him earlier that evening that she lived right above it and he was sure she was still awake. If he was going to consider her a suspect, he needed a bit more than Tyler's speculation.

He walked the few short blocks to Cat's studio and had to cross the crime scene tape to get there. The uniformed cops asked him if he had any leads yet.

"Not yet but it's early. Make sure no one but residents come through here," Luke reminded them and then walked past three buildings until he reached the building where Cat lived and worked.

Luke looked up to the second floor of the building. Light poured through the row of windows, so he knew Cat was still awake. He glanced down at his phone when it chimed. She told him to come on over. He texted that he was there already and she buzzed the door to let him up.

Once inside the small foyer, there was a heavy glass door off to the right with the name of her podcast *Rock City Killers* etched in it. Right in front of him were stairs that went to the second floor.

Cat pulled open the door before he hit the second-floor landing.

She had a cardigan wrapped around her that looked like it was a size too big. "Is there something more you need, Det. Morgan?"

"Mind if I come in?" he asked and she stepped out of the way. Her apartment had fifteen-foot ceilings and a wide plank wood floor that looked original. She had an eclectic style of decorating, which didn't surprise him given the flamboyant way she dressed and the purple in her short, bobbed hair. Cat stood about Riley's height at five-foot-seven. She had rows of earrings on each ear and a tattoo of a vine of cherry blossoms on her right arm. It was poking out from under the sleeve of her sweater. Luke had seen the full tattoo the day she interviewed him for the podcast.

"I had a few more questions," Luke said and pointed to her couch. "I know it's late and I'm sorry for dropping by like this. I thought if I can get this out of the way, I could hit the ground running in the morning."

"Certainly," she said and followed him over as he sat on the couch. Cat perched herself in a wide oversized chair that was upholstered in rich turquoise fabric. "How can I help you?"

"Is it common for you to not check your mail frequently?" It was too late to be indirect.

"My assistant is on vacation this week. We aren't slated to record new episodes for another couple of weeks. I'm currently researching my next case." Cat paused herself from rambling and smiled over at him. "That's a long way of saying my assistant opens my mail and without her, I'm a disorganized mess. The only reason I even checked the mail earlier tonight was because I was looking for a check from one of my advertisers."

It made sense to Luke. If Riley didn't get the mail and put what was important on his desk at home, he'd rarely see anything. "What happened after you found the note?"

Cat tucked her legs under her. "As I said before, I came to see you."

"The shooting had already happened and there were cops on the street out front. Did you look for me there?" he asked.

"No," Cat said without emotion in her voice. "It didn't occur to me. You had texted me earlier that you were going home to listen to the podcast. Did I do something wrong?"

"It's not that you did anything wrong. We are trying to understand your reasoning for not bringing the note to one of the cops on the street or calling 911."

If Cat was worried she had done something improper, she didn't show it in her expression. "I wanted to get it to you as soon as possible. I know you're the head of the homicide unit. I believed the note and the shooting could be connected but I didn't know for sure. I didn't want to hand off important evidence to just anyone."

Luke could understand and even appreciate that. "Why do you think the killer chose to leave the note for you? Have you done a podcast about Son of Sam?"

Cat pulled the cardigan tighter around her. "I haven't done a podcast about that case. I have mentioned him on the podcast in a general way. I don't know why I was targeted. I'm terrified, to be honest with you."

"Do you want protection?" Luke asked, wondering if he could authorize that.

"I don't see any point. You all have enough to do."

Luke asked her a few more questions, none of which yielded anything that could make her a suspect. "Are you planning to talk about this case on your podcast?"

Cat raised her eyebrows. "Is that what this late-night visit is about? You don't want me to talk about it?"

"I'd prefer you didn't, not until it's solved. I don't want the sniper feeding off the notoriety," Luke explained, which wasn't completely a lie. "I was more curious *if* you were planning to discuss it."

Cat paused several beats to answer. She was looking at Luke like she couldn't believe he was asking the question. Finally, she expelled a frustrated breath. "No. It's scary enough he targeted me. I don't want to draw attention to myself. I wouldn't do anything, Det. Morgan, to impede your investigation. It's frustrating you think I would."

"I don't think you would, Cat. I was only trying to understand your involvement."

"I haven't been involved," she countered. "The killer left me a note in my mailbox and I brought it to you. I have no idea why he chose me, other than the podcast."

Luke stood to leave. "I appreciate your time. I'll be in touch. Let me know if you hear from him again."

"You'll be my first call," Cat said dryly as she followed him to the door. "I wish I knew more to help you. Like everyone else, I hope there isn't another shooting."

Luke looked back at her and offered a sympathetic smile. "Keep yourself safe." He left knowing it wasn't a matter of *if* there was another shooting but *when*.

CHAPTER 3

Cooper walked Adele to her office in the morning to make sure she got there safely. The area in front of her office had been cleared, but the roadblocks on Scott and 2nd Streets remained.

Adele insisted she'd be fine to walk the few blocks alone. Her words and tone told one story, but her expression told another. Cooper knew they were feeling what everyone in downtown Little Rock was feeling that morning – who might be next? The fear was palpable in the air.

There had been shootings in the city before including what was considered a mass shooting at a nightclub. Those had been gang violence though. Most people reasoned if they weren't involved in that life, they'd be safe. Little Rock wasn't known as a safe city. It always made the list as one of the most dangerous mid-sized cities in America. The crime for the most part remained contained to the southeast part of the city.

A sniper striking randomly was something different.

After leaving Adele at her office, Cooper walked the few blocks to his local coffee shop and listened to the customers chatter about the shooting – each of them worried for their safety and that of their neighbors. A few noted people they knew were working from home today and wouldn't venture to their offices. Others, who lived outside of downtown, wouldn't be driving into the city that day either. No one knew what was going to happen next.

Cooper wasn't going to let fear get the better of him. As he stood there waiting for his coffee, someone called his name. He turned to see Cat standing by the door. He waved to her. "How are you this morning?"

Cat crossed the coffee shop, saying hello to people she knew as she passed. She dropped her voice low. "I think Luke believes I had something to do with what happened last night."

Cooper didn't understand. "How could you have something to do with it?"

Cat nodded to a woman she knew then stepped around Cooper so her back was against the wall. "He showed up at my apartment at one in the morning asking all kinds of questions about how often I check the mail and if I was going to cover the shooting on my podcast."

Cooper didn't think that it was unusual. "He's covering his bases. You were the one who received the note. You're involved whether you want to be or not. I'm sure he was trying to rule you out."

"You think?" Cat asked with uncertainty in her voice. "That's what he said. I wasn't sure."

Cooper knew Luke was doing his job. "I can't speak for Luke, but I don't see how you could be involved. How good of a shot are you?" Cooper meant it as a lighthearted joke but it fell flat. "Cat, I'm serious. You're fine. Luke is a thorough investigator."

Cat relaxed her body and leaned against the wall. "He wanted to know why the killer targeted me. I want to know that too. There are people more famous than I am in this city. He could have sent the note to one of our hot newscasters. They all have fan clubs and they'd be more than happy to share the gossip. I'm not going to be sharing it."

Cooper tried to hold back a laugh. She was right. Little Rock had a few attractive news personalities that had legions of fans on social media. The killer could have targeted any one of them and the message would already be all over the news. Targeting Cat meant the cops could keep the note to themselves for a while – which seemed the opposite of what the killer wanted in writing the note in the first place. She made a fair point.

"Why do you think he left you the note?"

Cat threw her hands up in defeat. "I've been wracking my brain trying to figure it out and I don't know. My podcast has been growing and I've gained some popularity. Maybe he's hoping I do a series on the shootings as they are happening. He left me the note and then killed someone right down the street from me. He wanted my attention and he got it. I'm not sure what I'm supposed to do now."

"Are there any cases you profiled with someone who could pull off crimes like this?"

Cat tucked strands of her purple hair behind her ears. "The first case I covered was of a guy in the Army who killed his family after he got back from Iraq. It was a clear case of post-traumatic stress disorder. He tried to kill himself too but the cops showed up and rushed him to the hospital. He had been a sniper but he's been in a mental health facility since then. Once he's cleared from there, he'll be sent to prison. It was a sad and tragic case and I covered it fairly. He allowed me to interview him and his psychiatrist even participated. I don't think it could be connected to that and that was the only case even close to this."

Cooper agreed it didn't sound like it could be coming from her first podcast case. "Has there been anyone you've encountered that has raised alarm bells for you or made you suspicious?"

"Luke asked me the same thing last night and there wasn't anyone. Of course, I don't remember every single person I've interviewed. Every case I cover is usually six to eight episodes and I take on five cases a year for an average of forty episodes. It's a lot of research and ground to cover on my own."

Cooper had an idea but he wasn't sure she'd be up for it. "I'm on my way to meet Riley. Last night, we were discussing how we might be able to help Luke with this case. Unofficially, of course. Maybe we can start by helping you to go through all your past cases to see if there's anyone who jumps out at us."

"You'd do that?" Cat asked with uncertainty in her voice. "I haven't gotten my money from the purchase of the podcast yet. I'm not sure how much I can pay you right now."

Cooper waved her off. "I don't need you to pay us. I'm willing to help you do this for free. The Little Rock Police Department doesn't have the manpower to take this on. Luke doesn't even have a partner yet." He leaned in closer to her and lowered his voice. "I was nervous walking my wife to work this morning. The fact that she allowed me to walk her to work says everything about how this case is already impacting the city."

"Understood," Cat said, her tone reflecting the gravity of the situation. "I'm going back to catch a few hours of sleep. Do you want to meet me around noon in my studio?"

"Sounds good to me. If there's anything changed on my end, I'll call you." He watched Cat walk off and then looked back to the counter to see the barista putting his coffee down on the counter along with the muffins he ordered. Riley was so much more amenable to suggestions with coffee and a treat. He wasn't sure how she'd react to helping Cat.

Cooper stepped out of the coffee shop and glanced up at the high building across the street. Downtown Little Rock had enough high buildings where a sniper could easily perch. On the walk back to his loft, Cooper noticed his pace was a little faster. A moving target was harder to hit.

Cooper made it back to his loft and found Riley sitting on the floor outside his door. "You're here early," he said as he made his way down the hall. He held up the coffee and the bag with the muffins. "I figured you'd be hungry. Did you eat this morning?"

"I didn't get much sleep last night," Riley said trailing behind him. "Luke didn't get home until two and he was too wound up to sleep. I saw four on the clock and then finally dozed off. This morning was a scramble to get out of the house." She took the coffee and bag from his hand so he could unlock the door. "Did you feel strange walking out there? Like you were going to be shot at any moment."

"It's been on my mind."

"I thought about it too. It's only going to get worse if the shooting continues."

"Let's make sure it doesn't." Once inside, Cooper tossed his keys on the kitchen counter and joined Riley on the couch. He sighed as he sunk back into it. "How's Luke doing?"

"About as well as can be expected." Riley took a sip of her coffee and groaned appreciatively.

"Did you ask Luke how we could help him?"

"I didn't get the chance." Riley turned her head so she could see him better. "Luke thinks Cat might be connected, even if she doesn't realize it. He said Tyler was the one who brought it up first. Luke felt like some of her answers seemed hesitant. He didn't think she was lying, but he wasn't sure she was telling the truth either."

Cooper took a sip of his coffee. "Cat found me at the coffee shop this morning. She knows Luke suspects her of something and she was freaked out about it. Her answers might have seemed hesitant because she was concerned with why Luke was asking questions."

"You mean other than because it's his job."

Cooper was trying to gauge how Riley felt about Cat. He couldn't read her. "What do you think about Cat?"

Riley turned her whole body so she was facing Cooper. "I don't know what I think about her. I didn't love that she started mentioning us in her podcasts without speaking to any of us. Then when Luke called her out on it, she invited him to be interviewed about his case. It seems to me if she was interested in sharing facts, she would have contacted us earlier in the process. We didn't even know she was doing a podcast until a stranger told us."

That was a fair statement and one Cooper couldn't argue against. "Does that mean you don't like her?"

"I don't know her but she seems to know a lot about us. That makes me suspicious of her." Riley took another sip of her coffee and dug into the bag of muffins. She pulled out the blueberry one and tore off a piece of it. "What did she want this morning?"

Cooper thought back to their interaction. "To be honest with you, I'm not sure. She told me about Luke suspecting her and she seemed to want reassurance she wasn't a suspect. I don't know what she thought I could provide in that regard. I told her not to worry about it and that Luke was doing his job. Would you be opposed to helping her?"

Riley scrunched up her face in disgust. "Helping how?"

Cooper ignored the look. "I asked Cat if any of her past cases could be connected. She said it's a lot of material to go through and I suggested we might be able to help her." When Riley didn't look convinced, Cooper stressed the point. "If she is a suspect, then maybe there's something in her past files we can find to help Luke. The more time we spend with her, the more we'll get to know her. Cat might slip up and tell us something. We'd also be able to keep an eye on her for Luke. I'm sure he's not going to be able to focus on her too much given everything he has to do. I'm not sure how else we might be able to help him."

Riley considered it as Cooper knew she would. All he ever had to do was make a good argument and she'd usually give in. "Do we tell Luke we are going through her files?"

"If you think we should. Otherwise, we can keep a low profile on it. If we find something, then we can tell him. Do you think he'd have a problem with it?"

"I don't think so." Riley stared down at her cup. "He's worried about getting a new partner. Tyler mentioned it last night and Luke thinks dealing with a new partner right now might be a distraction. He asked Tyler if he could wait."

"What did Tyler say?"

"He was noncommittal about it. I'm worried this might be a challenging transition for them both. Tyler is a great choice for captain, but Luke has outranked him for a few years. It might be hard for Luke to take direction from him."

Cooper had considered that too. "I'm sure they will work it out."

Riley nodded slowly, not fully convinced. "What time did you tell Cat we'd meet her?"

Cooper realized then she knew he had already told Cat they'd help. "Noon. It gives us time to go over a few of our pending cases." It was times like this when Cooper was happy they had hired a few investigators to work with them. It allowed them to take the cases they wanted without being bogged down with work that didn't interest them.

He was sure if he asked Riley to take one more surveillance case, she'd quit.

CHAPTER 4

By ten that morning, Luke had already been at work for four hours. He had met with the crime scene tech supervisor and they had gone over the evidence found at the scene. As he had told Tyler the night before, the sniper's location could only be one of a few places and they found it relatively quickly.

He had been perched on the top floor of a parking garage about a block away from where the victim was killed. The crime scene techs found the place because an eagle-eyed tech noticed dirt on one of the ledges had been brushed away. The pattern in the grime was distinct for a rifle bipod stand. There were half boot prints in the dirt on the ground that outlined the toes of the boot. It wasn't enough to figure out what kind of footwear.

There were no shell casings, cigarette butts, or garbage in the area – nothing that they could use to gather some DNA. The techs fingerprinted the wall and metal bars but they didn't expect to get much back.

Luke had stood in the same spot as the sniper. It was a clear line of sight and the shot wasn't as difficult to make as he had assumed last night. The distance from the scene also gave the sniper time to get out of the area before anyone was the wiser.

As Luke stood he considered what the sniper might have seen. What became apparent quickly was that he could have chosen anyone on the street below. He had a range of streets to aim his weapon at and there would have been a plethora of targets at eight-fifteen when the shots were fired.

Luke wondered if the victims weren't randomly chosen. He considered the sniper went looking for a pair of young women earlier in the night and then set up the location to aim. Otherwise, it was luck finding two twenty-year-old women – one of whom he killed and the other he wounded.

Wounding Teresa Jenkins had not been an accident. If he had wanted to kill Teresa, he could have easily. He had intended to shoot her in the thigh – an act which Riley had explained was exactly what the Son of Sam had done in his first shooting. Luke believed then, that even if nothing else matched up between the two cases, that did.

The thigh wound also went clean through, nicking the femur as it went. Teresa would recover but the damage to her leg might be long-lasting. Luke had stopped at the hospital right before heading to the police station that morning, just as she was getting out of surgery. He spoke to her parents but hadn't had a chance to interview her yet. She was still doped up on pain medication and in and out of sleep. An officer had taken her statement the night before but she had been in serious pain and shock.

In addition to finding the location where the shots had been fired, they also found out more about the ammunition and gun used. One of the crime scene techs found the bullets lodged in the building behind the victims. The ammunition that went clean through Gemma's head and Teresa's thigh was .300 Winchester magnum. After assessing the ammunition, Luke believed the gun was an M2010-enhanced sniper rifle. The manufacturer was selling the gun to civilians now so where he had obtained it was anyone's guess.

Luke had also stopped to see Ed Purvis that morning and had picked up the rushed autopsy report. The only thing not back was the toxicology report and that didn't matter so much in this case. He knew the girls had been at one of the local bars. One of their friends had shown up at the crime scene and indicated to a uniformed officer that they had been in the River Market. Luke didn't know if the girls showed fake IDs or if they just hadn't been carded. It didn't matter much at that point.

There were still many unknowns, but one of the biggest was figuring out if Cat was somehow involved. He had hoped speaking to her would erase any question. It only left him with doubts. He had told Riley as much when he got home. The worst part was he couldn't put his finger on why her responses bothered him. She had quickly gotten defensive. She also dismissed the notion that it could be connected to her. It wasn't so much in the responses she gave but the tone of her voice. It could be nothing. Then again, it could be everything.

"You look frustrated, Luke," Tyler said and waved him into his office.

Luke grabbed the autopsy and crime scene tech files off his desk and carried them with him. He entered the office and sat down. Luke needed to get something out of the way first. "Do you want me to call you Captain Tyler? I can if you want me to out of respect, but it feels a little weird to say."

"It would feel weird hearing it from you," Tyler said as he sat behind the desk. He put his hands on the top and felt the surface as if he couldn't believe it was his. Then he gave Luke a knowing look. "Around everyone else, it's probably a good idea. I'm worried the rest of the detectives won't take me seriously. If you can help set an example, that would be helpful. But when it's just us, please don't. While we are on the subject, I don't want to supervise you, Luke. Not in the way some captains can. I want to take a hands-off approach like Captain Meadows. You let me know what's going on. If I can give some input, great. If not, that's fine too. If you think something is going to be politically risky, run it by me so I'm aware. I don't want to get in your way or change how you work. We were partners for more than a decade. I trust your judgment. I trust you with my life."

That was all fine by Luke, preferable even. "It works for me and I appreciate the approach. I think that will work for the rest of them too. If there's an issue, let me know and I'll step in first. There will be bumps, but in time, it will all smooth over."

Luke put the files on the desk and gave Tyler a rundown of everything they knew to date. "There haven't been any surprises. The shooting wasn't that hard to pull off and they didn't leave much evidence behind. I think we have to assume the evidence left was intentional."

Tyler read through Luke's notes, flipping through all three pages. When he was done, he raised his head. "Do you think we are dealing with someone with a military or law enforcement background?"

Luke had been asking himself the same question since last night. "We can't rule it out. But I don't think they'd have to have special training either. An avid hunter or simply a good marksman could have taken those two shots. The thigh wound was intentional. He didn't shoot to kill her. He wanted to wound her. You or I could have taken those shots with the same accuracy."

Tyler nodded his head. "How did your interview with Cat go last night?"

Luke wasn't surprised Tyler knew he'd already interviewed her. They had been partners for too long for Tyler not to know how Luke operated. He probably knew last night that Luke was headed there. "I have more suspicions about her now than I did before. Maybe it was the power of suggestion. I considered what you said and when I went to speak to her, she seemed hesitant. She didn't give wrong answers, just slow ones that made me think she was thinking a little too hard about what she was going to say."

The truth was the jury was still out on her.

Tyler seemed happy with the assessment. "Don't put all our eggs in that basket but keep an eye on her. What's the plan for today?"

"I need to speak to the victims' parents and the girls' friends to see if anyone approached Gemma and Teresa last night and rule out definitively that there isn't someone in their lives who had a motive for killing Gemma. We don't have one solid lead at this point. As I said, he was smart enough not to leave a lot of evidence behind. What he did leave doesn't point in any specific direction."

"Let me know if you need anything." Tyler sat back in the chair. There was a hint of melancholy in his voice. When Luke asked the unspoken question with his expression, Tyler shrugged. "I want to be in the field with you with all the action. Don't get me wrong, I'm glad I took the job. It's going to take me a little time to adjust. I'll be spending the rest of the day with Captain Meadows meeting all the important people we used to avoid."

Luke didn't envy him for a second. "If you get done early and want to talk over what I learn today, call me. I can walk you by the sniper's perch if you want to check that out. It's only a small taste of what you used to have but it's something." They laughed together and Tyler told him he appreciated it.

Luke went back to his desk, grabbed a few things he needed for the day, and headed to the back lot to get his car. He drove the distance to West Little Rock where Gemma's parents lived off Chenal Parkway.

Luke pulled into the circular drive of the two-story home that was one of the bigger houses in their cul-de-sac. He parked and walked to the front door. Before he had a chance to knock, a woman in her late forties with a blonde bob and a pained expression pulled open the door.

She extended a cold thin hand to Luke and introduced herself again. "I'm Gemma's mother, Rose. Her father Grady is upstairs in his study. He said to call him when you arrive." She escorted Luke into a living room bigger than the entire first floor of his house.

He wondered if she didn't remember meeting him the previous night. Luke knew trauma could play tricks on the mind. "I'm sorry to bother you both again," he said as he sat. "I need some background on Gemma for the investigation."

"Of course," she said as she walked to the stairs. She called out her husband's name but her voice was as weak and thin as her handshake. "Let me go get him." She climbed the stairs and disappeared.

Luke took in his surroundings but there wasn't much personal in the space. The room was big and airy without any clutter or personalization. The furniture was well-made but stuffy. There was a painting of the sea and lighthouse above the fireplace. Other than that the walls were bare. A clean look as Riley would have told him. It was in stark contrast to their cozy home – neat but well-lived.

A moment later, Grady, wearing blue slacks and a white button-down shirt and tie, bounded down the stairs without Rose anywhere in sight. He joined Luke in the living room and shook his hand. "I'm sorry but my wife won't be joining us. She said she can't bear to speak about Gemma, as I'm sure you can understand."

Luke knew all too well. When his sister was murdered during his senior year of college, his mother barely held on. It was his father and him who handled most of the interaction with the cops. "You can relay the questions I asked and if she has anything she wants to add, she can call me."

"Very good then," he said and sat on the edge of the couch. He rested his hands on his knees. "I know how this works. I've been a defense attorney longer than you've been a cop. I never thought I'd be on this side of it though."

Grady's job raised the question whether someone in his life might have had something to do with the shooting. Luke asked, "Do you know what Gemma was doing last night downtown?"

"I always knew what my daughter was up to even if she didn't think I did," he said with a sad smile. "She was meeting friends for dinner and then a few drinks. I know she's not yet twenty-one, but her friends know the bartender at Mick's. She was spending the night with her friend, Teresa, who lives in a loft downtown. Gemma was a responsible young woman. We never had any issues with her. She didn't drink excessively and never any drugs. I don't know anyone in her life who might have wanted to harm her. She had the same small circle of friends she'd had since grade school. She was a good kid all around."

Luke went through several more questions but there was nothing in Gemma's background that indicated she could have known the killer or who had a motive to want her dead. Luke saved the most difficult question for last. "Given your profession, is there anyone you can think of in your professional or personal life who might have wanted to harm Gemma?"

"I heard the hesitancy in the way you asked that and I appreciate the sensitivity," Grady said to start. "It was the first thing I thought of last night. There's no one I can think of unless someone is holding a long-ago grudge."

Luke had not released any details about the letter sent to Cat – not to the public or the victims' families. If there was a time, this would be it. "We received some communication from the killer. He referenced the Son of Sam and finishing his work. Is there anyone you can think of who might have been obsessed with that case?"

Grady's complexion palled. "I do. It's a former client," he said slowly, almost in shock. He recovered quickly though. "He was recently released from prison. I don't represent him anymore. Let me get the information for you." Grady got up and promised he'd be right back.

It might just be the first break in the case.

CHAPTER 5

This was my first time in Cat's studio. There was a small reception area in the front where her assistant normally sat that connected to a conference room with a large window overlooking the street. Her office was down the hall and her recording studio was in a soundproof room in the back of the space. The very last room in the far back was a small kitchen with a two-seater table.

The recording studio had a U-shaped table with three microphone setups and a host of equipment I wouldn't know how to use even if someone showed me. It was professional and impressive.

I was doing my best to warm up to her the way Cooper had. It wasn't that I didn't like her. As I told Cooper, I didn't know her and she seemed to know everything about me and the people I cared about most.

Cat had done a podcast on the murder of Luke's sister and the other victims of the same killer from long before we ever met her. It was a serial killer case that took all of us across several states and even back to my hometown. It had been a long and complicated case but not one without resolution.

Luke finally solved his sister's murder and it brought Adele, the sister of one of the other victims, into our lives. Cooper had met Adele while he was investigating her sister's case in Atlanta. My sister was kidnapped in the process of the investigation. It was a case that touched all of us on a deep and personal level, and I hadn't quite gotten over the fact Cat had done a podcast without contacting any of us.

It was in the early days of her podcast career, long before she thought anyone was paying attention. She had apologized for not including us. Her excuse was she didn't think any of us would be interested. The podcast episodes had brought her international fame and it's why she had the deal with Justice Exposed, the podcast platform. I had done some research on the company while I was waiting for Cooper to get ready to go to Cat's.

They were only backing a few well-known and highly successful crime podcasts. Cat had landed herself a great deal off the tragedy of others. I wasn't sure how well that sat with me.

I sat down in a cozy chair in the corner of her office. Cooper had left to get us some lunch, leaving Cat and me alone together. I assumed he had done it on purpose to give us a chance to connect. "What made you decide to do a podcast?"

Cat sat cross-legged on the floor in front of a box of files she was sorting for us. She raised her head. "I was a journalist and had been freelancing for a long time. I had covered a few criminal cases and there was one about two missing girls in Chicago that bothered me for a long time. It wasn't far from where I had grown up and the case was never solved. I wanted to learn more and needed a legitimate reason to explore it. It started as a series of articles but a friend from college told me I should start a podcast. She thought I had enough content and the voice for it. My journalism background helped me craft a good story and provided me with the interview skills needed. That was the second case I covered." She paused for a moment and pursed her lips. "Did Cooper tell you I moved to Little Rock for a relationship that didn't work out?"

That was news to me. "Cooper didn't share much with me."

"I needed something to focus on besides the heartbreak," Cat admitted with her eyes sad. "I needed to connect with people and investigating a case, preparing it for the podcast, and recording each episode gave me purpose. It took my mind off my life and allowed me to do some good with my time. The case I mentioned with the two girls was solved three months after the last episode aired."

My cold heart softened. "I assume the cops had renewed interest in it after you started talking about it."

Cat nodded. "I was able to interview a few people who hadn't spoken to the cops when they went missing. A woman saw the killer take them. She hadn't realized it at the time, but with the other information I uncovered, we put the pieces together and handed all the evidence over to the cops. It was a sad ending, but at least the family had closure."

"I didn't realize you could do that much good with a podcast." To be fair, I didn't listen to any podcasts. I didn't have a feeling about them either way. They just weren't my kind of thing.

Cat assured me there was a lot of interest. "Listeners get involved in a way I didn't realize either. At first, there were only a handful of people listening but it quickly grew. I have a whole fan base on social media. You would not believe how invested they get in each of the cases. Some of them are good amateur sleuths. They are always posting theories and connecting evidence in ways that I don't see." Cat looked down at the box of files. "I thought I was doing something good and having a real impact. Now I'm not so sure."

I hadn't realized that her podcast covered cold cases. "I'm impressed with what you've created in such a short time," I said honestly. I was never one to hold back credit where it was due. "It must have been hard going through a breakup in a city by yourself. I moved down here not knowing anyone either."

Cat nodded but didn't want to say more. "It probably wasn't fair of me to go to Cooper after Luke came to talk to me last night. I was freaked out that he thought I could be involved."

I had the feeling she was baiting me either for reassurance or to tell her what Luke had confided in me about the case. I needed to let her know I wasn't going to be pumped for information. "If you're looking for information, Luke doesn't tell me much during an open investigation. I'm sure he was asking routine questions to rule you out. Cooper and I are happy to help with your files though."

Cat seemed disappointed by my answer. She went back to sifting through the box. "Luke asked me if I had any episodes where I mentioned Son of Sam. I covered a serial killer who was stabbing young female victims in Atlanta. I brought up the Son of Sam cases because the victim type was similar. If you want to start with that one, feel free." She slid a box full of files over to me. "It's everything I have from my research – everyone I spoke to and the notes. There are also audio files of all my interviews. The full interviews are there, not just the parts that made it to the podcast."

I looked down at the box that was so stuffed the lid wouldn't stay on. It sat crooked, perched on the rim. "Have you ever covered the Son of Sam case?" I knew the same question had been asked by Luke and Cooper but the third time could be the charm.

Cat sat back on her hands and stared up at me. "They really don't tell you anything, do they?" She waited for me to respond, but I stayed quiet. Finally, she shook her head. "It's not a case I knew much about. I knew the victim type and remembered the stories about the women with long dark hair. It was the same for Ted Bundy's victims. Honestly, it probably had more to do with the hairstyle at the time than a victim type."

I knew that to be true. I had seen photos of my mom and her siblings in the 1970s and they all had straight long dark hair. It was the style then. "Is that the context you mentioned – the victim type?"

"That was it. It was probably a five minute discussion where I mentioned a few serial killers including David Berkowitz, Ted Bundy, and a handful of others who all had similar victim types. That was my only reference. I can't imagine something as brief as that would be motivation for someone to *finish what he started.*" She stressed the last part and used air quotes about the killer's note.

Cat was right it wasn't enough. It still didn't mean that her podcast hadn't been the inspiration for it. "You said you have a lot of fans on social media who follow you and listen to the podcast. Have you ever had any threatening letters or fans that got a little too intense?"

Cat considered the question and nodded slowly. "There's been a few. Either they don't like the angle I'm taking in an episode or they don't agree with my theory in a cold case. I've had a few, mostly men, email us at the generic email address we provide and write me scathing messages that I'm an idiot, that I don't know what I'm doing, and in some cases, there have been threats of violence."

That didn't surprise me. "Have you turned those threats over to law enforcement?"

"No," she said with regret. "Maybe I should have but I didn't take it seriously. They were emails and nasty direct messages on social media. I've had to police my page for comments. I've kicked people off my page and blocked them. I've never taken the direct threats seriously."

"Did you save them at least?"

Cat pushed herself up from the floor and headed toward a filing cabinet. "A friend told me I should print and save them in case I have any repeat offenders. That way I could keep a record."

"How early on did you have threats?"

Cat turned her back to me and spoke over her shoulder. "Almost immediately. I think it was the second episode of my first case. I had speculated that one of the initial witnesses had changed their story and it was suspicious to me. Someone felt I wasn't being fair to that person. Given I had no law enforcement background, he insisted I was a stupid woman who had no place covering these cases. Why he couldn't just stop listening I don't know. This man's response was to write me and tell me that I deserved to be murdered for my stupidity."

I cursed softly under my breath. Cat had faced far more threats of violence than I had as a private investigator. When I was faced with danger, it was because I put myself in the line of fire. I made an executive decision before Cooper got back. "We should review the threats first and consider them before we spend time going through your podcast notes. I feel like we are far more likely to find a suspect among them than find a needle in the haystack of your research on cases that don't have anything to do with this one."

Cat agreed with me. "I should have thought of it sooner. Cooper mentioned my older podcasts and I thought it might be someone I had interviewed. It makes far more sense that it might be someone who had previously threatened me." She dug through the files until she came upon a thick folder. She tugged it out and held it in her hands for me to see. "I guess there are a lot more than I initially said. It's hard to remember them all."

The stack had to be two hundred pages deep. "Is that all individual threats or are they organized by the person who sent multiple threats?" Going through that many was going to be as time consuming as going through her podcast files.

"It's a mix of both," Cat said with a sigh. "I've had a few repeat offenders. There's one guy who doesn't like the sound of my voice but listens to every episode. He also told me I shouldn't have purple hair or earrings and I should devote myself to my husband and not be a public figure. I never mention much about my personal life. My photo is on the website and social media and we occasionally take photos of the interview sessions. Luke's photo was up on the website the day his episode aired. I don't post photos without permission." Cat shrugged and frowned. "You can't please everyone."

I stood from the chair and closed the distance between us. My opinion of Cat had changed in the short time I spent with her. Cooper was right that she was only trying to earn a living and help a few people along the way. I took the thick file from her. "Let's start with that guy."

"He's local too." When I put the file down on her desk and pulled the first stack of pages out, she added, "I put the local ones on top of the pile. They worried me the most."

"Have any of them ever come here to the studio?"

"Not that I know of. If they had, I might have called the cops then. They hid behind their keyboards." She looked up at me. "That doesn't mean I didn't use my research skills to keep an eye on them."

Cat was as smart as I had hoped and her research would save us precious time. "Let's dig in."

CHAPTER 6

Cooper walked the few blocks to the deli where he got sandwiches and chips and also used his absence as a chance to pick up lunch for Adele. He had texted her on the way to the deli and she told him she was back at her office after a bad morning in court.

He assumed she would be lamenting the outcome of her case for the rest of the day and would skip lunch. At her office, Cooper said hello to her assistant at the front desk and made his way down the hall to her office. He tapped on the half-closed door twice with his foot and then inched it open.

Adele sat at her desk resting her head in her hand. She raised her eyes when he said her name. Seeing all the things in his hands, she jumped up to help him. "What's all this?"

"Some of it's for Cat, Riley, and me, but I brought lunch for you too. I figured you'd forget to eat." He set all the items down on the small round table in the corner of her office then took her in his arms and kissed her. "Do you feel like talking about what happened in court today?"

She kissed him and leaned her body on him. "I made my opening statement and was heading back to the table when the defendant stood up and shouted at the judge that he was guilty."

Cooper had never heard of that happening in any of her cases. "Why did he do that?"

"He had considered taking the plea when it was offered but his mother had talked him out of it. He's looking at serving at least ten years given his prior convictions. The deal wasn't that great and his mother thought he might have a shot at trial. I guess hearing the prosecutor's opening statement compared to mine sent him over the edge." Adele clicked her tongue. "The truth is the evidence against him is compelling. They had a strong case and I didn't know if I could beat it. I had told him that before we got started. I wish he had told me so that I could have negotiated a plea for him at that point. Now, he's confessed in front of a whole courtroom and we are going into the sentencing phase. It all happened before I could stop him. The judge gave me time to confer with him, but he was adamant he was guilty and would take whatever sentence was handed down."

Cooper had no idea what to say. "I'm sorry, babe. It doesn't sound like he was making rational decisions. Do you think he was scared about something coming out in the trial?"

"Maybe. I asked him if anyone threatened him or his family and he said no. I believed him." She rubbed her fingers along her brow. "I should have seen it coming."

Cooper reached over and rubbed her back. "There's no way you could have seen that coming."

Adele didn't seem satisfied with that answer but she didn't get a chance to debate him. Her assistant, Gail, knocked once on her door and informed her there was a letter in the mail she needed to see.

"I didn't open it," Gail said. "It has some strange writing on the front, almost childlike. You know we get those letters from prison sometimes. I figured it best to let you open it in case it's client information. I can bring it in if you'd like."

"I'll come out there," Adele said and dropped a kiss on Cooper's lips. "I appreciate the lunch. Did you get me anything good?"

"Turkey and cheese on rye with two pickles and a bag of chips." He smiled wickedly at her and laughed. "I also got you two of those chocolate chip cookies you love but pretend you don't eat."

Adele laughed for the first time all day. "You know me too well. Let me sort this letter and I'll be right back."

Cooper waited while Adele went to the front. He pulled out his phone and sent a quick text to Riley letting her know he'd be back to the studio soon. He hit send as Adele called for him. She called his name once and then yelled it.

Cooper rushed out of her office and down the hall to find Adele standing with a letter in her shaking hand. She looked up at him with fear in her eyes. "This is from the shooter. He wants Cat to create a podcast about him and he's angry she didn't do that immediately after getting his message. He said if she's not on air in the next twenty-four hours talking about the messages he's sent us and the shooting, he's going to shoot someone else."

Cooper didn't take the letter from her. He peered over her shoulder and read it. This time the letter was typed as compared to the handwritten one Cat had received. It was addressed to Adele Baker and detailed everything she had just told him. That wasn't the whole message though. He wanted Adele to represent him.

"Can he officially retain you like that?" Cooper wasn't sure where attorney-client privilege would come in.

"No. He can't." Adele jabbed her finger on the paper. "What about his demand?"

Cooper didn't see that as an issue. He'd probably shoot someone else even if there was a podcast about him. The threat was meaningless. He explained that to Adele. "We need to call Luke and get this letter to him."

"I probably shouldn't have touched it," Adele said, holding it now between her index finger and thumb. "I got my fingerprints on it."

Cooper went to the back of the office where Adele had a small kitchen. He opened the first cabinet and found coffee supplies and dry food. When Cooper opened the cabinet underneath that one, he found large Ziploc bags. He tugged one out of the box and brought it to Adele. "Put the letter and the envelope in here. Luke said the sniper didn't leave prints behind on the last letter but we should do this right."

Adele slipped the letter in the bag and then picked up the envelope from where she had dropped it on the desktop. "Call him now. I don't want to delay on this." She turned to her assistant. "Did the mailman drop off this letter? It doesn't have any postage on it."

Gail leaned over the desk and peered down at the envelope. "I didn't even notice that. It was in the pile with all the regular mail." She pointed to the stack of mail sitting in the middle of her desk. "I've been sorting through it. Most of it is the usual junk mail. Then I came to that in the middle of the stack. I assumed the mailman put it through the mail slot with everything else."

Adele had a mail slot next to the front door where the mailman dropped the mail. It landed in an inside bin under the opening. It was a system that had worked well until now. Anyone could have walked by and dropped something in.

Adele looked at Cooper. "Are there surveillance cameras pointed at the office? If there are we might have an image of whoever dropped it off."

Cooper wasn't sure where the city had cameras. He knew some of the cameras were old or broken and not working anymore while some were dummies meant to give the appearance they were working as a deterrent. "It's something we can mention to Luke. I'm more concerned this man knows your name and where to find your office."

Adele stroked his arm. "It's okay. I'm findable online and my name has been in the newspaper recently with this case. It's not hard to find my office. If he's looking for a lawyer, he's found one but he can't retain me as he did."

Cooper furrowed his brow. "You'd represent this guy?"

"I've represented people accused of worse crimes." Adele put the makeshift evidence bag down on the desk and sat in a chair in the small waiting area. "He wants to communicate. Even if he retained me, I can't become an accomplice to active criminal activity. I won't obstruct justice for him. He's come to me though, so maybe I can open a communication channel with him."

"No," Cooper said his voice tight. "I don't want you involved in this."

Adele looked up at him. "This is my job, Cooper. This is what I do, and if I can help the accused and the police resolve this situation, then I will." She stood and straightened her skirt. "Call Luke for me or I can do it myself." Without saying another word, she headed down the hall back to her office.

Cooper looked over at Gail. "I guess I didn't handle that well." She offered him words of encouragement before he headed down the hall after Adele. He stopped outside of her door and called Luke but had to leave a detailed message. He knocked once on Adele's door and stuck his head in. "Is it safe for me to enter?"

Adele looked up at him from behind her laptop. "Are you going to continue to tell me how to do my job?"

Cooper put his hands up in front of him as a sign of a truce. "I didn't mean to do that in the first place. I was caught off guard that you'd be willing to defend this guy."

Adele nudged the laptop to the side and turned to face him. "Cooper, since long before I met you, I have taken on homicide and rape cases. I've taken on the worst of the worst offenders because I firmly believe people have a right to a fair trial. Does that mean I defend guilty people? Yes, all the time. But for every fifty I defend who are guilty, there's one who is innocent. They are being accused of something they didn't do and don't have anyone to help them. I remember a time not that long ago when you were suspected of doing something terrible."

Cooper didn't want to think of the morning he woke to find a dead woman in his bed. It was right at the start of his relationship with Adele and he had thought nearly the end of it. "I don't have a problem with your work. I'm only worried about your safety."

"I know," she said softly. "I'm more worried about yours. If he thinks I'm willing to help him, he's not going to shoot me."

"Until you can't help him anymore."

Adele didn't respond to that but her expression told Cooper she knew the reality of the situation. "It all may be a moot point. He hasn't officially retained me. He hasn't paid my very expensive retainer fee."

Cooper felt some relief about that. "I called Luke but he didn't respond yet."

"He's with one of the victim's parents," Tyler said from the doorway. "I didn't mean to interrupt. Luke forwarded your message to me and I was right near your office. I figured I'd just stop in."

"Come on in, Captain Tyler," Adele said with a beaming smile. "How's the new job going?"

"You don't have to call me captain," he said as his cheeks reddened. "I told Luke the same thing this morning. It feels weird from you all." He hitched his chin toward her desk. "The letter here?"

Adele stood from behind her desk. "It's in the front. My fingerprints are all over it and my assistant's prints are on the envelope. We touched it before we knew what it was."

"We can compare the prints and rule you both out, so that's not a problem. I can't believe he sent another so quickly."

Adele joined him at the door. "He said he wanted to retain me but didn't pay me and didn't provide me a name. I can't represent a ghost. His directive in the letter is clear though. You're going to need to address that quickly."

Cooper followed them down the hall to the front and waited while Tyler put on gloves and pulled the letter out of the bag. His expression changed to horror as he read the sniper's demands. He read it over again, saying he couldn't believe what he was asking. He slipped the letter back into the makeshift evidence bag and grabbed a Sharpie off Gail's desk. He made some notes on the bag.

Cooper didn't want to waste time. "Cat told me you suspect her. I'm sure this request brings up even more questions."

Tyler gave a curt nod of his head. "Luke had some concerns after speaking to her but *suspect* is a strong word. She assured Luke she had no intention of podcasting the case. He felt better after that but questions remained."

Adele asked, "Does this request make you suspicious of her?"

Tyler wouldn't commit one way or the other. "It doesn't help. You don't find it odd that this guy wants her to promote his crimes?"

Cooper shook his head. "Half the reason these guys contact the media is because they want notoriety for what they are doing. Podcasts are the new media. Before it was print letters from the killer in the newspaper. They can go on social media anonymously but know that law enforcement can trace that. I don't know how he wants Cat to tell his story if he's not going to come forward, but I don't think it's an odd request."

Tyler locked his gaze on him. "You aren't suspicious of her?"

"Not at all. I've spoken to her several times. I even suggested we go through her past cases to see if it might be someone she knows. She's over at her studio with Riley getting her files together for us."

"Let's go talk to them," Tyler said and turned toward the door.

"Do you want me to come with you?" Adele asked, uncertain. She looked at Cooper but he didn't know either.

Tyler turned back to her. "You're a part of this investigation now.

The sniper seems to have chosen you to communicate for them. I want your input."

"That's decided then," Cooper said not sure it was such a good idea. He couldn't argue with all of them. He followed Adele back to her office and gathered all the lunch items including her uneaten lunch. Together, the three of them walked the two blocks to Cat's studio.

CHAPTER 7

"Todd Hall," I said as I read over Cat's file of harassers. We had moved from Cat's small office to the conference room in the front of the building. The window provided some natural light and we had more space to spread out.

I had been reading through Hall's file for more than an hour. I hadn't been able to move on from him to the others who had been harassing Cat because there was so much information. There was social media information and public record search data as well as all of his communication with Cat.

Hall was forty-two and divorced. He had lost custody of his children due to domestic violence. He had never been arrested because his ex-wife decided twice not to press charges. I assumed she was afraid of him and didn't want more of a hassle. The judge had been less forgiving after hearing from witnesses including their family, neighbors, and friends. The divorce had been granted and the judge awarded sole custody to Hall's ex-wife. He chose not to attend supervised visitation and had never paid child support. His ex had a good job and didn't bother going after him for it. A year ago, she had taken the children and moved out of state with the court's permission.

Hall remained in Little Rock working odd jobs here and there. It looked to me like he spent most of his time harassing people online. He focused a lot of that attention on Cat. By the looks of the messages she had printed off from online chat groups, he was more than a little obsessed with her. His rhetoric was misogynistic and violent. I was surprised Cat wasn't more afraid of the man.

Hall had a gun permit and several weapons. He had been in the Army when he was younger and received a dishonorable discharge. His social media was full of photos of him with guns. They seemed to be the only photos and videos he took of himself. I didn't know enough about weapons to know if any of the photos included the type of gun used in the shooting.

I had raised my head to ask her a question when I heard the knock on the door. "I think someone is out front," I said, standing. I followed Cat out of the conference room and into the small foyer to the front door. Cat unlocked the main front door and we found Tyler, Cooper, and Adele with grim serious expressions on their faces.

"Has there been another shooting?" I asked and then my heart thumped in my chest. "Is Luke okay?"

"He's fine, Riley," Tyler said quickly, realizing what it might have looked like to me. "He's interviewing the victim's family. I went to Adele's office and picked up the sniper's most recent letter."

"He left another one?" Cat asked, stepping aside to let them in then closing and locking the door behind them. We filed into the conference room and Cat locked the inner office door too.

I gestured to the files on the table. "Cat's been telling me about the men who harassed her online. I figured since she had active threats against her, the best plan was to look at those first. There's one local guy who is a real piece of work."

"Any potential?" Cooper asked.

"I could see him being a suspect. I spent an hour on his file and didn't get a chance to look at the others. Cat was able to do a bit of research on him. It's certainly saved time, but she should have called the police about it."

"Hindsight," she said as she pulled in a few chairs from her office. When Tyler looked at her with a question on his face, she explained all the threats she had been receiving since starting the podcast. "I know I could or should have made a report. It seemed like such a waste of time. People get angry all the time."

"They don't send ongoing threatening emails, social media posts, and letters to a podcast host, threatening to kill her," I said with my tone firm. I wanted to stress the point in front of Tyler. I pointed to the stack of files at the end of the table. "Those are repeat offenders and not one-offs. Cat didn't keep track of those."

Tyler's eyes grew wide as he looked at the overflowing file folders. "I didn't know you had threats against you."

Cat looked at him in earnest. "It's all part of the business. Something as serious as this shooting has never happened before. It's been a wake-up call, to say the least. You're welcome to look through them anytime you like, Captain Tyler." He glanced back at the pile and then to Cat. She realized rightly she wasn't the reason they were there. They had said there'd been another letter. "How can I help you?" she asked as we all sat.

Tyler slid the bagged letter across the table to Cat. I peered over her shoulder and we both read it. I couldn't believe what I was seeing. "How can she possibly create a podcast about the shooting? Cat doesn't know anything about the sniper."

My concerns weren't shared by Cat. She seemed to understand better than the rest of us. "It sounds to me like he wants me to figure out who he is through the podcast. That's why he sent me the initial letter. That was my first clue. He says here that if I don't produce the first episode in twenty-four hours there will be another shooting. There's going to be another shooting either way."

Cooper agreed with her. "That's exactly what I said."

"He will continue no matter what we do." Cat studied the letter then raised her eyes to Adele. "Either he knows I'm connected to you or he wants to involve you as well. Do you have any past clients who you suspect?"

Adele shook her head. "I've been in the news because of a recent case. I assume that's how he heard of me. He could have walked by my office on the way to your studio. He dropped this letter off sometime today. It was mixed in with today's mail but doesn't have a postmark. He didn't mail it. It was hand delivered like your letter."

Cat took a deep breath, seemingly overwhelmed as anyone would be. "What do you want me to do? I told Luke I wasn't going to create a podcast about this and I meant it. This isn't what I do. I cover cold cases and summarize cases where the killer has already been caught. This is an active investigation. Anyone I interview will be a potential witness in your case while it's happening."

Even if Cat wanted to do it, I didn't know if it was logistically possible. "Could you get a podcast episode out within twenty-four hours?"

"My assistant is on vacation. I wasn't going to be recording anything until she got back. I'd need some help in the studio." Cat looked around the table at us. We were all still wondering if she could pull it off in time. She finally relented. "I have no idea what I'd say but it can be done. If I do one episode, he's going to want more. He will keep shooting people."

"It sounds like he's going to keep shooting people regardless of what you do." I wanted Luke's opinion. I trusted Tyler but I wanted to know what my husband thought of all this. I trusted his opinion more than anyone. He had been taunted by killers before and would know what to do.

Tyler read the expression on my face. "Riley, it looks like you've got something on your mind. Care to share it?"

It had been a long time since Tyler asked me that question. He humored Luke when we got involved in their investigations. "I was only thinking about Luke and what he would think. I know you're his boss now, but it's technically his investigation. I don't think we should make decisions without him. I'm inclined to agree with you though – Cat should create the podcast. Adele should keep lines of communication open with him. If we can open a communication channel, we might be able to mitigate some deaths."

"It could encourage him to kill more for notoriety," Cooper countered and he wasn't wrong.

"I don't think there's an easy answer on this one." I looked over at Adele whose opinion I trusted. She had sound logical reasoning in most cases. "What do you think? Are you willing to keep a communication channel open with him?"

"I told Cooper I would already. I believe I'd be more help from the inside. Maybe I can reason with him."

"There's no reasoning with a sniper," Cooper snapped back at her, his eyes leveling a look I hadn't seen before. I wondered if there was trouble in paradise.

If I believed in the evil eye, I was certain Adele was giving it to Cooper right now. She wasn't going to back down. "I reason with criminals all the time. This one seems like he's more rational and intelligent than the rest. His writing is that of someone in the middle of a breakdown. It's better than nothing."

Before a war broke out, Tyler told everyone to settle down. "Riley's right in that this is all a moot point until we can get Luke involved." He pulled out his phone and called him. He spoke in short quick sentences and asked him to meet them all at Cat's studio. When he ended the call, he said, "Luke is on his way."

While we waited, I wanted to check in with Cooper who wasn't even looking at Adele but the anger between them permeated the table. "Cooper, I want to show you the case file on Todd Hall in Cat's office."

I grabbed the file off the stack and headed for the door before he could tell me to stop. I had a feeling Tyler and Cat knew I was trying to lower the temperature in the room. Neither of them said anything to me about what I was doing. I walked to Cat's office and stepped inside.

A moment later, Cooper stood in the doorway. "I know you don't want to talk about the file. Why did you pull me away?"

I leaned against Cat's desk. "You need a break. What are you doing snapping at Adele like that? She's a criminal defense attorney and she's doing her job."

Cooper relaxed his shoulders and stepped inside the office. He closed the door behind him and took a seat in one of the chairs. "I don't know. This case has me freaked out and I'm worried about her getting involved. I snapped at her at her office too." He rubbed his fingers along his brow.

I didn't think I'd ever seen Cooper this rattled. "Is it possible that because you got hurt on a couple of cases you're being overly cautious about Adele's safety? Luke did this to me and it caused a lot of arguments between us. In the end, you're the one who talked to him and reminded him this was my job and I'm good at it. He could either accept it or we needed to break up. Do you remember that?"

Cooper nodded his head and lowered his eyes. "I guess if the advice is good enough for Luke, it's good enough for me." He raised his head and locked his gaze on me. "When I gave that advice, I didn't account for how much Luke loved you and worried about you. Being on the other side of it, I'm not sure I'd have given the same advice."

I couldn't help but laugh. "You'd have given the same advice. You're still healing from a few cases. You're being sensitive and owe Adele an apology. Arguing about this is only going to make her dig in her heels more. I know this because she's a lot like me."

"She's a better cook."

I put my hand to my heart like I'd been shot. "That's a low blow considering how many nights I cooked you dinner when you were single."

Cooper cracked a sly smile and pointed to the file. "What about Todd Hall? Do you think he could be a suspect?"

I put the file on Cat's desk and went through the details I knew about the man. "I don't know if he has the temperament to be a sniper. He certainly has the hair-trigger anger. I believe this killer is a lot more measured. Most of Hall's violence is off the cuff and he seems to have a hard time controlling his temper. I don't think we can rule him out. When I first saw all of this, I thought he might be at the top of the suspect list. Sending that note to Adele though was measured. I don't know if Hall could pull that off. We can go find him. He's local."

Cooper raised his eyebrows. "How close?"

"Just over the river in North Little Rock. He lives in an apartment in Argenta." Luke's voice echoed through the building as he spoke to Cat. I tabled the discussion for now and wanted to get out there and see him.

Before I left the room, Cooper had a question. "Tell me the truth. Do you think it's a good idea for Adele to talk to this creep and for Cat to do the podcast?"

I took a breath and bought myself some time. I knew lives where hanging in the balance no matter what I said. "I do," I said finally. "If there's a chance to get this guy talking, we need to take it. I don't like meeting his demands about the podcast but he might slip up if he gets cocky enough."

Cooper seemed satisfied with that answer and followed me back to the conference room.

CHAPTER 8

L uke's head was bent low over the letter. He had put on gloves and taken the letter from the bag to study it more carefully. I waited by the door and watched my husband. He was such a good man, a great detective, and sometimes I didn't always appreciate him as much as I should.

When he was done with his assessment of it, he glanced over at Adele and asked questions about the mail and how accessible the mail slot was to the outside world. She explained that anyone could have dropped it. She asked him about cameras, but Luke said there wasn't an active one in the area.

Luke's tone was measured and confident. "I know you're all waiting for me to agree or not with his demands. I'd like to know what all of you think. First, I'd like to know, Cat, if you're even willing to engage with him. Last night you said you wanted no part of a podcast about this shooting."

"I still don't." Cat wrapped her arms around herself. She retreated into herself and her eyes glazed over the way they did when she was thinking something through. I had noticed that about her earlier. After an uncomfortable amount of silence, she looked directly at Luke. "I don't want to do this podcast, but if you think it will help your case, I'll do it. I'll need some help though. I've never done a podcast during an active and open investigation. I want to make sure I'm saying the right things and not impacting your case. I'll also need some technical help as well to record."

"I can help with that," Cooper volunteered.

"Does that mean you agree Cat should do the podcast?" Luke asked him.

"Our consensus was that no matter what threats he's making, he's going to shoot someone else. That's his intent. Creating a podcast about one shooting isn't going to prevent him from shooting someone again. No matter what Cat does, he's going to continue. Adele made a good point that at least now communication channels are open. I'm not fully on board with it, but I don't disagree either."

Luke looked to Adele next. "I know he can't retain you like this. Are you willing to communicate if he reaches out again?"

Adele gave a brief nod of her head. She didn't say more though.

He looked at me next and gave me the look that told me to give it to him straight. I told him exactly what I told the rest of them. "It's a gamble either way, Luke. He wants to communicate even if it is a game. Let's hope he slips up along the way." I caught the look on his face and asked, "Have you found something?"

"I'll get to that in a moment." Luke looked over at Tyler. "What do you say, boss? I know you'll leave the ultimate decision up to me, but you're the one who is going to have to answer for it."

"I'm in," Tyler said, not hesitating. "For all the reasons Riley said. Plus, the more he talks, even through letters, the more we learn about him. I agree with Cooper that we'd be giving him fame he doesn't deserve. The truth is he's going to keep killing until we stop him. If Cat's willing, then I'm fine with it." He made eye contact with Cat. "We can offer you police protection if you'd feel safer."

"I'll think about it."

All eyes turned to Luke then. We had all voiced our agreement that the podcast should move forward. It was Luke's call now. I knew a lot was riding on his strong shoulders – almost more than any one man should have to carry.

"I agree with all of you. I don't like it and we'll need to set some parameters for the podcast. I don't want to see the victims exploited and I don't want to hype up any more fear than people have already. If this man has a story he wants to tell, then let's tell it and hope we catch him in the process."

It was the calm and measured response I had been expecting from him. I wanted to know his other news. "You said you had something else."

Luke looked over at Tyler with a question. "Can I proceed or do you want me to wait until we are back at the station?"

Tyler gestured toward us. "They are all involved at this point. I'll leave it to your discretion what you share."

"Raymond Bollin served in the Army as a sniper in Iraq and Afghanistan. He was a decorated soldier until his last tour when he suddenly started acting strangely. He became erratic, unreliable, and violent towards his fellow soldiers. He received a medical discharge and went back home to St. Louis where he proceeded to get arrested twice on battery charges. He served a short six-month stint in jail and then moved here to Little Rock where he was immediately in trouble again. This time he beat up a guy in the River Market. There was no apparent motive. Gemma Cullen's father represented him at his last court case. He told me Ray was obsessed with serial killers including the Son of Sam and Zodiac. He even commented that he liked the way those killers taunted the police and that Zodiac was the better of the two because he was never caught."

"Is he still local, Luke?" Tyler asked.

"He got out of prison three weeks before the shooting. He spent more than a year inside this time and that would have given him plenty of time to plot and plan."

I wasn't sure if Luke was saying this was a targeted murder on Gemma. "Do you believe he went after Gemma on purpose?"

"I can't say that. Grady said he wrapped the case with Ray on good terms and got him the best deal possible." Luke sighed loudly. "It's unlikely to be a coincidence though. Hard to say right now until I learn more about him. Grady thought Ray could have done something like this, but I need to know more."

People didn't suddenly become erratic though, especially not a decorated soldier. "Could he be suffering some post-traumatic stress or some other mental break, Luke? Do we know anything about his mental state? Someone somewhere must have done an evaluation."

"All information I still need to gather," he said evenly.

"I have someone too." I slid the file down the conference table and gave everyone the overview. "He's been targeting Cat for a while now. She did a great job of researching his background. I'm worried he might be too hair-trigger to be the killer though. He might not have the temperament, but he's targeted Cat before. Given the first note and the shooting steps from her doorway, I thought we might at least give him a once-over. If you don't want to focus on him, Cooper and I can go see him. We don't want to make more work for you."

Luke glanced down at the file and flipped through a few pages. His face distorted in anger as he read the threats. When he looked back up at Cat, he wasn't happy. "Is there a reason you didn't call us about these threats? They are specific and credible. You have enough here for us to arrest him for harassment."

Cat sank back in her chair, a worried expression coming over her face. "I didn't realize that. It was a nuisance to me. I figured calling the police might make him worse. I saved his messages and then started to do some background research on him. He's never approached me. I figured it would have to escalate before you'd do anything." She closed her eyes for a few seconds and then opened them. "I should have called you though. I'd feel terrible if there had been a chance for me to stop him and I missed it."

"You couldn't have known, Cat," I said. I didn't want her to feel badly that she might have been able to prevent the shooting. "I don't want to speak for Luke, but I think all he's saying is that the police could have helped you and you didn't have to live with these threats hanging over your head. There were resources if you wanted them."

I shifted my eyes to Luke and hoped he caught what I was trying to do. If we wanted Cat on our side, we couldn't alienate her already. She was the key to this killer communicating. Luke understood and echoed what I said.

He changed the subject and focused back on the podcast. "Time is ticking. What do you need from us to produce the first episode of the podcast?"

Cat's eyelids fluttered as she considered. "I've never produced and recorded a podcast in this short of a time. Does he specify anything in the letter about what he wants me to say?"

Luke shook his head. "I suspect he wants you to say you received his letter and give some information about the shooting from what you know. I'll give you a brief interview but not release anything more than we told the public at the news conference. I want to review your script before you record and make sure that you're not releasing anything you shouldn't. The name I mentioned is not to be made public. You shouldn't say anything about the man harassing you either. Anything related to suspects is off the table right now. Other than making sure you let your listeners know you've been directed to make the podcast."

"Can Cat ask him to communicate directly? I think if we are going to do this, maybe part of it should be directed right at him. It might also be a good idea for Cat to be sympathetic towards him and for Adele to say she's on board with opening communication with him. If they appear to be on his side rather than adversarial, he might open up more."

"I like that," Tyler said, agreeing with me.

We spent a few minutes crafting some content that Cat could use. Luke said he'd call Grady to see if he'd be willing to be interviewed to talk about Gemma. Teresa would be off-limits. Her name wasn't being released to the public at her parents' request. He was going to honor that for as long as possible. Cat didn't have a problem not using Teresa's name.

After they were done and Cat felt like she had enough direction, Luke and Tyler went back to the station. Cooper promised me he'd return soon. Adele had to get back to her office but would come back later to record her statement for the podcast. I walked Cooper out and reminded him to make it better with Adele. The last thing any of us needed was this kind of tension hanging over our heads.

When they were gone, I walked back into the conference room but Cat wasn't there. I went to her office and found her tapping the eraser end of a pencil against her desk and staring at a blank pad of paper. She either didn't hear me come in or was too lost in thought to break her concentration.

I waited a beat to see if she'd raise her head and when she didn't, I knocked once on the door. "I don't want to bother you but I thought you could use some help."

Cat pinched the bridge of her nose. "Even though we had that conversation with Luke and Captain Tyler, I'm not sure how to plan this podcast. They told me the points they wanted me to get in and what to avoid. I'm not sure about the rest of it though – the storytelling that keeps my listeners engaged. I have to record and edit it tonight for it to be on the air in the morning."

She finally raised her head to look at me. "I forgot to mention I need to run this by Justice Exposed and have them approve it. The content isn't all up to me anymore. I still have editorial rights and choose the cases I cover, but I need to run it by them. This is a bit different than the normal content I run."

"Do you think they will have a problem with it?"

"I can't imagine they will. It will get me some serious ratings, which is all they care about. More ratings means more money for them." Cat sat back and sighed. "I wonder if any of the advertisers will have an issue with it. I guess with Luke's interview, they will know the cops approved it. I'm sure some of my listeners will think I'm exploiting the situation."

I sat down in the chair. "Is that what it feels like to you?"

Cat seemed to stare past me as she spoke. "I'm not sure. I never meant to be in the middle of something like this. It's why I've never taken an active and open investigation. All the cases I focus on are cold cases the cops don't seem to care about anymore or they are all out of leads. Either that or the offenders have been caught and prosecuted. It feels weird to be in the thick of it. As a result, I'm stuck on how to start."

"Start with the letter," I suggested. Cat didn't seem convinced. "It's the beginning and the reason you're involved. Let your listeners know you didn't see the letter in time and how you ended up at our house. You have a great relationship with your listeners. They will care that you're involved."

"That's the thing, Riley. I've never been *involved* in any other case. I've always been the outsider looking in."

I could see the struggle on her face. She was scared and hesitant. "You have to do what you do best, Cat. Step outside of yourself and interview yourself. If someone else had received that letter, what would you ask them? Start there."

We spent the next hour planning the podcast. When we were done, it was a compelling narrative. Luke called before I left to tell Cat that Grady was willing to be interviewed and that he'd stop by the studio at the end of the day. Even though we had only a little time, it was shaping up to be one of the most compelling podcasts Cat had ever planned.

CHAPTER 9

At the end of the day, Tyler called Luke into the conference room. Captain Meadows had shown up at midday and the two of them had spent the rest of the afternoon in the office with the door closed.

Luke carried the case files into the conference room and closed the door. He hadn't had much of a chance to speak to Tyler after the meeting with Cat because when they arrived back at the station Captain Meadows was already there waiting for him. Luke hoped Tyler wasn't having second thoughts about the podcast. He sat down at the table. "Do you want an update about the case?"

"We want to discuss the podcast," Captain Meadows said.

Luke's stomach lurched and he shifted in his seat. "Do we need to call it off?"

Thankfully, Captain Meadows said no. "We want to discuss your thoughts on Cat."

Before Luke could say anything, Tyler added, "This is exactly what I had been concerned about. You spoke to her last night and cautioned her not to do a podcast about the case. Today, a note is sent to Adele supposedly from the sniper threatening to kill someone if she doesn't do a podcast. Don't you find that suspicious?"

Luke wasn't sure if Tyler had an issue with it now or was covering himself in front of Captain Meadows. He aimed for the most diplomatic response possible. "Cat didn't seem convinced she wanted to do the podcast. If anything, I felt like the rest of us talked her into it. I don't have any reason to suspect her of being involved. She has no connection to the victims, has never covered anything related to the Son of Sam murders, has no weapons registered to her and expressed no interest in doing anything other than helping us. Riley and Cooper trust her and neither of them trusts easily. She's been more than willing to work with us. Given her involvement now, we can more easily keep an eye on her."

"Sounds rational to me," Captain Meadows said and looked over at Tyler. "You made a good decision."

Luke shifted his eyes between them. "Was this a test?" he said with a nervous laugh.

It was Captain Meadows who responded. "Tyler gave me the overview of what was going on. I wasn't sure the podcast was such a good idea. Once we start negotiating with the sniper, who knows what he's going to request. I was suspicious of Cat, but Tyler assured me she was on the up and up. I wanted to make sure you were on board with this. I told Tyler to address it with you. I wanted to see how he'd do it given you were partners for so long."

"It was a test then." Luke relaxed back in the chair not sure how he was feeling about it.

"It was my test and you both passed," Captain Meadows said evenly and without regret. "I'm leaving you all in good hands. Now, tell me, Luke, do you trust Cat?"

That was an easy question. "I trust her as much as I can for someone I barely know. Do I think she's involved with the sniper? No. She's not doing this for fame. She got defensive last night with me and I was suspicious earlier in the day, but she looked positively freaked out by the note to Adele. I believe she thought her involvement with this case was over."

"What about the person of interest mentioned by the victim's family?" Tyler asked with eyebrows raised.

Luke needed his file for the most current notes. He pulled it off the table and rested it in his lap, flipping over the first page. "Raymond Bollin works construction here in Little Rock. I went by his apartment in West Little Rock but no one was there. I spoke to a neighbor who said Ray was quiet and kept to himself. I spoke to the office manager of the apartment complex and she said she knew Ray had been to prison but he had been a model tenant since getting released. He maintained a full-time job, was seeking help at the veteran's hospital for his mental health issues, and hadn't caused any trouble. His previous issues could have been related to post-traumatic stress as Riley mentioned. Given his connection to the victim's father, I'm going to bring him in for questioning. I don't want to call and tip him off though. I'll stop by there again this evening."

"You okay going alone?" Tyler asked.

Luke had considered this and had gone around and around whether it was a safe move to go it alone. "I don't want a full SWAT team going with me to ask him a few questions. I want to make this as casual as possible and build a little rapport with him. If I suspect it's him, I'll get out of there. If this guy did have post-traumatic stress, I don't want a full SWAT to trigger anything. It sounds to me like he's back on track."

Captain Meadows agreed with that assessment but they weren't done that easily. "We have a new partner for you. He is still working on some other cases and he needs to wrap those up first before we reassign him to you. He's been working without a partner for some time. He's a good detective, Luke."

Given he was the head of the homicide unit, he knew all the detectives in it. There was only one without a partner currently. "Det. Tyson Granger?"

"What do you think about that?" Tyler asked with hope in his eyes.

Luke didn't necessarily want a new partner, but if he had to have one, Granger would be a good choice. He had solved many homicides in the city, worked well with others, and would give Luke the space he needed to get things done. "I think we'd be a good fit."

Tyler looked relieved. "He'll take direction from you well and he has a solid closure rate. I was hoping it would be a good fit for you both. He hasn't had a partner since his transfer into the department but he's open to one. We wanted to run this by you first though, Luke."

Luke could see they were trying to do that. They didn't need to try so hard. He was used to change and didn't have as much of a problem with it as people might have suspected. He could roll with the punches. "Do you need to tell him officially or can I go mention it to him? I noticed he was still at his desk."

Captain Meadows gestured toward the door. "Feel free to tell him. The sooner the two of you can get acquainted the better. You only live a few blocks from each other in the Heights too."

"Is there anything else?" Luke asked as he gathered up his files. It had been less of a case conference than he'd expected. When he saw the looks of concern on their faces, he knew he wasn't done. "I know this case is going to cause you both a nightmare. It's the last one for you, Captain Meadows, and Tyler's first. You're going to get it on all sides from the community and city council to the mayor. There's not much more I can be doing. I hate to say it but it's going to get worse before it gets better."

Captain Meadows agreed. "The podcast isn't going to make it any better. Do you think we should get ahead of its publication and mention it to the media so they know we are on top of it?"

Luke didn't think that was a good idea. "The sniper mentioned the podcast. I'm sure he is aware law enforcement will be interviewed. I can make a statement on the podcast that will cover anything said to the media. After the fact, I think we hold a press conference. I want the podcast to lead the story. Grady Cullen has also agreed to be interviewed." Luke checked the time on his phone. "He should be over at her studio right now."

Tyler seemed surprised the victim's father was on board. "He didn't feel like the podcast would exploit the situation?"

"No. I explained to him about the letters and that we were giving in to the sniper's demands in a controlled and strategic way. He agreed with me that no matter what we do, there will be another shooting. Better to engage with the sniper in the hopes he slips up."

They talked for a few more minutes about the case then Luke was free to go. He left feeling better about the meeting and about having a partner. He found Granger sitting at his desk hunched over a case file. Luke didn't consider himself a small guy at six-foot but Granger was taller than him and had spent considerably more time in the gym lifting weights. The man's biceps and chest eclipsed Luke's by a long stretch. Granger was a wall of a man but surprisingly quick on his feet. His intellect and instinct rivaled any other detective on the force.

"Granger," Luke said as he approached the man's desk.

He stopped what he was doing and gave Luke his full attention. "How's that case going? It's a terrible thing that happened to that young girl."

While Luke hadn't planned on giving him a rundown of the case, Granger had opened the door. Luke figured if they were going to be partners, he should start confiding in him. He went over all the details to date. When he got to the end, Luke stressed, "I'm sure many will disagree but we are going forward with the podcast. Either way, this guy is going to shoot someone again. There's no right answer and the victim's father is on board."

Granger didn't even flinch at the news and didn't second guess the decision. "You have to get creative sometimes if you want to solve the case."

"I like that attitude," Luke said and glanced back at Tyler's new office. He focused back on Granger. "As you know, Tyler was promoted. He's been my partner for more than a decade. He and Captain Meadows suggested we partner up. What do you say?"

Granger relaxed back in his chair. "Are you sure you don't want someone with more seniority? Many detectives were hoping to be chosen as your next partner. I'm not sure the others are going to be so happy you picked me."

Luke hadn't realized anyone cared who he chose. He was sure some of them wanted to become his partner, in the hopes of taking over Luke's role as the head of the homicide unit should he ever leave. He was happy with the choice and reassured Granger. "There may be detectives with more seniority in the department but you transferred in. Your record is stellar and you've been closing cases faster than some of our longest-running detectives. You're already taking homicide cases and I don't have time to train someone else from another unit." Luke gestured toward the conference room. "Let's talk privately before I head out."

Granger closed the file and got up from the desk. He followed Luke into the conference room and closed the door. "Is there a problem?"

"Not at all," Luke said, sitting. He gestured for Granger to do the same. "I wanted some privacy to say what I need to say. I'm in kind of a unique situation. My wife, Riley, and my best friend, Cooper, are private investigators."

"I've met them. They are good people and good investigators."

Luke thanked him for that. "Sometimes they like to get involved in my cases no matter how much I try to keep them out. The truth is they often help get the cases solved faster. Cooper was a detective before deciding the paperwork and rules were too much for him. He didn't like the politics of it all and went private. Riley was an investigative journalist. They know what they are doing. Tyler tolerated it, but I'm concerned another detective wouldn't. I've heard some rumors you might be in a similar situation. I never addressed it with you because it didn't seem to be a problem and I'd be a hypocrite if I did."

"I wondered why you had never said anything." Granger took a breath and didn't seem to know what to say. Luke encouraged him to speak freely. "My sister-in-law, Harper, and her aunt, Hattie, have a bad habit of finding dead bodies. They have some interesting skills that have helped me with investigations. They can get me information that's not available to me otherwise." Granger ran a hand over his bald head and closed an eye as he screwed up his face. "Let's just call it otherworldly insight."

Luke had heard that about Hattie. She had a psychic shop in the Heights. Cooper had developed a relationship with her after she was robbed in a previous case. Luke didn't believe in all of that but he couldn't dismiss it outright. He hadn't mentioned it to Tyler or Captain Meadows, but Granger was the perfect partner for him for this reason above all the others.

"Then you understand how complicated it can get sometimes." Luke and Granger shared a look and words went unspoken between them. Neither one of them wanted to give up their sources – no matter how unorthodox they were. "What do you say then? Partners?" Luke extended his hand and Granger accepted it.

"What's the process? I still have a few pending cases that I'm wrapping up."

"Finish those off and join me when you're done. Tyler said you don't have to join me on this current case if you're busy with whatever else you have."

Granger said he understood but added, "If I can help you with this one, let me know. I do have a bit to wrap up but I'm certainly willing to pitch in. This shooting has everyone rattled."

"I hate to say it but there's going to be more. Tell your family to keep a low profile and watch where they go. It's anyone's guess what's going to happen next." Luke hated saying that but it was true. There was no telling what this killer had in mind.

Granger folded his thick arms over his chest. "I'll pass on the message. You think it's going to get bad?"

Luke sighed loudly. "I don't want to speculate. What he's threatening is beyond anything this city has ever seen, even with all of our gang violence issues. That at least is understandable. This guy's true motive is anyone's guess."

Luke could only hope that was true and his real motive wasn't the notoriety they were able to give him.

CHAPTER 10

I paced around the living room far too keyed up to sleep. After everyone else was done being interviewed, Luke came by Cat's studio and was interviewed for the podcast. After that, Luke said he was going to interview Raymond Bollin at his apartment. He wanted to catch him late in the evening when he was home from work and his defenses were down. That was more than an hour ago and Cat was going to drop the podcast at midnight.

She'd be well under the sniper's deadline and she hoped that by dropping it so late at night, fewer people would hear it. Her contact at Justice Exposed had been excited by the idea of doing a podcast about an open and ongoing case, given they had the police approval to do so. She did not share her reasoning for the timing of the podcast. They didn't question her about it either.

I stayed for the interviews with Adele and Grady Cullen while Cooper helped her with the recording. Adele's interview sent a powerful message. Grady seemed nervous but proud to speak about his daughter. He remained tense throughout the interview and kept his eyes focused on Cat as if he wasn't sure where else to look.

When they were done, Cat asked several times if he was on board with the podcast. The last thing she wanted to do was exploit a victim's family. He had assured her that if it would help to solve the case, he was on board with it. When he was getting ready to leave the studio, he asked Cat if he could speak to her privately. While she didn't look comfortable with it, they left for her office. They were gone about ten minutes when Cat came back and walked him to the door. She didn't tell me or Cooper what they had discussed and we didn't ask. By then though, her posture had stiffened and worry lines creased around her eyes. We had no idea what had happened in the exchange.

By the time Luke and I left the studio after his interview, Cooper and Cat were hard at work editing to create a smooth start-to-finish listening experience. Cooper had texted me a few minutes ago to say that the podcast was ready and she'd have it live by midnight.

At a quarter to midnight, I heard Luke's car in the driveway. I left through the front door and met him at the car, anxious to hear about the interview. "Did everything go okay?"

"He wasn't around," Luke said as he got out of the car and hit the button to lock it. He leaned against it and stared up at the sky. "I waited a couple of hours and spoke to two more neighbors who didn't have anything bad to say about the guy. He never came home though."

"Maybe he has a girlfriend and spent the night with her," I suggested and leaned up to kiss him. "I have some dinner I can heat up for you if you're hungry."

Luke thanked me but declined. "I grabbed something earlier. I probably should have waited because it's sitting like a rock in my stomach. Did Cat get the podcast finished?"

I told Luke how the whole evening went because we didn't get much of a chance to talk when he had given his interview. "Cat's great at what she does. Grady was able to share many stories about Gemma. He also made sure to leave Teresa's name out of it. He did say that the other young woman was wonderful, smart, and talented and he wished her a speedy recovery. To be honest with you, the podcast focused more on the victims than it did the sniper."

He either sensed my tone or caught a worried expression on my face. "You think the sniper's going to react to that?"

"He wanted Cat to do a podcast about him. I don't know how he'll react knowing the podcast is mainly focused on the victims and the law enforcement response. It's not like he gave Cat much to go on though." I had wondered for most of the evening if the sniper was going to send more information for the podcast. Nothing ever came and Cat had no way of interviewing him.

"She shared details about the letters and the shooting right near her?"

"She stuck to the plan. I didn't wait around to hear the final product because it was late and they didn't need my help. Cooper was able to help her with the tech side of things though." I checked the time again. "The podcast should be live right now. Do you want to listen to it?"

Luke wrapped his arms around me and pulled me into his chest. He dropped a kiss on the top of my head. "I don't want to do much of anything other than get some sleep." He pulled back, put a finger under my chin, and tipped my head up toward him. He kissed me on the lips, slowly and then more passionately right there in the driveway. Then he emitted a guttural groan that sounded like a man in the middle of a debate with himself.

"You're tired," I said saying aloud what he didn't want to admit.

"Do you know how much I want to take you upstairs…" his voice trailed off and he chuckled softly. "But yeah, I'm tired. I don't want to start something I can't finish tonight."

I put my hand on his chest. "It's okay. I'm a little too stressed to think about anything other than the podcast and the sniper's response."

Luke cursed softly. "We promised we weren't going to let work get in the way of our relationship. We've been passing by each other like ships in the night for weeks now. I don't see an end in sight." He looked right into my eyes. They were dark brown and filled with emotion. "Are we okay?"

"We're more than okay," I reassured him, wondering where this was coming from. "This is what happens with two working people. At least we are in the same city." I had been traveling to take a few cases in recent months and that left us living separately for weeks and sometimes even up to a month. It wasn't ideal but we were managing our relationship as best we could. "We'll have time to spend together soon. Let's get through this case."

"There will always be another murder case, Riley. It's how it works."

"What do you want to do?"

Luke looked past me. "I want to go in and take a shower and then I want to go to bed together and at the very least go to sleep at the same time."

"Sounds good to me," I said, even though I wanted to listen to the podcast. Luke's needs were more important though.

I got ready for bed while Luke showered and then we pulled the covers down, got into bed, and talked for about a half hour before Luke fell asleep mid-conversation. I lay there awake wondering if he'd notice if I got out of bed and listened to the podcast. I figured it would keep me up all night if I did. I needed the sleep as much as he did. I pushed all thoughts of it and the sniper from my mind and closed my eyes.

When I opened them again, Luke was getting out of bed. A phone, his or mine I wasn't sure, was ringing in the distance. I heard Luke answer the call, give a few short, clipped responses, and then promise whoever it was that he'd get back to them later in the day. They tried to keep him on the phone longer, but Luke was adamant he wasn't speaking to them now.

I rolled over and looked at the clock on the nightstand. It was five-thirty in the morning. The bed on his side depressed under his weight and he leaned his body against mine, wrapping one arm around me and nuzzling into my neck.

"Who was that calling so early?"

"A reporter with the *New York Times*. They wanted a statement from me about the podcast. When I told him I didn't have anything to say, he told me I better figure it out because the case is already national news."

"We knew that was going to happen." I knew Luke had hoped it wouldn't because it put far more pressure on him to solve the case, more than he was already carrying on his shoulders. "If anyone can lead an investigation like this, it's you. I only wish you had a partner."

"I do." Luke snuggled me closer to him and pulled the blankets higher around us. "I forgot to tell you last night Det. Tyson Granger is going to be my new partner. I think it's going to be a good fit. He needs to wrap up a few cases and then he'll join me. He told me yesterday that if I needed him on this case, he'd make himself available. Tyler and Captain Meadows are fine with you and Cooper exploring any of the people threatening Cat. I think you should run down whatever leads you find because I don't have many leads left."

"What have you done so far?"

Luke explained how he had called several local gun shops trying to track down sales of the weapon he believed was used in the shooting as well as the ammunition. He said he was looking for any unusual purchases or purchases of those materials close to the shooting date. The gun shop owners weren't all that helpful and a few demanded search warrants before they'd even consider helping him. All in all, it had been uneventful. Luke didn't even know if the sniper had obtained the gun legally. Luke told me about other leads he had run down but none of them had led to anything fruitful. All he could do now was hope something came through. If not, they'd be sitting there waiting for the next shooting.

The contents of the letters were out now and I wondered what kind of impact that would have on the community. When the phone rang again, Luke groaned and got up to answer it.

While he was doing that, I listened to the sound of traffic on my small street off of Cantrell in the Heights neighborhood. Lately, it had been louder than usual as a new swath of homeowners were moving in and tearing down the lovely Craftsman bungalows and erecting McMansions. I wasn't thrilled with what I saw as the destruction of the neighborhood, but I was an outsider to most, even though I had lived in the city for several years.

The noise was earlier this morning and louder than normal. I roused myself from bed and crossed the room to the window. I expected to find a construction crew. I was met with television news vans and more reporters than I could count parked on the street in front of our house. My neighbor across the street was in his pajamas yelling at one of the cameras to get off his lawn.

This wasn't going to win us any favors in the neighborhood. I rushed to the closet and pulled out a sweater and shimmied into jeans I had thrown over the chair in our bedroom that served as a way station for clothes out of the dryer. I twisted my hair into a knot on the top of my head and didn't bother to apply any makeup.

I could hear Luke arguing with who I assumed was a reporter as I made my way down the stairs and straight out the front door. I didn't know what exactly I was going to say. The fact that the media had camped in front of our house made me wonder how they had gotten our home address. It was easy enough to find but the media didn't normally target the homes of law enforcement.

I stopped at the reporter closest to me – a middle-aged man with a receding hair line and glasses. "What are you doing here?"

"Who are you?" he asked with the inquisitive tone of a reporter. I knew it too well. I had been on the other side of that notepad not that long ago. "We are here to speak to Det. Luke Morgan. We were provided with this address and told he'd be making a statement. It's about the sniper case."

"Who provided you with this address?" I demanded.

He shouted to a man standing not that far from us. He had a video camera pointed at my house. "It was called in around four. We were told if we got out here by five-thirty Det. Luke Morgan would be making a statement. I thought it was a bit unusual but stranger things have happened."

"Do you know who called?"

He shrugged. "I assume it was someone handling the logistics for the press conference. The call sounded official so here we are. Is there not a press conference?"

I knew Luke didn't have any plans to make a statement here. He'd never bring the media to our neighborhood let alone our front door. There was a press conference scheduled for later at the police station to discuss the podcast he hadn't even listened to yet. The reporter asked me again for my name. I ignored him and moved on to another. I was told the same thing over and over again.

Either there had been a colossal mistake at the police department or someone had purposefully leaked our address to the press. I stood among the sea of reporters and stared back up at my house. Luke was standing in the window of our bedroom with the blinds split apart. I knew he was contemplating what he should do. I had no idea how I could help him, but I wasn't much use to him standing on the street with the reporters.

I walked to my next door neighbor Emma's house, cut up her driveway into the backyard, and then went through the gate between our fences back into my house. Now that I had drawn attention to myself I wasn't going to walk in the front door of my house and give away that I was Luke's wife. As far as I knew, the reporters remained oblivious to my identity and I'd rather keep it that way for as long as I could.

CHAPTER 11

The distinct crack of a gunshot ripped through the morning silence and sent Cooper from sound sleep to sitting straight up in his bed. He instinctively reached for Adele beside him and found her eyes fluttering open from the sound.

"That was a gunshot," Cooper said as three more shots rang out. He clamored out of bed in search of clothes and his gun. Not that he was any match for whoever was out there, but the sounds were close – too close to his loft. "Stay there," he told Adele as he tugged on pants and went shirtless into the kitchen.

He made it halfway through the living room when a knock on his door made him jump. He cursed loudly and went over to the door to look out. He found his new neighbor, who lived across the hall, standing in the hallway.

Cooper pulled open the door to see Marissa tightening her bathrobe. She had bare legs and feet and an expression of pure fear. Without even speaking, Cooper stepped aside and let her into his apartment. As he slipped the bolt lock in place, he reassured her. "I heard the shots too. I don't know where they are coming from but you're safe here."

"It's him, right? The same guy who shot the girls on the street." Marissa stood away from the door and the windows near the island that separated his kitchen and living room. "Where's Adele?"

"I'm here," Adele said, shuffling out of the bedroom. She had her robe and slippers on and put her arm around Marissa. "I'm glad you came over. Do you want some coffee?"

"I don't know how you're both staying so calm. It sounded like it was right outside our building." The sirens blared a moment later, confirming what Marissa said. It was indeed right outside of their building.

Cooper told them he was going to get dressed and go downstairs. "I'll call Luke and let him know."

He finished dressing, brushed his teeth, and walked back into the living room to find Adele sitting on the couch sipping coffee by herself. "Where's Marissa?"

"I walked her back to her apartment. She said she had to get ready for work and was going to stay with a friend of hers in West Little Rock. She said she wasn't going to come back downtown until the sniper was caught."

"I hate to say it but I don't think she's going to be any safer in West Little Rock." Cooper grabbed a cup and filled it with coffee and a little sweetened creamer. He took the coffee with him when he left the loft and rode the elevator down to the first floor.

There was a wall of blue lights right outside the windows and door blocking his view. The sirens had quieted but their swirling lights were visible from inside.

"What's going on, Lou?" Cooper asked the building manager at the front desk where the doorman usually sat. He had his head bent over the newspaper and Cooper wasn't sure the man had heard him. He was close to seventy and Cooper suspected he had a little trouble hearing but was too proud to admit it. Cooper rapped his knuckles on the desk and Lou snapped his head up.

"I didn't even see you there, Coop. As you probably heard, there was a shooting outside the building. The cops won't tell me anything."

Cooper took a step toward the door and Lou cautioned him. "I think it's going to be a while before you can get out of the building. I've got the back door unlocked though if you want to go out into the alley. That's how everyone has been leaving for work."

Cooper didn't retreat. He walked right up to the door and opened it. He was hoping Luke was already out there. He hadn't been able to reach him on the phone. To the cop whose back was to him, he asked, "What happened?"

"Shooting," he said stating the obvious. He pushed Cooper back. "You need to go back inside. I'm not going to be able to let you out this way."

"Is Det. Morgan on the scene? I'm a friend of his and I'm connected to the investigation."

"He's not on the scene yet. He's stuck in his house because the media is camped out in front of it."

Cooper looked between the cop's legs to see if he could see anything on the ground. There was a pool of blood and the paramedics working on someone. That was all he was able to see, so he stepped back inside and called Riley. She answered quickly sounding out of breath and stressed.

"There's been another shooting, Cooper," she said instead of hello.

"I know, it's right outside of my door. The cop here said Luke was stuck in the house because of the media. What's going on?"

"His cellphone started ringing at a little after five this morning. It was different news organizations wanting a statement from Luke. He told them he'd be making a statement later this morning as they had planned. I heard some noise outside, thinking it was the ongoing construction but it's every local and national news organization you can think of. I even saw some news vans from Dallas and St. Louis. They said they were provided Luke's home address and he'd be making a statement from here. He had to go out the backdoor and Det.

Granger picked him up three streets over." Riley explained Granger was going to be Luke's new partner. "It's a mess."

"Granger is a good choice," Cooper said and then speculated, "Do you think it was the sniper who called the media as a way to block Luke from getting to the scene?"

"I don't know if he was trying to keep Luke from getting to the scene or sending a clear message that he can get to us anytime. Our home address has never been disclosed in a case before. It's easy enough to find but no one has ever done anything as brazen as this. I don't know what to do. Luke told me to wait here because there were still news vans outside. I assume they would have heard about the shooting by now."

"Did you tell them Luke wasn't going to be making a statement?" Cooper asked what seemed like an obvious question.

"Luke told me not to engage with them at all. If they don't see him, he was hoping they might think they have the wrong address and not return."

Cooper hadn't thought of that.

"Do you know anything about the shooting?"

He peered over at the front windows hoping to see something but the line of cops was still blocking his view. "I can see someone deceased on the ground. I'm not able to see anything else though. The cops are blocking my door and the wall of windows." He explained what Lou told him about using the alley entrance.

"Luke was told it was a man and a woman. Both were injured. There was no one pronounced dead at the scene. That was the initial call though. I don't know if anything has changed."

"The paramedics are here and were working on someone. They aren't there now but there's a sheet over the person. I assume they didn't make it."

"If the sniper is following the Son of Sam script both people should live. He shot the male victim and the female victim only had superficial wounds from broken glass. I guess we'll know if he's following the same pattern later."

Cooper thought the little bit he saw outside looked far more serious than the scene Riley described. He could still hear the echo of the shots ringing in his ears. It would take him a while before he would be able to shake that. "Cat published the podcast at midnight as we planned. I'm surprised he struck already."

"Have you listened to it all the way through?" Riley asked him with an edge in her tone. Cooper said he hadn't listened to it at all after helping Cat edit. "It was heavily victim-focused like almost all of Cat's podcasts. I'm assuming he might be angry that it wasn't more about him."

"She didn't have information about him," Cooper reasoned. The previous night Cat had stressed about what she should say about the sniper. She had given a brief overview of the letters and the connection to the Son of Sam cases and she speculated about what kind of person could commit a crime like this. She had no real facts to give about the man.

Cooper didn't know what more she could have said. They were both worried about angering him. As Cooper had said the previous day though, the sniper was going to kill someone no matter what they did. He just didn't think it would be this soon.

After a few beats of silence, Riley finally said, "There is no right answer. We are going to have to wait to see if he communicates with us again."

Cooper dreaded the thought of that. He wondered if the sniper already left another message for Adele. If he considered her his attorney, he might have left something for her. She had no way of informing him that he couldn't retain her anonymously. As far as he was concerned, Adele had given the message to Cat and she had produced the podcast. "I'm going with Adele to her office. I'll be in touch when I know more." He clicked off without waiting for Riley's response.

When Cooper opened the door to the loft, he was surprised to see Adele standing at the kitchen island dressed and ready for the day. "Are you going somewhere?"

She turned her head to him. "I thought I'd go to my office to see if he left me a message. The news is reporting a man and a woman were shot, both of them are deceased at the scene."

Cooper winced and expelled a breath. "Someone gave Luke's address to the media. Riley said they had media camped out there all morning."

Adele's mouth fell open and her eyes got big and round. "That's terrible. Who would do something like that?" She said it and then it occurred to her like it did for Cooper that it was probably the sniper. "Why would he do that?"

"I don't know. Why does he do anything?"

Adele grabbed her work bag and keys off the table. "You can come with me if you want. I'm headed to the office now. I told my assistant to stay home for the day. She was a bit freaked out yesterday with the sniper's letter and I didn't want to make her come downtown today. I'd like to keep her employed."

"She needs to toughen up if she's going to work for a defense attorney." Cooper went down the hall to his work office and grabbed gloves from the box and an evidence bag. If there was a note, he wanted to be prepared.

They left the loft through the alley and made it the few blocks to her office. They were able to avoid the crowds on the street and the cops who blocked off some of the roads. Adele unlocked the front door and poked her head inside. She flipped on the light as Cooper's heart raced.

Riley had mentioned that the violence he witnessed in previous cases might be getting to him and he was starting to think she was right. His neck and shoulders were the tightest they'd ever been. Since getting hurt, he hadn't been able to fully relax.

They stepped inside the office and peered into the mail bin. Sitting right on top of the pile was a small white envelope with block-style handwriting. It almost looked like a note from a child.

Cooper pulled the gloves from his back pocket and tugged them on. He lifted the letter from the pile. It was heavier than he thought it would be. Cooper noticed the small bump at the side of the envelope. There was something more than a letter inside. He carried it over to the desk, used the letter opener to make one clear slit at the top of the envelope, and pulled out the sheet of paper.

The letter was addressed to Adele.

I can't hold you accountable for the podcast. You delivered the message as I instructed. You are safe for now. Tell Cat the podcast was not to my liking. She must focus on my life. I've provided an audio file she can use for the second episode. If she doesn't get it right, she will be the next victim. I rarely give second chances so tell her how fortunate she is – for now.

"This guy is a psychopath," Cooper said as he shook the envelope and a small detachable drive fell into his hands. "For as much as I want to listen to this, I'm calling Luke. He might be able to get data off this to connect directly back to the sniper."

"I don't think it's going to be that easy. He's had this planned for a long time and came prepared." They shared a look that said more than words.

CHAPTER 12

Luke balanced on his haunches over the body of the woman. The sniper had killed her with a clean shot to the head. The man beside her had been the first to go based on the blood spatter evidence on her face. Luke imagined she had enough time to scream. She was silenced moments later.

Based on witness statements, there had been four shots. There were still two unaccounted for at the moment. Techs would go through the scene.

While Luke waited for Purvis to collect the bodies, he read the few text messages Cooper had sent. There was an initial one letting him know of the shooting and then two more alerting Luke to the fact the sniper had left another message for Adele – this time threatening Cat for not getting the podcast right. Cooper indicated the sniper had left something, a detachable drive.

While it might lead to a break in the case, Luke didn't think the sniper was stupid. He was starting to believe he was one of the more intelligent criminals he'd ever come across. Right after the announcement of the second shooting hit the news, Tyler and Captain Meadows were called into the mayor's office for a meeting.

Cat's podcast had already garnered some nine million listens, eclipsing even her most popular podcast episodes. There'd be questions about whether Luke had made the right call in allowing her to do the podcast at all. The shooting wasn't a surprise to Luke nor should be to anyone else. No one believed there wouldn't be another shooting. The quickness of it though was a slap in the face.

The medical examiner pulled to the curb and got out shaking his head. "What is this city coming to?" Purvis asked as he went around to the back to pull out the first stretcher. Purvis and his assistant tugged the stretcher up the curb.

"It gets a little worse every year," Luke said without any emotion in his voice. The truth was there weren't more murders, they just got more strange and complicated.

"What do you have for me, Luke?" Purvis said as he squatted down and pulled back the sheet on the woman. "Clean shot to the head but a lot of blood spatter on her face."

"The man was in front of her as he was shot. I assume he was shot first and then her."

"Reasonable assessment." Purvis covered the woman back up. He went to the man and took a look. "Were these two people walking together?"

"I don't know. I waited until you arrived before I went through their pockets. I wanted you to take a look before I did anything. The mayor is already all over this case and I want to make sure we are doing what we can to lock down the crime scenes. We can't have any mistakes." He'd never known Purvis to make a mistake, but Luke didn't want to take any chances.

Purvis gestured for his assistant to take photos of the bodies as they normally did. Some detectives waited for the medical examiner while others let the crime scene techs get to work.

After the photos were taken, Luke reached a gloved hand into the man's pants pocket and found a wallet. Bennett Crawford was forty-three and lived in Cooper's building on the second floor. He had a few credit cards and twenty-three dollars in cash. He had a security pass for the federal building a few blocks away. Luke tugged down the man's collar and found what he was looking for. He wore his badge on a chain around his neck.

Bennett was an environmental lawyer for the government.

Luke moved to the woman and found a similar badge around her neck. Kristy Hamilton was also an environmental lawyer but her badge listed a Dallas federal building.

Luke had already looked for a purse by her body or any kind of workbag but had found none. He didn't have a wallet or cellphone or any personal items for her other than the badge around her neck. He wondered if the shooting was politically motivated given their work. Luke could only assume the two people were together, possibly headed to a work meeting or maybe Kristy was coming from a nearby hotel to meet with Bennett at his residence.

There was no way of knowing based on the position of their bodies. It would take some calling around to figure out where Kristy was staying. He'd need to find next of kin for them both.

Luke raised his head to Purvis. "I have a few things to do before I can make the call to next of kin. Make sure their identities don't make it to the media."

Purvis's office never had leaks. Both of them knew he was saying it to have it said. If anything, the police department was the one that routinely leaked information. It had more holes than a sinking ship, especially when the leaks benefited the department. Luke was proud to say it rarely happened in the homicide unit.

Luke left Purvis to do what he did best. He told the uniformed officers to keep the scene secure while he went to collect more evidence. It was a short walk to Adele's office and he was able to avoid the throngs of media and onlookers that had already gathered. He still had to figure out how all the media ended up at his front door that morning. Riley was sure it was the sniper who had tipped them off. Luke wasn't so sure.

Adele and Cooper were sitting in the front office near the door when Luke arrived. "You found it quickly," he said as he made his way to the desk where Cooper had laid out the note and drive.

"We assumed he left more communication," Adele explained as Luke examined the note. "As you can see, he's made a direct threat against Cat this time and he left us a recording."

Luke could see that. "Have you played it?"

Cooper went to stand near the desk. "I didn't want to destroy any evidence the tech guys might be able to get from it. For all we know, he's set it up to play once and then self-destruct."

Luke side-eyed him. "I don't think he's a spy, Cooper. I'm fairly certain this guy wants everyone to hear what he has to say."

"Fair enough," Cooper said with an embarrassed laugh. "Still, I'm trying not to overstep."

"I appreciate that." Luke asked Adele if he could use her computer and the three of them marched down the hall to her office. Luke went behind her desk as she typed the password to her laptop. He raised his head to her. "Do you have anything on here you mind losing if there's a virus on this?"

Adele shook her head. "I keep everything on a secure cloud with triple security and a firewall. If there's a virus on that, you're not going to get far. My laptop will kill it before it gets a chance to do any damage."

"You're more prepared than the police department," Luke said as he slipped the drive into place and clicked on the only file. As he clicked play, a man's deep voice crackled to life. Luke listened to the recording that started with the man's life in high school and the first time he had an urge for violence. It went on to describe crimes he committed in college and then into his later life. He didn't say where he was from or give any information that could identify him or the area of the country where his crimes had been committed.

The audio file was a full two hours in length. Luke didn't want to stand there and listen. He could do that back at the station. He clicked stop. "I don't think this is his real voice. It sounds artificial."

"The technology for that is getting better, Luke. I have an expert if you want more information. I'm sure he'd be willing to help you out on anything you need," Adele offered. "I don't know what kind of expert help you have at the police station."

"Our techs are good but possibly not that good." He took the name and phone number of Adele's contact then pulled the drive out of the computer. "Adele, could you come down to the station with me? If this guy thinks you're his lawyer, then you need to listen to this. Cooper, you can come too."

Luke didn't wait for either of them to respond. He assumed they would follow. He couldn't imagine offering Cooper the chance to listen to the evidence and him turning it down.

"Give me time to wrap up here and I'll be over," Adele said as Luke headed for the door.

He walked the distance from Adele's office back to the station in record time. He went directly to his desk, unplugged his laptop from the power source, and carried it to the conference room. The detective's bullpen was quiet with only one detective from the robbery division on the phone at his desk. The light in Tyler's office was on and the door was closed.

He knocked once then opened it without being told to enter. "How many calls from the mayor have you received this morning?" Luke asked when he found Tyler staring at his desk phone.

"Five," Tyler said, holding up his hand. "They started before I made it to the office. It was shortly after the shooting. Captain Meadows is with him now. He didn't want to speak to me, he wanted Captain Meadows. They are probably second-guessing their decision to promote me."

Luke closed the door. The last thing the case needed was Tyler having a lack of confidence. "You didn't make any decision Captain Meadows wouldn't have made. He said so himself yesterday. If you were still a detective, would you have been on board with the podcast?"

"Yeah," he said without hesitation or any trace of doubt in his voice. "We didn't have a choice. We had to take the risk that if he got the podcast, he'd stop shooting. It was also important to keep him engaged."

"It's still the right call. Just because you're the one who made the ultimate decision, it doesn't suddenly become the wrong decision. We all knew what we were risking." Luke sat down without being asked. "I'm surprised there was a shooting this soon, but he communicated with us again."

"There was another message?"

Luke pointed toward the conference room. "I have an audio file that he sent to Adele. She and Cooper went to her office this morning assuming he would have communicated again. If there was a mistake made it was not putting video surveillance across from her office yesterday. We need to get that done discreetly today in the hopes of catching him next time. I considered the communication yesterday a one-off. During all the chaos, I didn't consider he'd go back to her office and drop off something else. I asked Cooper and Adele to join us to listen to the full audio file. It's two hours long. Do you want to listen in?"

Tyler reached for his phone. "Let me call the tech to get the video surveillance in. I don't think I'll have trouble pushing that through. Is there any place inside Adele's office where we could place the camera?"

Luke didn't think inside would work. "We need a view of the street. The drop box is built into the building. There wouldn't be a clear shot from the inside. I'd like to see where he's coming from and where he's going after the drop."

Tyler understood and made the call. He relayed the information, side-stepped any issues the city government might have with setting up a camera on the street, and convinced the tech to get it done as soon as possible. When he hung up, Tyler sent a text to Captain Meadows. "If the mayor has a problem with my decision, he can fire me."

"Are you feeling better?" Luke asked surprised at the quick turnaround.

"Not really but what am I going to do? Captain Meadows told me the same as you, not to sweat it. I'm not going to create any more stress for myself than I already have." He got up from his desk and headed for the door with Luke right behind him. "If I get fired, my wife will be happy. I can retire to Key West like she wants."

Tyler already had twenty years in the police department and could retire with full benefits if he wanted to. It hadn't occurred to Luke he was even thinking about it, but it made sense to him. He might be thinking the same thing at that point.

Luke was opening the audio file when Cooper and Adele walked in.

As Cooper sat at the table, he asked, "Given the threat against Cat, I told her to stay inside and wait for you to reach out to her."

Luke hadn't forgotten about the threat and was glad Cooper had taken the initiative. "I'll reach out to her as soon as we listen to this audio."

Luke put a lot of work on hold to listen to the sniper's words, most importantly finding the victims' next of kin and making the death notifications.

He was working on borrowed time but believed the audio was most important.

CHAPTER 13

At two that afternoon, long after the media departed from the front of my house, I met Cooper at Cat's studio. Cooper and Luke had arrived together to tell Cat of the threat against her and let her listen to the audio recording. Together, the three of them hatched a plan for the next podcast episode.

I hadn't listened to the recording yet, but Cooper had given me the gist. The sniper blamed his poor childhood and his mother for his crimes. His mother had abandoned him early in life. He lived with his father who was physically and emotionally abusive. He was sent to live in a juvenile facility and then later made a life for himself. His misogyny was the undercurrent throughout the entire audio recording. He had hatred for women and their ability to exert their control on him and now they needed to pay.

The sniper didn't say anything about ever being married or having children and did not indicate his age. Luke assumed he was late forties to early fifties based on the juvenile detention center he described.

By the time I got to Cat's, Luke had already left to track down the victims' families from the morning shooting and deliver the news of their murder. So far, the media remained unaware of their identities. Luke knew that would only last for so long. When I asked him about what we were going to do now that our address was public with the media, he told me we'd figure it out. I couldn't blame him for not wanting to focus on that now. It was the least of his problems.

Cat had been uncharacteristically quiet since I arrived. We were camped out in the conference room as she was trying to put the finishing touches on the script for the podcast.

I wanted to find a way to ease her fears. "Luke was serious that he could move you to a safe house and give you police protection until this is all over. You don't have to stay here by yourself."

Cat stared at me with an expression I couldn't read. She stayed silent for a few moments. When she answered me, there was no doubt in her tone. "I'm not going to be driven out of my home by this psycho. I'm willing to continue with the podcast as he requested. Luke said I could take snippets of the audio file or play the whole thing. At first, I thought why bother giving him that much air time. Now, I'm going to play the whole thing. I'll do an intro and a wrap-up at the end. He wants his story told, let's tell it."

Cooper didn't disagree with that. "As Luke said, we have no idea if he's telling the truth. This could all be some elaborate made-up story about his life. For all we know, he has no juvenile record or the hard life he described."

"That's not my problem," Cat said with an edge to her tone. "I'll say at the start that we have not been able to substantiate anything."

Changing her podcast hadn't been what Cooper meant. "I was suggesting we listen to it and pull out any facts we might be able to substantiate. Not for the podcast but for the investigation."

"Was there anything we could substantiate, Cooper?" I asked not meaning for my tone to sound cynical. "From what Luke said, the voice sounded to be artificial intelligence and he didn't say what part of the country or dates. What can we substantiate?"

"I don't know," Cooper said with frustration. "He took the time to record it so even if he didn't tell us the truth, what he chose to tell us might hold some clues. Maybe there's something in his subtext he didn't mean to let slip."

"There could be that," I conceded but still felt like it was a waste of time. "Cat, are you up for listening to the whole audio file?" Luke hadn't played her the whole thing just a clip at the start and then showed her the note.

"I'm going to have to listen to the whole thing if I'm going to publish it on my podcast. I need some coffee before we get started." Cat stood from the table.

Cooper gestured for her to sit and that he'd go to the coffee shop. "Luke is right you need to keep a low profile. I hope you'll reconsider the police protection or safe house. If you won't, the least you can do is stay inside until you publish the next one."

"If he kills me, then there is no podcast. Who will he turn to then?" Cat shifted her eyes to me and then to Cooper. "I don't think he's going to bite the hand that feeds him." Even though she argued the point, she sat back down and let Cooper go for her.

I asked Cooper to grab me some coffee too and then he left Cat and me alone together.

She sat stone-faced across the table from me. I wasn't sure there was anything I could say to make it better. I couldn't sit in the silence with the tension that hung in the air. "I want to be able to tell you I understand how difficult this is for you, but the truth is I don't know. When the media showed up at my house this morning, I felt violated. I still feel that way. Whether it was a media source who found our house or the sniper shared our address, I don't know. I do know how sick it made me feel."

"I feel like a performing monkey," Cat said with a sigh. "First the threats from Todd Hall and now this. All I wanted to do was start a podcast and do a little good for victims of crime. I didn't expect to be part of a case."

"Have you heard anything else from Hall?"

"Nothing in email. I haven't checked the discussion boards about the case. He usually posts on there first."

I made a mental note to check that out later. I wasn't sure if Hall was even a viable person of interest in the case. Luke didn't seem to be too keen on the guy other than the harassment against Cat. We chatted while we waited for Cooper to come back with coffee and snacks.

"Any update from the street?" I asked as he handed me my coffee.

"People are upset and freaked out. The coffee shop wasn't even sure they were going to open this morning. The manager said she wasn't sure it was safe for her employees. Many of them park in the garage near my loft and walk the few blocks to work. The media is all over the place out there. I'm surprised they haven't shown up here at the studio yet, Cat."

While she had a small sign with her business name out front, someone casually walking by probably wouldn't notice it. "They will find me sooner or later. There have been calls but I haven't answered. I set it up so the calls go directly to voicemail and my cellphone isn't listed anywhere."

Cooper cautioned, "That's probably a good idea, but we'll need to go through those messages. A listener could have called you instead of the tipline."

"I didn't even think of that. I told them to call the tipline with information but listeners tend to trust me." Cat looked over at the laptop. "The one thing I agree with Luke about is that we have to assume everything this guy tells us is a lie. He said he wouldn't shoot someone and then he did, not even six hours after I published a podcast episode. I'm inclined to agree we can't believe everything in his audio file. From what Luke said, the guy takes no responsibility for anything in his life. He blamed his mother and other women. Nothing was his fault. He sounds like a narcissist to me."

A few months back, I had grown to hate the word narcissist. It was being overused by nearly everyone. The real diagnosis of narcissistic personality disorder wasn't as pervasive as people seemed to believe. That said, it was hard to disagree with her.

Cat clicked the start button on her laptop. "Let's get this sickening display over."

I admired her resolve. I didn't know that I'd be doing the same faced with the kind of threat the sniper had written. We sat there for the full two hours listening to the deep male voice provide his story. Cooper stopped it a few times to jot down a note. He didn't tell us what he was writing down or why. I assumed once we were done, he'd explain.

We got to the end of the recording and there was one glaring bit of information missing for me – the motive for the current shooting and any mention of the Son of Sam cases. He didn't give any reason why he was terrorizing Little Rock. He also didn't make any further demands.

Why this city and what was his connection? It was all missing from the recording.

He didn't explain enough about his juvenile detention time for me to believe he was telling the truth. What he described could have been read in a book. It lacked emotion and authenticity. That could have simply been the artificial voice he used to tell the story but even in his word selection, emotion was missing.

When Cooper clicked stop at the end, he asked, "Do you believe him, Riley?"

"I don't," I said evenly and explained what I had been thinking about the lack of emotion. "He told a story that could have been in a book or movie. Every serial killer blames their parents or poor childhood. He's also blaming women but never mentioned anything about his relationships that sounds authentic." I shifted in my seat to look at Cooper. "Do you believe it?"

"I didn't believe a lot of it the first time. This time around, I believe even less." Cooper jabbed his pen on the pad where he had taken notes. "I wrote down a few things I thought we could check. You were right that there wasn't much. He described murdering three women when the urge to kill became too much for him when he was in his twenties. He saw the women walking alone and the urge to kill overcame him. That doesn't sound out of the realm of possibilities but he also gives no context. He didn't even say how he killed them. He also didn't say anything about later murders. Most killers don't just stop."

That had struck me as odd as well. "What else did you write down?"

"The details he provided about the juvenile facility. He mentioned the landscape which didn't sound like anything around here. It sounded more like the northeast." He locked his gaze on me. "I wondered if you caught that."

It had been the only authentic thing he described about the place. "It sounds a lot like the Adirondacks, particularly how he described the pine trees near the river and the backdrop of the mountains. I'm not out in nature much around the rest of the country so it was hard for me to know if that landscape is anywhere else."

Cooper agreed with that. "What he described sounded a lot like the case we had in Lake George. That's what I was imagining when he said it. It's the first thing that jumped out to me." He glanced over at Cat. "What about you? Do you know that area?"

"I don't but it didn't sound like anything here or in Chicago. Like Riley, I'm not out much in nature. If you think it could be an area in the northeast, run with it. We have nothing else to go on."

"Do you have any contacts up there with juvenile facilities?" Cooper asked me.

"A few but many of them are closed. The kind of work camp environment he described has been long gone in the northeast. A few are remaining out west. I only know that because the news has done stories about the abuses that happened there. I'll see what information I can dig up though."

Cat pointed to her laptop. "What should I do about the podcast?"

"I thought your idea was a good one," I said, agreeing with her earlier plan. "Do a brief intro and explain the sniper sent this to you after the murders this morning and wanted it played. I'd even mention that he threatened to kill you if you didn't. Then do a wrap-up at the end. I think it's fine for you to say no one has been able to substantiate the information. I think that covers you. The sniper didn't give you a directive either way of how he wanted the audio used, only that he was providing you the information for the podcast since you couldn't interview him and he didn't like your focus on the victims."

"Don't focus on the victims this time," Cooper cautioned. "I wouldn't mention them at all. Luke hasn't released any information about their identities so best to focus solely on the sniper."

Cat asked Cooper if he'd help her later when she was editing again. They planned to meet later in the day. "Are you both going to work here today?" Her tone indicated she wanted to be alone.

"I'm going back to my home office." I raised my eyebrows to Cooper. "I think Cooper is going back to his office as well."

Cooper caught my meaning and agreed.

Before I left though, I gathered information from Cat about access to her social media platforms and where I should search for Hall's comments. I also had her check her email but there was nothing from him.

Cat stared at the laptop screen. "You know, it's strange. I usually get at least one email a day from him and there was nothing yesterday or today."

"Nothing since the shooting started?"

"Nothing."

"Maybe we will pay Todd Hall a visit today," Cooper said and I agreed.

I wanted to rule him in or out as quickly as possible. I also wanted to let him know he needed to stop harassing Cat because we were all watching now.

CHAPTER 14

Cooper worked at his home office until late in the afternoon. He lost a few hours searching the internet for a series of three murdered women in one city but came up with so many possibilities that he had to let it go. Without knowing how the women died or a little more about the victims, there simply wasn't enough to do a decent search – which Cooper assumed was the point.

The sniper didn't tell them enough to confirm anything he said. Without being able to confirm it, they couldn't say it wasn't true either. They were stuck with the sniper's narrative about his life without any way to prove it.

Just as he was growing frustrated, Riley called him to let him know that she couldn't find any messages Todd Hall had left after the most recent podcast episode. She explained Cat found it odd given the slew of messages he posted after every episode. She had found messages going back to the first episode of the first case Cat ever covered. Since the first sniper shooting, there was nothing from him.

Riley explained where he could find everything and how to access Cat's emails, which was what Cooper wanted to read first. As he dug into the content, he was a bit surprised and caught off guard by what people would say sitting safely behind a keyboard. He assumed the majority of them would never say the same in person. Cooper shouldn't be surprised given the history of social media and the anonymity it allowed. Reading the messages turned Cooper's stomach. He wasn't sure how Cat could tolerate knowing people were out there who seemed to hate her so much.

When he was done with his research Cooper called Riley back and convinced her to allow him to go alone to see Hall. He had a sense from the messages he wouldn't open up in front of a woman and the last thing he wanted to do was put Riley at risk. Not that Cooper could match the misogyny in the messages – he wasn't even sure he could fake it for the sake of conversation – but he assumed he'd be better off going alone.

The man's address wasn't hard to find. He lived in a similar style loft as Cooper's across the Arkansas River in North Little Rock's Argenta neighborhood. He had found out that Hall was a mechanic for the City of North Little Rock and posted on social media more than once that he was so glad when three o'clock came around. Cooper assumed he worked the seven to three shift. He also posted more than once about a bar in Argenta that he frequented after work.

Cooper checked his phone and figured he'd make it to the bar right around the time Hall might be showing up. He'd check the bar first and then the loft. For a man who spewed such vitriol on social media, he did nothing to hide his personal information online.

Not sure what he'd encounter or if he'd need to go anyplace else, Cooper drove over the bridge instead of walking. He found a place to park on the street outside of the bar and went inside. The place was filled with older guys, some of whom looked like they'd been there for a while.

He made his way up to the bar, perched himself on an open stool, and ordered a beer he probably wasn't going to drink. Cooper had learned early in his career that if he wanted a bartender to talk, it was easier if he ordered a drink and left a sizable tip.

"I'm looking for someone," Cooper said as the bartender put his beer down in front of him.

"We don't get many women in here this time of day. In the evening, the clientele changes and you might have better luck then. Try a Saturday night too."

Cooper laughed and held up his left hand to show his ring finger. "I'm looking for a guy named Todd Hall. I heard he comes in here often."

The bartender, who had tattoos up and down both arms, nodded. "He comes in here just about every day." He glanced up at the clock. "He should have been in here by now."

"When was the last time you saw him?"

It took the bartender a moment and then he shrugged. "Come to think about it, he hasn't been in here the past two days either." The bartender turned toward the end of the bar and yelled to a group of men. "You see Hall in here the last few days?"

Two older men shook their heads.

One of them said, "Maybe he's on vacation."

The other laughed. "He doesn't go on vacation."

The bartender focused his attention back on Cooper. "Is there something you want with him? He's a bit of an odd duck."

"Have you heard of the *Rock City Killers* podcast?" Cooper asked, which drew the attention of nearly everyone in earshot. "Hall seemed to be obsessed with the podcast host, Cat O'Conner. He sent her threatening emails and spent considerable time posting hateful comments on some discussion feeds and social media. I wanted to chat with him about that. Has he ever mentioned the podcast to you?"

One of the men who sat in the middle of the others hopped off his bar stool and came over to Cooper. He extended his hand. "Bobby," he said.

"Cooper Deagnan. Private investigator. Do you know him, Bobby?"

The man sat down next to Cooper and ordered himself another

beer. "I've known Hall a long time and he's been a bother to a lot of people for a long time. He mentioned Cat and the podcast. He had a real bee up his butt about her too."

"Do you know why or what set him off?"

The bartender put down the beer for him and he knocked back half of it in one sip. He wiped his mouth on the back of his hand and put the bottle down. "Hall is like that. He gets focused on something or someone. More than focused," he amended as he narrowed his eyes. "Obsessed. He got on a kick of listening to podcasts a few years back while he was working and then he started listening to *Rock City Killers*. I've heard a few episodes and thought she did a good job. People seem to like her too. She just got that deal with Justice Exposed. Hall didn't take to her. He said she was fake and a big phony. He said she didn't have any experience in crime and she didn't know what she was doing. I told him to stop listening if she bugged him so much. He said he hated that she was getting such a big following and needed to be knocked down a peg or two."

Cooper would have disagreed with Hall on that. He thought Cat did a fine job of presenting the evidence. It didn't matter though even if she were terrible no one deserved to be treated like that. "Do you know what he said to her?"

"I don't and I'm not sure I want to know."

Cooper wasn't going to hold back. "Hall told her someone should rape and kill her and he detailed a few scenarios of her death he thought were fitting."

Bobby sucked in a breath. "I didn't know he said things like that. He never said anything like that to me about her. He only told me that she wasn't smart and she didn't know what she was doing. Then he'd argue points in her podcast with me. I didn't listen to many episodes, as I said, and I just listened to him ramble on. No point arguing with someone like that."

"Does Hall have any background in law enforcement or anything that would have made him an expert in the subject?"

Bobby sipped his beer. "He's an expert on everything if you ask him. He reads all kinds of books about serial killers but he has no real experience. It doesn't stop him from running his mouth and thinking he's right about everything." Bobby rolled his eyes. "He's difficult to talk to. I consider him a friend and he grates on my nerves most of the time."

Cooper wasn't surprised by that, but he couldn't get a read on Bobby's impression of the threats. "Does it surprise you Hall's threatened her like that?"

Bobby stayed quiet for a few moments, nursing his beer. Then he exhaled a breath. "Truth is he doesn't think much of women. I never heard him make threats like that, but no, it doesn't surprise me that he did. He hates women."

Cooper could believe that. "I want to know more about his relationship with women. Is he married or does he have a girlfriend?"

"No," Bobby said with emphasis. "It's not for his lack of trying, but the way he speaks to women pushes them away. He's not someone with a lot of charm. Not a ladies' man, if you know what I mean. It's his fault though. I tried to tell him that. He comes across as arrogant and argumentative. Who wants to deal with that? It's not like he has a lot of money or has a lot to offer a woman. My wife can't stand him. The only time I see him is here at the bar. She won't let him come to the house."

That intrigued Cooper. "Is there a reason why?"

"He told my wife she shouldn't have a job and that I should be the head of the household. He said if I didn't have the balls to tell her that, then someone should. Then he called her a fat old cow."

Cooper tried to imagine anyone saying anything close to that to Riley or Adele. He assumed they might not make it out of the house alive. Cooper didn't ask Bobby's response to that because he worried he might lose the little respect he had for the guy. "I can see why your wife would rather he not come around. Was Hall ever violent with women?"

"Not that I saw." Bobby took another sip of his beer and toyed with the bottle in his hand. "The truth is I never see him around women other than when he's hitting on them and that doesn't turn out well for him. I can't say what he'd do with a woman if he ever got one. I don't know much about his past. I've only known him a few years, mostly from in here."

"Understood," Cooper said and considered how much he wanted to share. Bobby seemed to be open to talking. It hadn't taken any prodding so he might as well go for it. "What do you think about the recent shootings?"

"Terrible. I don't know who would do something like that." His tone was sincere and his body language remained open. "I hope the police catch the guy fast. People around here are scared. My wife didn't want me to come here after work. She wanted me to come straight home."

Cooper leveled a look at him. "Given the threats against Cat and the sniper wanting her to do a podcast about his crimes, is there any chance Hall is the one responsible?"

Bobby pulled back in surprise. "For the shooting?"

"I saw guns and ammunition in his photos on social media. He's made credible threats against Cat, not just on the internet but to her directly in email. It's a logical question. The sniper dropped off a letter to Cat forcing her to do the podcast. His second communication threatened her life, just like Hall did. It's not too far a stretch."

Bobby considered what Cooper said and then shook his head. "I don't know, man. Hall is crazy but I'm not sure he's a psychopath. This sniper is demented. I don't know if I could see him pulling this off. Besides, I think if he was going to do something like that, he wouldn't do it where a lot of people know him."

There was enough doubt in Bobby's tone that Cooper pushed on. "It's possible though?"

Bobby didn't answer. He tipped back the rest of his beer, paid his tab, and looked at Cooper with his eyes wide. "Let's go visit Hall. If you're with me, there's a chance he'll talk to you. Without me, he's going to slam the door in your face."

"Fair enough," Cooper said and paid the bartender for the beer he didn't touch. He walked out of the bar and they walked a couple of blocks to Hall's loft. Bobby typed in the security code to get through the fence and then the code for the building.

"I've been to his place before," Bobby said as an explanation for having the code. He led Cooper down one hallway to an elevator and then took it to the fourth floor. Hall's door was a short walk down the hall. Bobby rapped his knuckles against the door and called out for his friend.

The man didn't answer but the next door neighbor poked his head out. "I don't think he's there and there's a strange smell coming from his apartment. I called maintenance this morning but they haven't checked it out yet. I figured he went away and forgot to take out his trash."

Cooper glanced over at the man. "You mind if I come into your apartment and see what you mean?"

"Come on in," the guy said, stepping out of the way. "It's a terrible smell and it's worse in the bathroom. We share a vent or something because it's bad."

Cooper only made it a few feet into the man's apartment and the smell knocked him back. "That isn't garbage," he said, his stomach churning. "That's the smell of death."

CHAPTER 15

Luke had managed to find someone at the federal office in Little Rock who was able to come to the morgue and identify both bodies. After a firm confirmation, Luke tracked down Kristy Hamilton's family in Texas to deliver the bad news. Her husband, Chris, was now on his way to Little Rock.

After positively identifying the victims, Luke searched for next of kin for Bennett Crawford and came up blank. His co-workers said he kept his life outside of work private and few knew much about his friends or family. Someone speculated he was originally from Baton Rouge, Louisiana, but wasn't sure.

Given they lived in the same building, Luke called Cooper and asked if he knew much about Bennett. Other than passing him in the lobby and a neighborly hello, Cooper knew little about him.

Luke had to go through the building's security to get a key to Bennett's condo. Once inside, the place looked nearly identical in layout to Cooper's. The only difference was Cooper had a view of the street and Bennett's faced the alley that ran in the back of the building. He kept his loft tidy but there were two plates, two coffee cups, and two sets of silverware from breakfast in the sink.

Luke noted women's cosmetics and toiletries in the bathroom and her clothes hanging in the closet. The bed had been hastily made. The indent of heads on both pillows told Luke that Bennett hadn't been sleeping alone the night before he was killed.

Luke searched the apartment for any trace of family or friends he could contact. The techs were still working to access Bennett's phone, which had a passcode Luke hadn't been able to break at the morgue. He had turned it over to his tech team to let them get to work.

Luke walked back out into the living room and stood with his hands on his hips as he considered what he should do next. The phone would hopefully give him the information he needed.

A key in the lock of the front door drew Luke's attention. He turned in time to see a woman enter and let out a startled yelp. "Who are you? What are you doing in here?"

Luke held up his badge. "I'm Det. Luke Morgan. Do you know Bennett Crawford?"

The petite woman with shoulder-length blonde hair dropped her bag on the floor. "I'm Joni Lewis and I've been Bennett's housekeeper for the past five years."

Luke hated to deliver death notifications. "I'm sorry to tell you but Bennett was killed outside this building this morning on his way to work. Did you hear about the shooting?"

Joni gave a slight nod of her head. "I heard two more people were killed. Bennett texted me last night and told me he was leaving early for a morning meeting and I was free to come any time after six. He knows I'm never here that early but I guess he wanted me to know he'd be gone all day. What happened?"

"That's what I'm trying to figure out," Luke said. "He was wearing his badge when he was shot. He was killed with Kristy Hamilton. Do you know her?"

Joni's hand went to her throat as she sucked back surprise. Her eyes grew wide and she bit her lip. "I'm not sure I should say."

Luke needed her to say it. "I need to know if Bennett had any family and friends I can notify. That's why I'm up here looking around. If you know something about Bennett's life, I need to know."

Joni went to the brown leather sofa and sat down. She raised her head to Luke. "Bennett and Kristy were having an affair. Well, it was an affair on Kristy's end. Bennett was single. He has a sister and a brother in Louisiana. I'm not sure how to reach them."

Luke flashed back to the women's items in the bathroom and the closet. He had thought maybe Bennett's girlfriend hadn't fully moved in because there weren't that many items of clothing. He hadn't seen a suitcase around so he hadn't immediately connected the two. "How long has the affair been going on?"

"At least a year that I knew." Joni grew quiet for a moment, seeming to process her thoughts or maybe take a moment to grieve. "He was a good man despite sleeping with a married woman. I walked in on them here about a year ago and Bennett told me about the affair. I'm not even sure why he confided in me. He didn't have a lot of people in his life. I wouldn't say he was estranged from his family, but he didn't have a lot of contact with them. He worked long hours and was dedicated to his job."

"What about friends here?"

Joni shook her head. "He never spoke about friends. He was working seventy to eighty hours a week for the government. Sometimes he had to travel if he had a case pending."

"Was there anything in particular he was working on now?"

Joni closed her eyes for a moment and took a few slow breaths. She opened her eyes and looked at Luke. "I'm sorry, this is such a shock."

"Take your time."

"Bennett was working on a case against Ezo Technologies. I'm sure you've seen it on the news. They are accused of dumping waste in the Arkansas River. It impacted communities in Arkansas, Oklahoma, Kansas, and Colorado. There is a federal case pending against them as well as a private lawsuit that could end up in payouts in the hundreds of millions for the families." She pinched the bridge of her nose. "Does this shooting have anything to do with that?"

Luke was familiar with it. Most people in the impacted states were, but he had only followed bits and pieces in the news. "Do you happen to know if Kristy was the other attorney on the case?"

"They have been working together for the past two years. That's how they met and the affair started. They were spending so much time together that the affair was inevitable. Kristy is from Dallas. That's where her husband lives. They don't have any children, which I guess is a blessing given..."

Luke understood the sentiment. He hadn't mentioned that Kristy had also been killed in the shooting. He told Joni that now. "I've notified her husband about her death. I didn't know about the affair then. I'm not sure..." Luke didn't know how to finish that thought. Delivering the news that his wife had been murdered was hard enough. Luke had no idea how he was going to tell him that his wife had been involved in a yearlong affair with her work partner.

Joni read his thoughts. "It's going to be inevitable that you have to tell him. All of her belongings are here. She was initially staying down the road at the Marriott. Once the affair started, she moved in here with Bennett."

"Do you have any idea why Kristy was assigned to the case if her office was in Dallas?"

"She's from Colorado and only moved to the Dallas office a few years ago. She had a previous case against Ezo Technologies that she won and was brought in for her knowledge and expertise." Joni locked her gaze on Luke. "I know your instinct is probably to judge her for having the affair. She was a good person though and worked hard on this case. I don't think either of them intended for the affair to happen. They were pushed together through work. As I said, it was bound to happen."

"I wasn't judging them," Luke said but he wasn't being completely honest. He didn't care how much he was working or how long he had to be away from Riley, he wasn't going to cheat. It wasn't in his nature to do so and a part of him judged Kristy and Bennett for being weak. He kept those thoughts to himself. "I stopped by their office and their boss came down to the morgue with me to identify them. He didn't mention anything about the case. Do you know if Kristy or Bennett faced any threats because of the case?"

In response, Joni gestured for Luke to follow her. They walked past the kitchen and down the short hallway to the bedroom. She went into the closet and moved a row of shirts over to reveal a safe. "This is where Bennett kept his gun. When he started the case, he said there had been a few threats made against them but nothing that worried him too much. He said he wanted protection at home."

Luke would have to go back and speak to their boss about the case. He couldn't rule out that it was connected. "I have Bennett's phone. Do you happen to know the code?"

"4212. It's his football jersey number and his date of birth. That's what it was a few months back anyway. I don't know if he changed it. He had left his phone at home, and while I was here one day, he needed me to relay some information from a text. That's why I know it. He might have changed it after that."

Luke texted the code to the tech working on it. He waited for a response and was glad to hear back that the code worked. "I appreciate the information," he told Joni. "Is there anything else you think I should know?"

"I don't envy your job. You have to tell Kristy's husband she was having an affair and then track down Bennett's family and let them know all the while trying to stop this awful madman." She reached out and patted Luke's arm. "You're a good man but please stop this killer. I didn't even want to come down here today. I'm glad I did though."

She pulled Bennett's key from her pocket and put it in Luke's hand. "I don't need this anymore." She left the bedroom and went back to the living room with Luke right behind her. She took one last look at the place. Before she left, she said, "Bennett was a good man and that's how I'll remember him."

Luke thanked her again before she closed the door. He took one last look around the place before he headed out, locking the door behind him. Luke would wait until after Kristy's husband arrived to tell him about the affair . It was the kind of news he wanted to deliver in person.

Luke received two texts before he made it down the hall to the elevator. One was from the tech who had the phone numbers of Bennett's brother and sister and the other was from Cooper who said he was standing outside of Todd Hall's apartment and there was the distinct smell of death. Cooper wanted to know if Luke wanted to handle it or if he should call 911. Luke had to be reminded who Hall was and once Cooper said he was connected to the threats on Cat, Luke told him to wait and that he'd be right there.

Not that Luke had time to take on anything else. If there was a chance it was connected to the case, he wanted to be first on the scene. He headed out of Cooper's building, past the section of the sidewalk still blocked off with crime scene tape, and walked to his car parked at the curb. He sent off a quick message to Tyler that he was getting closer to notifying Bennett's family and they'd soon be able to update the media with the victims' identities.

Luke drove the short distance to North Little Rock and found the apartment complex Cooper mentioned. He had given him the gate and door codes and Luke made his way to the apartment.

As soon as the elevator doors opened, the smell reached him.

Luke didn't even need to get a visual on the scene, he knew by experience there was a dead body somewhere on this floor. He gave a head nod to Cooper and the two men waiting outside of the apartment door and then sent a quick text to Purvis that he was still in the process of uncovering what was happening but that he most likely needed him at the scene. He provided him with the same information Cooper had given him.

"Give me the rundown, Cooper," Luke said as he introduced himself to the two men, one of whom was Bobby, Hall's friend, and the other was building maintenance who wanted no part of whatever was on the other side of the door. He slapped keys down in Luke's hand and headed down the hall to the elevator without looking back.

Cooper explained how he'd gone to the bar in search of Hall and met Bobby. The two of them decided to come over to speak to Hall directly. "He hadn't been seen in a few days, Luke, which even the bartender said was unusual. The neighbor came out when we knocked on the door. I went into the neighbor's apartment and could smell it right away. We called maintenance to get the keys for you and have been standing here ever since. The smell has only been getting worse."

"I don't know I can take it much longer." Bobby swayed on his feet.

Luke didn't need anyone throwing up and contaminating the crime scene. "Head downstairs and wait in the lobby. I'd like Cooper to stay up here with me." He raised his eyebrows to his friend who he knew didn't have the strongest stomach. "You okay with that?"

Cooper put a hand to his belly. "Let's get it done quickly. I'll do my best." He looked a little green. "I don't have gloves or booties though."

Luke pulled pairs of each for both of them. He handed them to Cooper as Bobby happily retreated down the hallway. He glanced back at them once and then stepped into the elevator.

"You met that guy at the bar?" Luke asked.

"He came over and started talking to me when I asked the bartender about Hall. He said it was conceivable he made those threats to Cat but didn't think he could have pulled off the shootings."

Luke used the key to unlock the door then nudged it open. He pushed it wider and stuck his head inside, the smell making his eyes water. He had to step inside because he couldn't see much from the doorway. Cooper followed right behind him.

They made it a few steps into the apartment and stopped cold. The rotting corpse of Todd Hall sat upright in an armchair with a bullet wound to the forehead. Given the markings around it, Luke assumed the barrel of the gun had been pressed against his skin.

His brain and blood peppered the wall behind him.

A note was pinned to his chest. Luke took a few steps to read it.

A gift for Cat O'Conner. I better have your full attention now.

CHAPTER 16

Luke had four murders on his hands and no evidence that pointed to any viable suspect. After discovering Hall's body and the note, Luke and Cooper left the apartment and he called in a crime scene team and confirmed with Purvis that he needed to get over to the scene. There was another body from the same killer.

Luke took a formal statement from Cooper and sent him on his way to Cat's studio. He instructed him not to tell Cat what was going on but to make sure she was okay. Luke believed Hall had been the first murder. He assumed the killer anticipated someone would suspect Hall of the shooting and go to question him or the neighbors would notice the smell and call the cops.

Luke contacted a relative of Hall's from the information Bobby provided and made the death notification. Then he called Bennett's family and made that death notification. His brother was stoic on the phone, but Luke could hear the emotion breaking in his voice. He told Luke he'd be in Little Rock as soon as possible.

Before Luke could make it to Cat's studio, he had to stop at the police station and provide an update to Tyler and Captain Meadows. He hated that he only had an update about another murder and nothing to indicate even a person of interest.

While both understood, worry lines creased their foreheads. After that difficult discussion, Luke had to inform the media, who had been camped outside of the police station, which was far better than his front yard. Reporters had more than a few questions about Bennett and Kristy's work. Luke wasn't able to provide any information, particularly because he'd only had a brief conversation with their boss.

Andrew McNamara had been in meetings all day trying to find suitable replacements for the pending criminal trial against Ezo Technologies. The case would move forward, even though the lead prosecutors had been gunned down.

The only thing Andrew had told Luke was that if the sniper believed the case would end with the deaths, they had another thing coming. Nothing would stop the prosecution or the pending civil litigation against the company. The federal office was more determined than ever.

Bennett and Kristy would be mourned but their work would carry on.

Luke was reminded once again how replaceable they all were – no more than cogs in the wheel of justice. He had a meeting set up with Andrew for later to discuss the case and any potential leads that Andrew could provide him.

After the press conference, Luke made his way back to his desk. Before he reached it, Tyler called him into his office. He thanked the detective who shouted he did a good job at the press conference then closed Tyler's door behind him.

Luke sat down across the desk from Tyler. "The media attacked the environmental angle. They are already speculating this could be someone connected to Ezo Technologies. I don't have any solid evidence to show that."

"Good work on that," Tyler said and echoed the congratulations on the press conference. "Captain Meadows has calmed the mayor down for now. We have a little breathing room. I wanted to discuss what happened with the media this morning. We've never had an incident like that."

"I wouldn't call it an incident," Luke said, downplaying it. He had been trying to forget it had ever happened.

"The media showed up at your front door under the guise you had called in a press conference. I've confirmed with all three local news stations and the two newspapers that they all received the call. They were suspicious because of the address given but weren't going to miss an opportunity for an update on this case."

Luke knew what was coming next. "You're concerned because the sniper has my home address."

"Aren't you?" he asked with an arch of his right eyebrow. "Luke, you have to take this seriously. At no point in the history of our cases has your address ever been breached like that."

"That's not true," Luke said and reminded him of the case where Riley and their neighbor had been kidnapped and the case where one of the suspects had snuck into his backyard to speak to him. "It's not the first time, Tyler, and it won't be the last. Social media only makes is easier. It's the nature of the beast. Riley and I live in a popular Little Rock neighborhood. We aren't going into hiding and aren't going to change our lives."

"It's the first time the media has gotten wind of where you live."

That was no more concerning for Luke than the previous incidences. "If you're worried about me going off script or giving an unsanctioned press conference, I'll remind you how much I hate speaking to the media. I went out the back door and through the neighbor's yard to the next street over. They didn't even see me, so maybe they aren't even sure it's my home."

Tyler leveled a look at him. "I'll ask to ask. Do you want police protection at the house or to move to a safe house for the duration of this case?"

Luke didn't even need to think about it. "I don't want to. Even if I did, I don't think I'd be able to get Riley to take you up on that. She's stubborn like I am. Any move would be seen as capitulating to a madman."

"I'd rather you do that than end up dead."

"It's a scare tactic."

"The bullet to the head of Todd Hall wasn't a scare tactic, Luke. The sniper sent a direct message." He leaned forward on the desk and pointed at Luke. "I'll concede you and Riley can stay at home for now. We aren't giving Cat an option. With the threats made against her and the little gift he left her, I want her in police protection this afternoon. Got it?"

Luke liked this new confidence Tyler was showing. "No problem, boss. I agree with you and will have it squared away by this afternoon. We might need to make some accommodations because she will need to be back in her studio to record any future podcast episodes. I will ensure she has protection and someone will sweep her office before she goes back into it."

Tyler provided the address of an open safe house where Cat could stay. With that squared away, Luke went back to his desk to return a few phone calls and then left for Cat's studio. He arrived at the same time as Riley, who had brought snacks.

"I brought you a sandwich even though I wasn't sure if I'd see you," she said as she raised to her toes and kissed his cheek. "I figured you didn't have time to eat today."

Luke didn't want to say that he had skipped lunch because the sight of Todd Hall in his recliner had voided out any hunger he was feeling. His stomach betrayed him now by growling in response to food. No matter what he had seen, Luke couldn't deny he needed food. Luke told her how much he appreciated the gesture.

He wanted to speak to her before they were in front of Cat and

Cooper. "Before we go in, I want to talk about what happened this morning. Tyler wants us to stay in a safe house."

Riley shook her head before he could finish. "I don't want him to drive us from our house."

"That's what I told him. I only wanted to make sure. They offered us police protection too."

Riley screwed up her face in disgust. "What are uniformed cops going to do for us that we can't handle ourselves?"

Luke kissed her again. "That's basically what I told him. I don't want to send any message that the sniper got to us. If he's going to shoot us, he could do that right here on the street. If he's the one who called it in, it's a scare tactic and not one I'm going to give into."

With the mention of being shot on the street, Riley instinctively ducked her head. "Let's go inside. I'm not looking to hedge my bets out here."

Luke tried to take the food she was carrying but logistically it was easier for him just to open and hold the door for her. Cat and Cooper were in the studio finishing up the editing for the most recent podcast episode and asked them to wait in the conference room.

Cooper had texted him letting him know the podcast was going to publish right at five. It was four-thirty and he had an hour before he was going to meet Andrew McNamara at the federal office building.

He and Riley unloaded the food and drinks in the conference room and chatted about the case until Cat was done with the podcast editing. Cooper joined them first and she followed a few minutes later.

"It's set to publish automatically at five," she told them as she sat at the table. Her skin was paler than it had been and she had dark patches under her eyes. "I stuck with my plan of providing an intro to explain the sniper had left me his statement on an audio file and then played the full thing. I wrapped up at the end with a disclaimer that we have not been able to independently verify anything the sniper said. I didn't go as far as to tell my listeners not to believe a word he said but it was implied." She looked over at Luke. "Cooper said you were coming back to speak to me. Is there something more you wanted to know?"

Luke was glad Cooper had withheld the information about Hall as he'd been instructed. "I have some news for you. Todd Hall was found in his apartment earlier today with a gunshot wound to his head. He's dead, Cat. His threats are done and he can't hurt you." He watched as her reaction went from shock to confusion to relief.

"I don't understand." She looked at Luke and then at Cooper and Riley. "I don't know what to say. I can't in good faith say I'm not glad he's dead. His threats were getting more than I could handle. Who killed him?"

Luke didn't know how she was going to take this next part. It was why he was glad Cooper and Riley were there with him to support her. "The sniper killed him for you." She winced and pulled back. "The sniper left a note on Hall's body. He said it was a gift to you and wanted your full attention. I believe the sniper is someone obsessed with you like Hall was. Do you have anyone else that was harassing you?"

It took Cat a moment to process everything he told her. "Did the note say anything else?"

"No. Is there a reason you're asking?"

"I thought maybe he said how he knew Hall. There is a big online community and social media where people post about the podcast. I'm assuming the sniper learned about Hall that way. He had to have known I was being harassed. I was trying to see if he left a clue to that in the note."

It was a logical question, but Luke didn't have an answer. "I have no idea how he knew Hall was harassing you. I assume he must have read the messages in the online community or social media. He might have posted in there too and we'll be looking into that. Did you mention any of the harassment on your podcast?"

"Not on the podcast. Some of my loyal fans noticed it online. How could they not? It was obvious what Hall was saying. Anyone could have seen it. The community and social media aren't closed groups. But there are thousands of people who post there and I'm sure thousands more who read the messages without ever posting. I'm not sure if you're going to be able to find him that way."

"I have the stacks of threats made against Cat that were sent to her email. We could start there," Riley suggested. "If he was that focused on her, it's possible he sent her messages."

"Those are threats though," Luke said, considering. "I was thinking we might find posts where the sniper was defending Cat against Hall. Given he wanted podcast episodes about himself, he must think she's credible and doing a good job. He's threatening her now because he's not getting his way. There was something that drew him to her from the start."

"Do you have any obsessed fans that love you?" Cooper asked the question more in line with Luke's thinking.

"There's been a few who I'd consider obsessed with me. None of them made threats against me though. I considered them just a little over the top in how much they said they liked me. Most of my fans talk about how much they like the podcast. The ones I'm talking about were solely focused on how much they liked me. They said little about the podcast as a whole."

Cat got up from the table and went to her office. She came back with a small stack of pages and dropped them down on the table. "These are from five people. They each sent me a handful of messages. They started posting on social media, leaving glowing comments about me. Three of them then sent me direct messages. When I didn't respond, they resorted to emailing me. I thanked each of them initially for the messages and told them I was happy they were fans of the podcast. I don't think that was a good thing to do because it only encouraged them to message me more."

Luke didn't have time to go through all of them. He asked Riley and Cooper if they'd be willing to go through the pages and do a little research to start. They agreed to help. "Are any of these people local to Little Rock?" Luke asked Cat.

"I didn't research them the way I did Todd Hall. As you'll see, there were never any threats but they are over the top. It didn't occur to me to worry too much about them. It happens sometimes, right? People get a little overly enthusiastic about someone they consider famous." She put the word in quotes. "I never considered myself famous. I'm just the voice behind the microphone."

Luke pointed to the pile. "I'd consider the sniper obsessed with you – enough he was willing to kill a man making threats against you. He wants your attention, which is why we want to move you to a safe house."

"He's got my attention," she said dryly. "I want to argue with you about the safe house, but honestly, I didn't get any sleep last night. I'll pack a bag and will be ready when an officer arrives."

"I'll be sending someone not in uniform. We'll figure a way to get you out of here so it's not obvious you're leaving. I know you'll need to come back to record."

"I can bring my podcast equipment with me," she informed him. "The sound quality won't be as good but I'll make do."

That was even better. "Cooper, you'll stay here until the officer arrives?"

"I won't let her out of my sight," he promised.

Luke grabbed the sandwich Riley had bought him for the road and left feeling like at least Cat had been handled.

CHAPTER 17

After Luke left us with Cat, I dug into the stack of messages from her admirers. What I soon realized was that the emails from the admirers were nearly as terrifying as the ones from those who had made threats. They were all from men who claimed they were in love with Cat and knew they were destined to be with her romantically.

Three of them had left their phone numbers and full names. Two of them only signed off by their first names. I read through each series of emails and then compared them with the copy of the sniper's notes saved on my phone. I was looking for similar word usage and style of writing. None of the three men who left their full names seemed like a match.

One of the emails was from a man who called himself Harvey. There was no last name and the email address had his name and a few numbers after it. He sent eight emails in all – the first letting Cat know she was doing a great job and that he found her attractive.

I glanced up from the note. "Cat, have you always had a photo of yourself online?"

"Since the start. It's on my website bio page and social media. We also take photos during the podcast and those get posted as well." She gestured toward the pages. "I assume you're asking because they reference the photos."

I confirmed I was. "I didn't know if you had photos from the start. It makes sense that it was more than professional photos and included candid photos too. Some of these reference what you're wearing and even suggest they like you better in skirts and dresses rather than pants."

"I considered not posting photos for a while but I didn't want to give them that much power."

I pushed a few of the pages I was most interested in over to Cooper. "Read these and tell me what you think." I was focused on the last email in the series. Harvey had come right out and told Cat he wanted her to meet him for lunch. He said that he was giving her a week to let him know where she wanted to meet. He hadn't phrased it as a question. He didn't ask *if* she wanted to meet for lunch. He wanted to know when. There wasn't an *or else* but it was implied. His tone was commanding, firm, and more than a little controlling. I hoped she hadn't encouraged him. "Did you ever reply to this request for a lunch meeting?"

"Harvey?" Cat asked and when I said yes, she said no. "I didn't want to meet him. He kind of creeped me out."

I agreed with her about that. I looked up at the top of the page to the email header. The email was sent three weeks ago with the date of the suggested lunch two weeks before the first shooting. That stood out as significant to me. "Did you hear from him after this last email about meeting in person?"

"No, and I was glad for it. I thought he had given up."

I had a sinking feeling in my gut it wasn't that easy. A man didn't go from obsessed with a woman to retreating that quickly. "Did you have any interaction with him either online or in email since his first message to you?"

"I had some back and forth with him early on in my comments," Cat explained her voice full of regret. "Had I known I was encouraging him, I wouldn't have done that. Back then, he was saying nice things about the podcast and wishing me well on my new journey. He seemed like a loyal fan at first."

"Then it changed?" Cooper asked, looking up from what he was reading.

"Yeah." Cat turned her head away from us and stared out the window. When she looked back at us, her mouth was set in a firm line and the corners of her eyes were pinched. "He direct messaged me a few times and I left them unread. I figured fans would just assume I wasn't able to get messages that way. That's when he turned to email. I keep the generic email address on the website for tips about cases, if anyone wants to suggest a case and so forth. He used that email address to reach out and told me he hoped he wasn't bothering me but he was sad that I wasn't responding to him. My email sends an auto-response thanking the person for the message and letting them know if a reply is needed, I'll get back to them as soon as I can. A reply is not promised. Usually, my assistant processes the tips on cases and suggestions. Emails like that she keeps in a separate folder and prints them off. We don't respond."

Cooper shook the pages in his hand. "You didn't respond to any of these? He makes it sound like you're in regular correspondence. He even said *since we last talked*. It sounds like you're saying it wasn't a two-way conversation."

"That's exactly what I'm saying. Other than those initial messages back and forth in the comments on social media and the auto-response that everyone gets sent, I said nothing to him. That's why I started having those pages printed. They were creepy and overly familiar but not the threats like the others. I didn't know what to do with them."

"These could be far more serious," Cooper said with an edge in his tone and then regretted it when he saw Cat's face. "I'm sorry. I know this was all new to you. I'm not sure how I would have responded to it either."

"I didn't know what to do with it," Cat admitted, leaning back in her chair. She tucked strands of purple hair behind her ears. "I started this as a side project to keep my mind off a breakup. It spiraled quickly into something more and with that came…" She gestured with her hand to the pages of emails. "There's no protocol for how to deal with all of this."

We were lulled back into silence as I read more of the emails. Cooper continued to pour over the ones sent from Harvey including the last one that I handed over. I didn't see anything in the others that were as serious as what Harvey was sending her. They were admiring emails and some were a little creepy pointing out things Cat was wearing in photos or how they liked her hair on certain days. They didn't have the same controlling and delusional tone that Harvey's emails had.

The name was tripping me up, like a memory I couldn't recall sitting in the far reaches of my mind. It was right there. I just couldn't access it. I pulled out my phone, hit the internet app, punched in a few search phrases, and came back with nothing relevant.

"What's the matter?" Cooper asked, sensing my frustration. It was either the look on my face or the fact that I was cursing softly under my breath because I couldn't figure it out.

"The name Harvey is stuck in my head. I feel like it's connected to something."

Cooper suggested a couple of searches but they came up blank too. I was stumped.

"What about searching with the keywords *Son of Sam*," Cat said, throwing it out there.

I tried the search and blinked rapidly at the screen in front of me, not sure I was seeing this correctly. I reached the first few search results and then scrolled through more to make sure.

"Harvey was the name of Sam Carr's dog," I said finally when they were both staring at me.

Cooper had the same confused expression as Cat. "Sam Carr as in Son of Sam?"

"Right." I rested my phone on the table. "Remember when I said David Berkowitz said a demon dog was telling him to kill people? That was Sam Carr's black Labrador Retriever Harvey." I picked up the pages from in front of Cooper and shook them. "There is no way there's a coincidence this big. Harvey must be the sniper."

"Possibly," Cooper said slowly and turned in Cat's direction. "You still have the original emails?"

"Yeah, there is a folder in my email. I can pull them up right now."

"The email headers," I said mostly to myself but they both heard me. It was exactly what Cooper had been thinking. The cops could trace the IP address. "Maybe he wasn't careful then because he didn't know he was going to go on a shooting rampage."

We were all so focused on the potential lead that the knock on the front door caused us all to jump. I held my hand to my heart and let out nervous laughter. "Are you expecting someone?"

"No," Cat said standing but Cooper gestured for her to sit.

Whoever it was knocked again and Cooper walked to the front door, opened it, and said a few words of thanks. He came back into the conference room carrying a large bouquet of white lilies. "Were you expecting these?" he asked as he put them on the table and stepped back to admire them. "I didn't dig through them for the card."

If Cooper wasn't paying attention to Cat's expression, I certainly was. Her eyes were wide open and she had pulled back from the table as if the flowers were a bomb about to go off. "Throw those out." She stood and backed away from them. "Please, get those out of here."

I grabbed the flowers off the table and carried them to the far back of the building where she had a small kitchen. I put them in the sink and dug through the stems to find a card. It was on the other side of the bouquet in the plastic wrapping around it.

"What's wrong with her?" Cooper asked as he came into the room. "The flowers are pretty."

I glanced over at him. "You mean other than an obsessed fan killing a man threatening her, forcing her to do a podcast about his shooting rampage, and threatening to kill her? It doesn't take much to wonder if the flowers are from the sniper."

Cooper bit the inside of his cheek. "Do you think he'd send her flowers? He just threatened to kill her. I figured they were from someone who knows she's going through a rough time." He ran a hand through his hair. "I honestly didn't think it was the sniper."

"We'll see in just a moment," I pulled the small square card from its entanglement and opened the envelope. I read the words aloud so we both heard it at the same time. *"You have done well, Cat. You did exactly as I wanted. I may spare your life after all."*

I tossed the card down on top of the flowers.

The look on Cooper's face said it all.

"We need to get her out of here," he said as he pulled his phone from his pocket. Cooper snapped a few photos of the flowers and of the note. He texted them to Luke. "He has more than enough to handle right now. I'm asking when the cop will be here to bring her to the safe house."

"Let's give her a few minutes to calm down and then we can talk to her. I don't want to confirm her worst fear though. Let's not even mention the flowers." We stayed there in the kitchen waiting for Luke's response. While we were talking, I asked, "What do you think the sniper wants from her? Just the podcast episodes?"

"I'm not sure what the sniper wants," Cooper admitted. "He's obsessed with her one minute and wants to kill her the next. He's obsessed with Son of Sam and then goes off that script and kills two people in the morning and Todd Hall. I can't make heads or tails of any of this."

"The Son of Sam case was never a sniper so he never seemed to be on script," I reminded him. "He was thinking about this long before he started. I don't think choosing the screen name Harvey was a coincidence."

"Is there any chance it's his real name and not connected to the Son of Sam at all?"

I didn't think there was a chance. I picked up the card from the flowers. "Look at the words he chose to use. This is someone intelligent. He's shot five people already and there isn't even a witness to any of it."

Cooper stared out the doorway of the kitchen. "The sniper was in Todd Hall's apartment. It means he went inside and there's a chance a neighbor or someone saw him. Once we know the details about the date and time of death, there might be someone who remembers him."

I shook the card. "The company that delivered the flowers might know something too."

"Let's wait for the cops to take Cat to the safe house and we can decide what we'll do." He decided we had given Cat enough cooling down time. I followed him to the conference room but it was empty.

We backtracked down the hall to check her office and studio. Both doors had been closed. He stuck his head into the studio space. "Riley, look in here. Is there something missing?"

I moved around to the side of him. I hadn't spent as much time in the studio as he did. I wasn't sure what was missing but it did look like something was gone. There was an area of the table near her microphone where I thought there had been something before. I pointed to the empty space. "What did she have there?"

"Portable recorder," Cooper said. "Maybe she's going to bring it with her to the safe house."

"She told Luke she could." I went out into the foyer and up the stairs to her apartment. "Cat," I said and knocked on the door. It inched open under the weight of my knock. "Cat," I called her again and then a third time, louder.

I entered her apartment and quickly went through the rooms looking for any sign of her.

I made it to her bedroom in the back of the apartment and found the room was a mess. There was a pile of clothes on the bed, her closet door was open, and two empty dresser drawers pulled out. There was a row of empty hangers in the closet. An open window sat on the far wall, the sheer drapes fluttering in the stiff hot breeze. She wouldn't have left a window open with the central air on.

My heart thumped in my chest as I raced to the window. There was a fire escape that went directly to the alley below. "Oh, Cat, what did you do?" I said aloud.

"Where is she?" Cooper asked as he rushed into the room.

I angled my head to look over my shoulder. "She's gone, Cooper. She took off."

"How is that possible? We were only talking a few minutes."

"She must have had a bag ready to go."

"Let me text Luke again. We have to let him know."

Luke was already dealing with so much. I worried that this would push him over the edge.

CHAPTER 18

Luke had been talking to Andrew McNamara for nearly forty minutes but still didn't feel like he was getting anywhere. The man used more legalese than plain English. When he felt like his head would explode if he had to listen to it a moment longer, Luke finally asked the man to stop.

"I understand your office is under a tremendous strain. You've lost two of your best attorneys in the middle of a high-profile case." Luke acknowledged the attorney's dilemma. "All of that is important but that's not why I'm here. I need to know if they had any threats made against them. I'm trying to solve this case as quickly as possible so no one else has to die."

McNamara leaned back in the chair and then rocked it as he stared over at Luke. "Who do you suspect?"

Luke hated to admit it but he didn't know. "I'm pulling at any threads here. I've had one man shot at close range in his apartment who was threatening the podcast host. I have two young women shot – one of whose father is a defense attorney. Now it's your two employees who are working on a high-profile case against Ezo Technologies. None of the victims seem to connect to the others. I need to know if Bennett and Kristy were under any kind of threat because of the case."

Andrew gestured with his hand as if to say it's all part of the game. "There's always a risk in these kinds of cases. They were skilled attorneys who would have won the case. Getting rid of them plays in Ezo Technologies' favor. That's the fact of the matter." He clicked his tongue. "They already called to see if we are willing to settle the case with a slap on the wrist. If we did that, it would help their private civil case as well."

"Are you going to settle?" Luke didn't care one way or the other, except he hated to think a company like that would walk scot free. It also went to the motive of the sniper. It might be exactly why Bennett and Kristy were murdered. Only McNamara wasn't answering. Luke pushed him. "Whatever you say won't go outside of this room."

After a few beats, McNamara admitted, "I don't know what we are going to do. I have to ask the judge for a continuance to see if I can get other attorneys up to speed. It's going to be a process. In the end, we might have no choice but to settle the case."

"Have there been threats against them?" Luke asked again.

"Yeah," he said, his voice gruff. "Not because of the case though or maybe it was. I don't know. What I do know is that the two of them were having an affair and someone found out. Someone was using it to blackmail them to drop the case. If they didn't, it was clear the information would come out publicly."

This was exactly the kind of information Luke was asking. "How did you find out about the affair?"

"Bennett came to me after he received a letter in the mail. It had a Little Rock postmark and we tried to figure out who sent it but we weren't able to. The letter was simple and straight to the point. If he and Kristy continued with the prosecution of Ezo Technologies, their affair would be made public. It was sent to Bennett's loft. He had no choice but to tell me. They admitted the affair but weren't going to stop prosecuting the case."

"What was your response to it?"

"I was angry. We all know better than to cross the line like that, especially since Kristy was married." McNamara threw his hands up in frustration. "It happens though more than you think. They are consenting adults. I wasn't going to fire them over it. There wasn't sexual harassment or anything like that. They said they were in love. The plan was once the case was over, Kristy was going to leave her husband and they were going to be together."

"What about the letter?"

"We didn't put too much stock in it. They continued doing their jobs."

Luke wasn't sure he would have either. "Did you confront the defense team?"

"We went to the judge and had a conference. The defense swore up and down that they didn't have anything to do with it. Ezo Technologies swore they didn't have anything to do with it. Bennett and Kristy didn't admit the affair to any of them. I don't think the judge wanted to know. He saw it as a real cross-the-line kind of moment and told the defense they'd better keep their client in line. As I said though, we weren't able to prove where the letter came from so there wasn't much the judge could do. The case proceeded forward."

"Was it just one letter?"

McNamara nodded. "Just the one and then nothing happened until this."

"How long ago was the letter?"

"Two months ago and not a peep from anyone after that. Nothing was ever made public and the case settled back down into its usual rhythm. We were prepared to go to trial at the end of the summer. We had a September 23 court date for jury selection."

Luke didn't know if that letter had anything to do with the murders. "Do you have the letter?"

"I'll get it before you leave," McNamara promised him.

"When do you think the case will resume?"

"The court date will be pushed back. I'm sure given the circumstances the judge will give us time. I can't say for sure when the trial date will be."

Luke needed McNamara to level with him. "Do you believe that this shooting had anything to do with your case?"

Andrew leaned forward and rested his arms on his desk. "Listen, Det. Morgan, Ezo Technologies has been involved in shady business practices since the beginning. I don't know of any direct murders. We can certainly say all the toxic waste they are dumping will kill people. That's why this case is so important. But cold-blooded murder? I can't point the finger at them. I simply don't know."

"Gut feeling?" Luke knew he was asking the attorney to speculate.

While his words didn't say yes, his expression did. "It certainly is convenient for Ezo Technologies. I have a hard time believing this random sniper happened to target them. If I were you, I'd be questioning if these murders are connected to the others."

That was Luke's main problem. "The first murder and the two young women could be connected. These murders, I agree that I'm not so sure."

"Has the sniper taken credit for them?"

"He left a note for the podcast host that he shot them because he wasn't happy with the first episode. He even sent an audio file she included in the next episode. It should be live now. I won't have more of a confirmation until the medical examiner is done. It appears the shooting is connected to the others, but as you said, there are more complications here."

"Your guy's a letter writer too," McNamara said evenly. "I don't know. Maybe it is all connected."

"That's why I'm here," Luke said with frustration. "I'm trying to rule out all other options. Is there anyone in Bennett's or Kristy's life that might have wanted revenge on them?"

"I don't have information besides what I told you."

Luke believed him but that frustrated him more. "What about Kristy's husband? Have you met him? Is he capable of something like this or paying someone to do it?"

McNamara gave an emphatic no. "He's a mild-mannered teacher who didn't know about the affair. Kristy was sure of that. It was one of the questions I asked. He'll be devastated to know the truth."

"He never came up here to Little Rock while Kristy was working?"

"Not that I know of. Kristy went home every other weekend. She said she loved him and he was a good man but that they had grown apart. I don't think he's your guy."

Luke didn't either. "What about anyone in Bennett's life?"

"Nobody. Before Kristy, I didn't even know him to date. He was singularly focused on the job. He was one of the best attorneys I ever worked with in this office. They both were, and I have no idea how I'll ever replace them."

Luke asked a few more routine questions and thanked him for his time. He left the office with the original letter, promising to return it after it was analyzed. There was no way to tell now if it was connected.

After the meeting was over, he checked his phone and cursed a blue streak right in the middle of the federal office building lobby. He got raised eyes by the doorman.

"Sorry," Luke said as he left and headed directly back to Cat's studio. He cursed his luck the whole way. "You had one job to do. Keep an eye on her was all I asked."

Riley had never heard him have his voice raised like that. Neither she nor Cooper said a word while he dressed them down. Luke got it out of his system then joined them at the table. He listened while Riley told him about the flowers and how freaked out Cat was by receiving them.

"She didn't read the note. She assumed correctly it was from the sniper," Riley explained. She then backed up and explained the rest. "We had been focused on the threats, Luke. That seemed to make the most sense. When Cat told us about a few of the men obsessed with her, I wondered if we were looking at it from the wrong angle, especially when the sniper killed Todd Hall and said it was a gift to her." She picked up a stack of printed pages off the table and handed them to him. "There are five men who were obsessed with her. These are even creepier than the threats."

"We have concerns about one of the senders," Cooper pulled off the top pages. "He writes in a similar style as the sniper and he asked Cat to meet with him."

"He didn't *ask*. He told Cat to pick a place where they could meet for lunch," Riley corrected, stressing the point. "He didn't give her the option of saying no. The tone was controlling and it bothered Cat, as it should have. He's also using the name Harvey."

Luke wasn't sure if that was supposed to mean something to him. He looked at Riley with a question on his face. Her response floored him. "Are you serious that Harvey was the name of Sam Carr's dog?"

Riley was sure. "You can look it up yourself. I knew it sounded familiar to me so I looked it up. Sure enough, it was right there in black and white. Getting the flowers when she hadn't been expecting them along with that sent Cat right over the edge."

Luke had been back and forth several times about Cat's potential involvement in this case. Tyler had made a persuasive argument for her involvement and then backed off the narrative. With her taking off like this, Luke's suspicions rose all over again. "If she didn't know who sent the flowers, why'd she run?"

"She's scared, Luke," Cooper said and Riley agreed. "This has taken a toll on her. Based on the number of threats she's had and the creepy admirers, it sounds to me like she's been dealing with a lot for a while."

Riley shifted in her seat to look at him more directly. "Given you suspected her of being involved, I'm not sure how much she trusted you to keep her safe."

Luke understood but it was more than that. "It also makes her look guilty. What are we going to do if the sniper wants more podcast episodes? We can't make it public she took off. That's only going to put a target on her back if she's not involved."

"She's not involved, Luke," Riley said with emotion in her voice.

"Yeah," Luke said, not sure what he should be feeling. He rubbed his bald head and groaned in frustration. "I can't worry about Cat. We offered her protection and she jumped ship. Captain Meadows and Tyler aren't going to be happy about this. I'll deal with it tomorrow and for now, we can only hope she knows what she's doing."

"What about Harvey?" Cooper asked.

"If you have the email header, I'll see what the tech team can do." Luke held out his hand and Cooper gave him the page. He glanced down at it. "This case gets weirder and weirder."

As Luke stood to leave, Riley asked, "Are you headed home?"

He shook his head. "I'm going to try to track down Raymond Bollin again. Then I have to tell Kristy's husband his dead wife was having an affair."

Luke was past his breaking point and he didn't mean to sound so cold and detached. He just desperately needed a break in the case.

CHAPTER 19

While Luke sat outside of Raymond Bollin's apartment, he called Tyler to let him know Cat had taken off. Before he gave his boss a chance to react, Luke added, "I share your frustration and suspicion that she could be involved. Riley and Cooper aren't convinced and discovered some information they think might be helpful. It's a guy who has been sending Cat obsessive emails. He calls himself Harvey, as in Sam Carr's dog from the Son of Sam case."

"Did those emails start before the shooting?" Tyler asked, not sounding nearly as angry as Luke had expected.

"Riley said Harvey has been messaging Cat since the start of her podcast. He first messaged her on social media. When she didn't respond to direct messages he sent, he found an email address on her website and emailed her several times. My understanding is that she didn't engage with him other than some basic niceties in the comment section on social media early on." Luke also explained his meeting with Andrew McNamara. "I have the letter that was trying to blackmail Kristy and Bennett. Do we have an expert who can compare the letters for us?"

"Handwriting?"

"I was thinking forensic linguistics and handwriting. The first sniper message was handwritten. The second was typed. It's a long shot but we don't have much."

"I'll see who I can find," Tyler said and then paused. When he spoke again, his voice was filled with concern not for the case but for Luke. "Are you doing okay?"

Luke stared straight ahead at the apartment building. "I'll be okay after this loser is caught. Right now, I'm only focused on catching him." The answer wasn't what Tyler was looking for but it would have to be good enough because Luke didn't have anything else.

"Is there anything I can do to help?"

Luke thought of a laundry list of things but nothing he would have ever said to Captain Meadows. It was things he would have told a partner, but didn't want to bog down Granger with yet. "What do you want me to do about Cat?"

Tyler didn't even hesitate. "You don't have any evidence to arrest her and she can't be in trouble for refusing police protection. She knows the risk she's facing. Don't waste any resources on it. If you find evidence against her, then we'll utilize resources to find her."

"What if he requests another episode?" That was a bigger concern than finding her. Tyler was right they had no real evidence to suggest she was involved. As with nearly the whole case, his suspicion of her was pure speculation.

"Not much we can do. If Riley or Cooper can contact her, maybe they can keep her in the loop. I'd have one of them keep checking her studio for any messages if they have access."

Luke hadn't told them to do that specifically. He wasn't even sure they had a key to lock up the place. "What about this Harvey guy who was emailing her? I have the email header and need tech."

"Drop it off when you can and I'll put someone on it. For now, if Riley and Cooper feel like they have any leads, let them explore it. You don't have the resources to chase your tail."

That's how Luke felt about the whole case. "How's the mayor's office treating you?"

"It's better, Luke. Captain Meadows smoothed things over and assured them I was making the same decisions he would have made. If we can get out of this case successfully, I might just have a career as a captain."

Luke wrapped up the call with Tyler and then sent a quick text to Riley asking her to see if she could find a key to Cat's place or to send her a text and ask what she wanted done in her absence. He explained he was going to get a tech to look at the email header and encouraged Riley to go after any leads she and Cooper had. At the end of the text exchange, he apologized for his grumpiness earlier and told her he'd be home as soon as he could.

She confirmed with a heart and kiss emoji. Luke appreciated that she understood his earlier frustration. Luke sent a heart emoji back and then put his phone back in his pocket.

He sat in his SUV for the next hour waiting for Raymond to arrive home. When he was just about to give up for the night, a rusted old Ford truck pulled into the parking lot and a man fitting Raymond's description got out. His arms were dark brown and weathered like he spent considerable time in the summer sun and his overalls and beat-up work boots shed dust and caked mud as he walked to his building. He looked like he had put in a hard day of manual labor.

Luke waited until he started his ascent to his second floor apartment and then got out of his SUV and followed. Raymond reached the landing of the second floor when Luke called his name.

The man turned around and glared at Luke. "What do you want?" Raymond asked with the voice of a man who wanted nothing more than a shower and a cold beer.

"I need a quick word with you." Luke climbed the rest of the stairs, introduced himself, and flashed his badge.

"I haven't done anything in a long time. You can call my attorney if you have questions about my past."

"This isn't about your past," Luke said, leaving out that it was his former attorney who had provided his contact information. "This is about the recent sniper shootings."

"Hassling the veteran." Raymond rolled his eyes and took it in stride. "Come on in. You'll only find a reason to do it anyway if I don't do it voluntarily." He walked to his apartment, unlocked it, and went inside. In the small square foyer, he kicked off his boots and left them on a mat. "Take a seat in the living room and I'll be right there. I can change my clothes, right?"

"Do you have any guns in your possession?"

"I've got a handgun in a locked safe in my bedroom, which I have every right to have." Raymond headed down a narrow hallway while Luke waited in the living room. He unlatched his holster and kept his hand on his gun. He'd give Raymond the benefit of the doubt for now.

A few minutes later, Raymond returned wearing shorts and a tee shirt. It looked like he had washed his face and splashed water on his hair. He went into the galley kitchen and pulled a beer out of the fridge. "Do you want one?" he asked and Luke declined. He came into the living room and dropped down into his recliner.

Luke took a seat across from him. "I stopped by the other night but you weren't here."

Raymond nodded but didn't explain. "What do you want? You said this was about the sniper shootings."

"One of the victims was Grady Cullen's daughter," Luke said.

"I saw that on the news. What does that have to do with me?"

"Grady Cullen was your attorney, right?"

"He did the best he could for me. I had no problem with him. I certainly wouldn't hurt his daughter."

"You ever meet her?"

Raymond shook his head. "Never even saw a photo of her. I'm sorry he lost his kid. Nobody should have to go through that." He pinched his eyes closed until they were mere slits. "What's this got to do with me though?"

Luke didn't want to come out and say he was the only decent lead in the case. Instead, Luke sidestepped the question. "I heard you were interested in the Son of Sam case. Do you know a lot about it?"

Raymond raised his shoulders in a shrug. "I know a fair amount. I took some criminal justice classes in community college. I had thought about being a cop but I went into the Marines instead." He gestured toward the television. "There was a documentary about Son of Sam on one of those streaming channels when I was going through my trial. I probably talked about it a bit at the time – a way to focus on something other than what I was going through. I'm still not connecting the dots here. What's this have to do with me?"

"The sniper is sending letters saying he's going to finish what Berkowitz started in New York."

Recognition took hold on Raymond's face. Luke thought he might get angry but he seemed only resolved. "You thought because of my interest in the case and the fact that I was a sniper and Cullen's daughter was the victim that it might be me." It was a statement, not a question. When Luke didn't respond, Raymond shook his head. "I didn't do it. I have an alibi for the night of the first shooting and the one this morning too."

"You don't seem angry that I'm here talking to you?"

"Why be angry? I had some issues in the Marines and after. I ended up in jail because of my temper. I was a sniper. I'm as good a suspect as any. I didn't do it," he said again. "I'm trying to turn my life around. I go down to the veteran's hospital and have a good doctor who helps me out. She's got me on some medication for depression that I take regularly. I talk to her every other week about what's going on in my life. I talk to my probation officer too. I've got stable employment, an apartment, and even a girlfriend. Life is finally getting back on track. I wouldn't mess it up now. I definitely wouldn't be shooting random people in downtown Little Rock."

Raymond's story seemed as plausible as any. Luke asked a few more questions that he answered reasonably. When he was done, Luke asked, "Can you provide me with the contact for your alibi?"

Raymond didn't argue. He gave Luke his girlfriend's name and phone number. "I told you I have a handgun in my safe. I haven't shot that thing in months. You're free to test it if you'd like. I don't have any others, and I'd be happy if I never had to touch a gun for the rest of my life. I'm trying hard to put the past in the past. I'm not one of those vets who want to relive their glory days. I did what I had to do and it messed me up. If I had to do it over, I would have been a cop."

"You probably would have made a good one too," Luke said, feeling for the guy. "What do you think of the shootings? Do you think he had training like you had?"

"I don't know that much about them, to be honest with you. I caught a little on the news and some guys at work were talking about it. I can't say for sure."

Luke found himself wanting to tell Raymond about the logistics of the shootings. He allowed himself to share the details and watched for any signs of recognition on Raymond's face but found none. Raymond had listened dispassionately and didn't seem to react to the information. "What do you think?"

Raymond asked a few clarifying questions and then answered. "It doesn't sound like he'd need to be a military-trained sniper to make those shots. He has some skill but he didn't need the level of training I had to make them. You can't rule it out. I'd widen your search."

Luke had been waiting for a slip up or for Raymond to ask a question or give away information only the sniper would know. He didn't – there wasn't one hint of suspicion Luke could find. He stood and shook the man's rough calloused hand. "I appreciate the information."

"Tell Grady Cullen I'm sorry about his daughter," Raymond said with sincerity in his voice.

By the time Luke got to the parking lot, he had the girlfriend on the phone. She confirmed that Raymond frequently stayed at her apartment and that he was there the night of the first shooting and had been there early that morning. They woke to see the morning shooting on the news. Raymond had gotten out of bed, showered, and left for the day.

When Luke asked her if she had any concerns he might have been involved, she said there wasn't a shred of worry in her mind that Raymond was involved and then gave him a play-by-play of their time together during the shootings right down to what she had made him for breakfast.

Luke even asked if Raymond had talked about Son of Sam or any serial killer cases. His girlfriend assured Luke it had never been a topic of conversation and nothing he read about or watched when he was with her.

Luke ended the call satisfied Raymond wasn't involved. His best lead had dried up.

CHAPTER 20

Cooper woke the next morning to his phone binging with an alert. He rolled over in bed and lifted the phone from the bedside table to read it. The heat index was going to be 117 degrees today, two degrees higher than the previous three days. The city had cautioned there might be rolling blackouts. It wasn't that unusual to see these temps in the summer on an odd day here or there. This was days and days of oppressive heat at the end of a scorching summer and everyone was tired of it.

Adele was in the shower already, which meant he had slept longer than he planned. He checked the time and it was nearing seven. He thought about joining Adele in the shower but then thought better of it. It would only start something Adele didn't have time for. He knew she had to be in the courtroom by eight. She had a meeting with her client, the prosecution team, and the judge. Her client had requested the meeting before his sentencing. Seeing he had already taken the plea, they didn't see any harm in the meeting.

Cooper closed his eyes and breathed deeply, wishing he could stay in bed all day. His thoughts drifted to Cat. He had received a text from her at midnight to let him know she was safe but that she didn't trust the cops to keep her safe. She had gotten herself into this mess and she was going to rely on herself to get out.

When Cooper asked about any further podcast episodes, Cat said she had her recorder with her and it would be enough to record and publish if needed. She told him where he could find a spare key and he promised to keep an eye on her place for her. He had wanted to ask her where she was but Cooper assumed she wouldn't tell him. He had tried a few times to get some clues to her location without asking outright. She gave nothing away.

Cat said she was safe and that was all he could hope for given the situation.

"What are you thinking about?" Adele asked as she walked into the bedroom in her purple silk bathrobe.

"I was thinking about joining you in there but figured you didn't have time."

Adele walked the short distance from the door around to his side of the bed and kissed him sweetly. "I would have made time. But you're right, I need to get to the courthouse." She went to the dresser and applied lotion to her arms and legs before getting dressed.

Cooper watched her go through her morning routine feeling lucky he had found such an amazing, beautiful woman. "I bet you'll be glad when the case is over."

"It's no different than any other case. This is how they go. You win some, lose some, and sometimes your clients make completely nonsensical decisions. I learned a long time ago to roll with the punches."

It was a little how Cooper felt about his cases sometimes, even when his clients insisted he should be able to get evidence that either didn't exist or was impossible to get. Adele had been asleep last night when Cat had texted him and he hadn't told her yet.

"I heard from Cat last night," he said as Adele fastened her favorite pair of turquoise earrings in her ears. Cooper told her about the short exchange they'd had and was surprised Cat had reached out at all.

"Do you think she's still local?"

"I don't know. She might have gone back home to her family in Chicago. If I were her and was faced with the situation, I'd want to get out of town. I haven't heard anything about another shooting. He must have been satisfied with the podcast last night."

"It won't be the last," Adele said with seriousness in her tone. "I'm going to stop by the office first thing and see if there was any communication from him overnight. Luke said those cameras are fully operational. Hopefully, we caught him on video if he did."

"Isn't that a conflict of interest for you – to hope they caught him? Won't make much of a case for you if they did."

Adele saw the teasing smile on his face. "Don't try to get me going this early in the morning. We both know I want this guy caught as much as anyone else. If he wants me to represent him after that, I'll do my best to protect his rights. He's not my client, no matter what he thinks." She finished getting herself ready for work and left the room, leaving Cooper to stretch and get himself out of bed.

He'd swing by Cat's studio to see if the sniper left any communication there and then go to Riley's house to see what she had planned for the day. She had told him she was going to work from home for as long as she could. Given how hot it was, she didn't want to leave unless she had to.

Cooper still wanted to review some of the other communication from both the threatening men and the men obsessed with Cat. He figured maybe the sniper wasn't going to be so obvious as to sign his communication with the name Harvey.

Cooper got himself ready for the day, locked the door to his loft, and was halfway down the hall when a call from Adele stopped him in his tracks. In the meeting with the judge that morning, her client Buster Thomas had admitted to knowing the identity of the sniper. He said he'd spoken to someone in county lockup who admitted to knowing the sniper. He wanted to share it with the judge in exchange for a lighter sentence in county lockup rather than going to state prison.

Luke had been called in and Buster had provided a name – Clayton Dalton. He had served time in the Army at the start of the Iraq war. He'd been dishonorably discharged and had been living in a camp on the outskirts of Little Rock that was filled with radical survivalists who were anti-government. Buster explained the goal was to shake up Little Rock and have it hit the national news. The goal was fear. If something like this could happen in the middle of the country, it could happen in larger cities.

Cooper only had one question. "What's the connection to Cat?"

"None," Adele told him. "The best Buster could figure was Clayton was toying with Cat and using the podcast to spread their national message."

That didn't make any sense to Cooper. The sniper hadn't provided any anti-government message. It hadn't been political at all and he never mentioned being a survivalist. "Who did Buster say he got the information from in jail?"

"He wouldn't tell us that part," Adele said with frustration in her voice. "Luke was annoyed by it but he had the potential name of the sniper and that was all that mattered. The court is going to wait to see if the information pans out and then the judge will sentence Buster. It was why he wanted the conference with the judge this morning, Cooper. He said he'd been provided the information yesterday and spent the whole day wondering what he should do."

"I don't like this, Adele. It's too easy."

"That's what Luke said when he left the courthouse. He said to call you and let you know what's going on. He's got the whole SWAT team headed out to that camp."

Cooper's heart thumped into his chest and thought back to the other times law enforcement walked into similar situations – Ruby Ridge and Waco. Cooper couldn't rule out that Clayton Dalton wasn't the sniper and wasn't doing this to draw law enforcement there. Even so, it didn't feel right in his gut. "I don't like this at all especially because Buster wouldn't reveal his source."

"I'm only relaying the message. Luke said he'd be in touch as soon as he could. He asked that you connect with Riley if you can."

Cooper couldn't shake the nervous feeling in his body – a million little pinpricks telling him the situation wasn't as it seemed. "What connection does Buster have to this group?"

Adele yelled to someone on the other end of the phone that she'd be right there. "What was your question?"

"Why was Buster given the information? Of all the people sitting in county lockup, why him?"

"I'm not sure that it matters. Someone shared it with him and he did the right thing by coming forward."

Cooper wondered if that was true or if Buster was just a good patsy. "Will the court let me speak to him?"

Adele let out a gasp. "Cooper, there is no way you are getting anywhere near Buster. He's sitting in protective custody until Luke and his team bring in Clayton. I know you're nervous for Luke but what other choice did he have? He's only going to know for sure once he brings Clayton in for questioning."

"Did he speak to the ATF? If they are in a survivalist camp, then I'm sure the ATF or the FBI has been monitoring them."

"Cooper," Adele said his name in an exasperated breath, "Luke has the whole thing under control. He called in both the ATF and the FBI. He knows what he's doing. He said he had no choice but to run down the lead and he's doing it as safely as possible." Adele told Cooper she loved him and rushed him off the phone.

Cooper stood in the hallway and stared at his phone. He wasn't even sure why his gut somersaulted at the news and his skin felt like it was on fire. The sniper could be Clayton Dalton. There was no reason it couldn't have been him and yet Cooper was sure it wasn't.

He left his building and walked the few blocks to the coffee shop. He ordered a coffee and a blueberry muffin. While he waited, he spotted the young barista with the nose ring and asked for Cat's key. He didn't know when Cat had started keeping a spare key to her studio with the young woman at the coffee shop and he wasn't sure why. She handed it over to him without question.

Cooper stood at the side of the counter to wait for his order as his phone rang.

"I'm nervous about this raid," Riley said after he answered.

"I'm worried about it too. From what Adele said, Luke's taken every precaution."

"That's what he assured me. He also said he's not sure he trusted Buster. He interviewed him for more than an hour this morning. Buster insisted that's what he'd been told yesterday. He said he had to pass the message forward."

Had to. Cooper rolled the words around in his head. "He said *had to* specifically?"

"What do you mean?"

"Did he feel like he was going to be in some kind of danger if he didn't tell Luke? Did someone threaten him if he didn't bring the message forward to law enforcement?"

Riley sucked in a breath, understanding his meaning. "I don't know, Cooper. There's nothing we can do about it now. Luke left an hour ago and the camp is about an hour outside of the city. I'm sure they are there now."

Cooper still had no proof that anything was wrong. It could have been any one of a thousand things. It's possible someone was out to get Clayton and saw the first opportunity to do that but wanted to remain anonymous in the process. It was also possible someone was trying to set up Clayton and found a good patsy in Buster. It was also possible this was a setup for law enforcement. That's what worried Cooper the most.

"I'm going to stop by Cat's and I'll be up to see you soon."

Cooper got his coffee and muffin and walked a couple of blocks to Cat's studio. They had only been able to lock the handle lock on the downstairs door and had to forgo the deadbolt the previous night because they hadn't had a key. Cooper was glad to see the studio still intact and the office space fine. He climbed the stairs to her apartment and found that secured as well.

After scoping out the place to ensure he was alone, Cooper went back down to the front of the building and checked the mailbox for mail. There among the flyers and junk mail was an envelope addressed to Cat in black ink. The handwriting looked familiar and he was sure it was from the sniper. There was no postmark and no address. The only thing there was Cat's name.

Cooper should have turned it over to Luke. He held it in his hands for a few precious seconds debating what he should do. In the end, he pulled gloves from his back pocket and went to the desk for the letter opener. He made a single slit across the top and tugged out an index card. The message was simple and clear.

Cat shouldn't have left. Now everyone must pay. While the cat's away, the mice will play.

The sniper knew Cat was gone. There'd be another shooting and Cooper had no idea who to warn.

CHAPTER 21

I spent the morning reading and rereading Harvey's emails, looking for any hidden clues and meaning in what he said. I skimmed through the podcast episode of the sniper's statement and tried to match any similarities in phrases or word usage and found two.

In the podcast episode toward the end, the sniper said he'd given his story to the "darling Cat" and in the email, Harvey referred to Cat as the "darling Cat" too. The second reference was the use of the word *balmy*. In the podcast, the sniper said he enjoyed a good balmy day, and in the email, Harvey said he was enjoying the balmy weather. It wasn't a commonly used word in my circles.

I finished the search more convinced than ever that Harvey was the sniper. I didn't think Clayton Dalton, a declared survivalist, was going to be sending emails to a podcast host, chatting her up on social media, and calling her darling.

When I couldn't go any further with the search, I tried to focus on a child custody case I had been working for Cooper before the shootings started. I had written half the report for the attorney and the other half sat there as a blank screen beckoning my findings. I normally didn't mind writing the reports. I just wasn't in the mood and it wasn't due for another five days. I had time.

I sat back in my chair and looked out the window of my second floor office. What I needed was a break. It was burning hot outside. I didn't want to walk the two blocks to Kavanaugh Boulevard where all the shops were, but my desire for a frozen mocha won out.

My fair Irish skin didn't do well in the southern sun so I slathered a fine layer of sunscreen on before I left and threw on a baseball cap. I walked the distance to the coffee shop and said hello to a few of my neighbors who had dared to venture out with me in the heat.

There were more people on the street than I would have assumed. It was nearing lunchtime and it looked to me like business people were heading to some of the local restaurants. No one wanted to work in this heat. It made everything feel the pace of a crawl. Even in the short distance from my house to the coffee shop, beads of sweat had pooled at my lower back.

The wave of cold air hit me as soon as I entered the shop. I breathed a sigh of relief and let the cool wash over me. Given the street traffic, I was surprised to find the shop empty. I made my way to the counter and placed my order, chatting with Johnny, the young man behind the counter. He asked how Luke was doing and I assured him things were going as well as could be expected. Luke frequented the shop, usually in the mornings on his way down to the station. We often stopped in together after a visit to the farmer's market if schedules allowed us to spend a Saturday morning together.

As I stepped to the side while he made my drink, I looked out the front window to the sidewalk at the people gathered. I allowed myself a brief moment of calm while I kept my thoughts focused on Luke and hoped he was doing well. A few moments later, the shop bell rang and a young woman holding the hand of a little girl, who had a halo of blonde curls around her face, entered the shop. I didn't think the little girl was more than four or five. She complained about being hot and her mother told her she'd be cool soon enough.

The mother saw me looking at her daughter and smiled. "I thought we'd get out and get some fresh air before the afternoon sun. We only made it a block."

"Same," I said laughing with her. I was admiring the little girl's yellow dress when a shot rang out. I've heard in situations like that everything moves in slow motion and that was true this time too. No one reacted to the first shot. The woman had a confused expression on her face and I instinctively ducked my head low.

I turned to the window to see a man get hit by the second bullet and the third pierced through the window of the coffee shop, shattering glass all around. I dove toward the woman and little girl taking them both to the ground with me. More shots rang out, coming now in quicker succession.

"We need to get behind the counter," I shouted. She kept her eyes focused on me. The shock had frozen on her face. Her little girl wailed in fright. "Now!" I shouted again when there was a break in the shooting.

We bellycrawled behind the counter. I made sure they both got behind it and then searched for Johnny but didn't see him anywhere. I crawled back to look out toward the sidewalk as the shooting began again. The young girl's screams pierced through the gunfire. I threw myself back behind the counter. I turned to look at the woman who sat huddled with her daughter against the wall.

"Are you okay?" I shouted to the mother.

She was still too stunned to speak or process my words.

I scooted over and patted her down making sure she hadn't been hit. I repeated the motion with the child and both, thankfully, appeared to be fine. That's when I turned and scanned the whole space behind the counter and finally saw Johnny backed up against the far wall with his hands over his head. I called for him but he didn't move other than the rocking of his body in fear.

"You're bleeding," the mother said, finally speaking. "Your arm. It's bleeding," she repeated, pointing to my left arm.

I cast my eyes down to my side and there was deep red blood running down the length of my arm and dripping on the floor. I didn't feel any pain but the blood was enough to know I'd been hit.

"It's okay," I said, trying to assure myself as much as her. "It's going to be okay." While I said the words for her benefit, I didn't know if what I was saying was true. The gunfire in front of the shop continued, sounding like it was hitting everything in front of the building.

The woman started crying causing her daughter's screams to be even louder. Johnny shrieked for his mother. The sounds of glass shattering and people yelling poured through the broken window of the shop.

As the shooting continued, I knew the counter wasn't going to provide us much cover. I assumed a bullet could easily pierce it. I bellycrawled over to Johnny and shook him hoping to break him free from the shock. "We need to get in the back of the shop. Come on."

I tugged him with me toward the double swinging doors, holding it open as I gestured for the woman to crawl to me. When she didn't move, I crawled back to her and pushed her and the little girl through the doors.

Once I got them all in the back of the shop in a far corner of the kitchen, I called 911.

"Someone is shooting along Kavanaugh Boulevard in the Heights." I told her my location and who was with me. "We have access to the alley but I'm afraid to go outside. The gunman can enter the shop. What should I do?" I felt like I was seeing the world through a wavy plexiglass and time stood still.

I didn't know our best course of action. We were sitting ducks if the gunman came inside but going outside could put us at risk as well. The 911 operator told me to remain where I was and I relayed the message to the others. She assured me that there were already cops and paramedics on their way. She asked me if any of us were wounded.

"I am. My arm. I don't think anything life-threatening." I kept my thoughts focused on the present. I didn't want to think of the carnage outside.

The 911 operator asked me if I was okay to hang up or if I wanted her to stay on the line. I let her go. I was sure she had more calls to handle and possibly some from people more injured than me.

The gunfire continued and we sat there huddled together not sure if we were going to live or die for what felt like hours. In reality, it was probably only twenty minutes from start to finish. I tried to offer soothing words. There was nothing I could say to make this any better. I reached up for some paper towels on the counter and wrapped my arm. There was too much blood to even see where I'd been hit. I had been shot once before and this time it felt different. Then, I'd been knocked unconscious.

Now that the shock was wearing off – this time, I felt it all. The burning, searing pain.

As the siren's wail grew closer, the gunfire finally subsided. I still didn't want to move from our position. The four of us sat on the kitchen floor of the coffee shop until a cop entered the building. He called for any survivors to come out with their hands up. I slowly rose from my position as he entered the kitchen.

He asked again for me to put my hands up and instructed the others to do the same.

"There are four of us." I raised my arm as high as I could. "I've been injured," I said as if he couldn't see the wound on my arm or the blood dripping to the floor. "I'm Det. Luke Morgan's wife. Please focus on them first. I'll be okay."

I wanted the woman, her child, and Johnny to feel safe and avoid seeing any of the destruction. The sooner we could get them to safety, the better I would feel. My only solace was the young girl would probably never remember any of it. At least, I hoped that was true.

The cop radioed for a paramedic and focused on the others as I had asked. He escorted them out of the kitchen towards the back entrance into the alley.

I slumped down against one of the refrigerator doors, my legs feeling like they might not hold me any longer. As he headed for the back door, I asked, "What happened out front?"

"Don't worry about that now," he said to me but I could see it all on his face. "Stay there and wait for the paramedic."

I remained there on the floor until the paramedic found me. He was working to wrap my arm when I heard Cooper's voice echoing through the shop. Cops told him not to enter but he didn't heed the warning.

"Riley!" he shouted my name.

"Tell him I'm okay," I whispered to the paramedic. He ignored me and kept working on my arm. I was sure I'd pass out at some point. The pain grew unbearable and I winced at the paramedic's touch. He was talking to me but I had no idea what he was saying.

My ability to process information had long since passed.

"Riley," Cooper said my name with relief, and then his voice droned out to the same dull background noise as the paramedics. I finally allowed myself to close my eyes, knowing I was safe – at least for the moment.

CHAPTER 22

Luke stood at the property edge of the Dalton compound. It was clear they didn't want visitors by the large no trespassing sign and the threat that those who entered would be shot. Luke had called the home several times. There was no voicemail and he wasn't even sure the phone number was still operational. It rang and rang and rang. What he knew about the Daltons was minimal too. Clayton was forty-seven years old and lived with his wife and three children. His brother and their parents lived on the compound too.

The ATF had a file on the Daltons that would have taken Luke all day to read. They were known to be survivalists and lived off the land. They rarely ventured into the neighboring town except for some supplies. They also had more weapons than the entire police department – all bought legally as far as Luke could tell. Still, the sheer size of their arsenal had put them on ATF's radar.

While Clayton had a dishonorable discharge from the Army, he didn't have a criminal record. His father had an old assault charge from the sixties but nothing since. The brother's record was clean. Neither of the women in the family had criminal records. There were no pending charges against any of them. As far as Luke could tell, there was no crime other than the speculation about the number of weapons they owned.

ATF and the FBI were looking for any reason to breach the

compound. Luke didn't want to play their game though and figured cooler heads could prevail. The last thing he wanted was a firefight or heaven forbid a standoff of some kind. Those didn't bode well for the federal government.

As far as Luke was concerned, all he had was the word of a convicted criminal who was looking to have a reduced sentence. He wasn't putting too much stock into it all.

"What do you want to do?" the lead ATF agent asked him.

"I want to go alone to the front door and ask a few questions."

The man shook his head. "We can't let you do that. You don't know if the land is rigged with explosives or what they have going on."

Luke turned his head to look at him while trying to control his temper. "What do you suggest then? We don't have a search warrant or a warrant for anyone's arrest. We have no reason to go on their property. We are operating only on the word of a criminal who could have been motivated to make up something to reduce his sentence."

Luke didn't think that was why Buster had come forward. He had interviewed him for more than an hour. By all accounts, he was telling the truth and looked freaked out to even have to share the information. Buster acted as if he had no choice but to share the information about the Daltons. It made Luke curious whether someone was threatening him.

It left Luke backed into a wall. It was a lead he had to run down.

"It's your call. Let us know what you need," the ATF agent said with an air of disappointment. It was clear to Luke they were itching for a fight he wasn't going to give them – if he could help it. Little Rock's SWAT team was there with him too and he had cautioned them about their response. Luke's only goal was to get eyes on Clayton and have a conversation. That was it.

He stared at the shack away in the distance and wondered if anyone was home. There were two beat-up old trucks in the driveway. In total, there were five structures on the property that he could see from his vantage point. Three small houses looked in need of a good paint job, a shack, and what looked like an old barn. The Daltons had more than thirty acres – most of it looked like overgrown grass and shrubs. The family had been living on the property for the last fifteen years.

Off in the distance, Luke watched as the old dog meandered his way toward the group of them. He had taken an interest but hadn't barked yet. Luke felt bad for the pup whose coat had turned gray and his right hind leg had a limp. Luke assumed there was a touch of arthritis.

The dog walked right up to the fence and stuck his nose through the barbed wire. Luke squatted down and rubbed his nose. "Where is everybody?" he asked him as he scratched his face.

The dog looked up at Luke with curious eyes then turned and started his walk back. Luke took it as a sign and swung the latch off the fence and opened it. He'd walk with the dog back toward the houses. He turned once and waved off the agents who started to follow him. Luke knew SWAT was set up around the perimeter. The last thing he wanted to do was start a fight.

Luke walked with the old dog for a few hundred yards when he spotted a man in dusty overalls hunched over the engine of a four-door silver sedan parked at the side of the house. "Clayton Dalton," Luke yelled and the man raised his head.

"Did you not see the sign?" the man asked as he wiped the grease from his hands onto a rag that looked like it had once been red. "We don't take too kindly to trespassers around here." He stepped to the side, looked past Luke at the range of police vehicles, then stepped back with a nervous expression on his face.

Luke kept his body loose and his tone calm. "I'm Det. Luke Morgan with the Little Rock Police Department. Don't worry about the rest of them out there. It's only for my protection. I have a few questions for Clayton." The man still hadn't identified himself and, with his disheveled appearance, he could have been Clayton or his brother.

He still looked uneasy about the police presence at his gate. "I'm Clayton. What do you mean you're from Little Rock? Why are you way out here talking to me?"

"Your name came up in an investigation and I needed to ask you a few questions." Luke took a step toward him. "I'm going to level with you. One false move on your part and they are going to take that as a sign and breach the property line."

"They have no right to do that." Clayton furrowed his brow and looked between Luke and the law enforcement standing at the fence.

"If my life is at risk, they will do it."

"You don't have any right to be here either." Clayton looked uncertain about what to do. He stared off at the contingent of police and thought better of any action he might have taken. "I got two chairs by the side of the barn. They can see you from there. How about we sit and talk?"

"Sounds like a good decision on your part." Luke turned and gave an all-clear sign and then walked with Clayton and the dog to the side of the barn. He sat down in a rocking chair that looked older than him. The wood creaked under his weight as the dog brushed up against his leg wanting attention. Luke reached down and scratched his head. "He's a friendly old guy."

"Not much of a guard dog. Then again, don't need one out here. The sign usually takes care of it for me." Clayton tucked the grease rag in his pocket. "What's this about? You said my name came up in an investigation. I don't see how. I haven't been to Little Rock in years."

"Did you hear about the shootings that have been happening?"

He chuckled. "Little Rock is a violent city. You're going to have to be more specific than that."

It seemed as if Clayton didn't know what was going on. "Do you watch the news much?"

He shook his head. "It's all lies. Why would I bother? I don't have a television out here. I listen to the radio sometimes but don't get much Little Rock news."

Luke explained about the sniper shootings. "There are four people dead and one badly injured. There's been a few letters left for a podcast host and a defense attorney."

Clayton had confusion on his face. "You think I know something about it? I don't understand."

Luke believed him. "I was provided your name from a criminal sitting in county lockup. He was told you were responsible for the shooting."

"Who told him that?"

"He didn't provide us with the name," Luke said, feeling slightly foolish that he hadn't been able to get that out of Buster. They had asked the correctional guard about who Buster was in a cell with, but that hadn't helped any. It could have been anyone in the yard. "As I said, I only had a few questions. I'm sure you can understand I needed to follow every lead."

"I don't know anyone in county lockup that would have provided you my name. We have guns out here for our protection. I didn't shoot anyone." He turned to lock his gaze on Luke. "When did you say these shootings took place?"

Luke gave him the date and times. "Do you have an alibi?"

"I was here. I drove into the next town over for a few groceries with my wife the other day but haven't been off my land since then. She's not here right now but you can talk to her when she gets back."

Luke would get that alibi but spouses weren't often the most credible. "What about your brother and father? Have they been here too?"

Clayton nodded. "My mother and sister-in-law too. We don't leave the land much. We have everything we need."

"You were described to me as an anti-government survivalist. Is that a fair assessment?"

Clayton shrugged. "I don't much care for labels, and I don't much care for the government. Lots of people don't like the government though. Look at the state of them. I'm not looking for trouble."

Luke could appreciate everything he was saying. "I'm still trying to figure out how your name came up in this. Is there anything you can think of why someone would point the finger at you?"

"Why does anyone do anything?" Clayton looked as confused as Luke felt. "I don't know anything about podcasts – don't listen much to those kinds of programs. I don't know anyone in Little Rock and don't know anyone in jail. I can't tell you what I don't know."

Luke released a frustrated sigh. "What about people out here? Do you have visitors out here?"

"No one but you has been dumb enough to cross the fence line," he said with a laugh and then considered the question. "About two months ago there was a man who came out here looking for a gun range. He got turned around and thought there was one out here. He said he heard shooting, which we do in the back of the property."

That didn't necessarily mean anything. Luke could see someone making the mistake right up until they saw the signs on the property. "Did you turn him away?"

"That was the plan but he showed me the gun he had. It was a 1940s Lugar in perfect condition. He said it had been his grandfather's in the war."

That didn't sound like the sniper. "What about other weapons?"

"He didn't show me any other. Although there could have been some in his truck. I told him we weren't a shooting range, didn't want a stranger shooting on our property, and that was it. I sent him on his way."

Luke's phone buzzed on his hip but he ignored it. "Do you have any idea why someone would send me out here to talk to you?"

"Distraction, maybe." Clayton gestured toward the cops on the other side of the fence. "This could have easily turned into a bad situation. Not many cops would have ventured onto my property alone to talk to me man to man. It was good that you did."

"I didn't want any trouble with you. I only wanted to see your connection to the sniper shooting." Luke looked around the property and wondered if Clayton had people hiding out waiting for trouble. He chose not to ask the question. "I didn't have any evidence you were involved and I had no evidence that you had done anything else wrong. I saw no reason for a fight when we could sit down and talk. I am going to need to double-check that alibi though."

Clayton rattled off the phone number and his wife's information. "I know spouses probably make suspicious alibis," he acknowledged. "It's all I got out here. You're going to have to take me at my word that I didn't shoot anyone. That's not an interest of mine. I want to live off my land and keep the government out of my life. Shooting up a place brings the government to my door. Seems like competing interests to me."

Luke knew he wouldn't have much of Clayton's time left and considered what else he might want to ask the man. "If you hear about anything regarding the shooting, could you let me know?" He handed Clayton a business card with his information. "All I want to do is catch this guy and restore order to Little Rock."

"Little Rock hasn't had order in a long time. Maybe never." He gave Luke a look.

Luke wasn't sure if he was referencing the gang violence problem, the city's long racial history, or even its political choices over the years. It was a medium-sized city in the middle of the country but had often made national news, usually not for anything good.

Luke stood and extended his hand to Clayton who took it. "I appreciate the information and your time." He bent down and gave the dog another head scratch and then headed back toward the fence.

Luke made it about halfway to the edge of the property and saw the constrained looks on the faces of the ATF and FBI agents. One of his SWAT team members had a phone in his hand and the man's face paled as he heard the person on the other end. It made Luke stop dead in his tracks. Something was happening. He looked back at Clayton who was back bent over the engine of the car. He didn't think it had anything to do with the Daltons.

Luke quickened his pace to the fence. "What's going on?"

The SWAT team member extended the phone to him. "It's Captain Tyler. There's been another shooting. This time in the Heights on Kavanaugh Boulevard. Someone fired along the street and into the shops. There have been casualties."

Luke's stomach dropped and he could tell the SWAT guy had more to say.

"I'm sorry to tell you, Det. Morgan, but your wife has been shot and is in the hospital. She's been taken into surgery."

Luke didn't hear much of anything after that. All he cared about was getting to Riley.

CHAPTER 23

My dreams were lucid, a kaleidoscope of color and confusion. I relived the shooting and watched the people in the shop die around me. I woke up at some point and heard that there were five dead. I slipped back into the dream state so fast I wasn't sure if what I had heard was real.

Later, I opened my eyes slowly and woke to a swirl of confusion. There were wires on my chest and running down my arm. My mouth felt like it was stuffed with cotton balls.

"Luke," I said barely above a whisper. My words remained trapped in my mouth. I swallowed the dust and took a deep breath that hurt in places I didn't know I had. "What's going on?"

Cooper appeared at my side. I had a brief memory of Cooper going with me in the ambulance to the emergency room. He reached out and touched my hand. "You're in the hospital. There was a shooting. Do you remember?"

I couldn't understand what he was saying and he had to repeat it. "I remember it," I said finally but was still piecing it together. I thought it had been a dream. "They are all dead, aren't they? Just tell me." I started to cry and my voice cracked as I tried to speak. "Johnny and the mother and girl. They all died."

"No. No, Riley, you got them to safety. You got shot in the arm in the process. You had to have surgery. It's going to take a little time to heal but you'll fully recover." Cooper explained that the bullet had shattered part of my humerus. In the meantime, I might be in considerable pain.

I cast my eyes down to the side and saw my arm bandaged and wrapped in a sling. I tried to raise my head and Cooper adjusted my pillow. He got me a cup of water to sip and it took care of the cotton in my mouth.

I put my head back and closed my eyes. "Is anyone else hurt?" When Cooper didn't respond, I turned my head to him and opened my eyes. I repeated my question.

Cooper pinched the bridge of his nose. "You should get some rest. We can talk later."

I struggled to sit up. "Tell me, please. I need to know."

Cooper nervously licked his lips. "There are twelve injured and five dead. Nine of those twelve are being treated and are expected to make it. Two remain in critical condition. One is in intensive care and they aren't sure he'll make it. It's a mess, Riley. I've never seen anything like it."

"What about Luke? Where is he?"

"He was out with Clayton Dalton when the shooting started. He got here while you were in surgery. He was here for a while. When you went into recovery and he knew you were going to be okay, he went to the scene. He said he'd get back here as soon as he could."

I understood why he wasn't here. "Is Adele safe?"

"She's fine, Riley. She's at court trying to get the truth out of Buster. We believe it was all a ruse to get Luke and the SWAT team out of Little Rock. The attention was focused out there and it gave the sniper time to move around freely."

"There were still uniformed cops," I said, trying to make sense of it.

"I know. But the focus was on Clayton Dalton. It's all a game to the sniper, Riley. It's just a sick, sick game." Cooper sat in the chair next to the bed. He looked like he'd aged a few years since I saw him last. "I don't know how we are ever going to stop this. He left a message for Cat, angry that she left. He indicated that while the cat was away the mice would play. Someone got Buster to plant a fake lead on Clayton Dalton. The man wasn't guilty. Luke was with him when the shooting was happening."

I didn't care about all of that now. I wanted to know who was dead and if I knew them. "Do you know the names of the deceased?"

"It's not anyone we know," Cooper assured me. "All the shops were shot up and it's a mess of broken glass and blood. The cops are still processing the scene. Once they are done, the community is ready to clean up. Everyone is strong, Riley. There's been a lot of people asking for you." He told me about all of my neighbors he'd spoken to and that had asked about me.

I closed my eyes. "How's Johnny – the young employee at the shop? He looked like he was in total shock, Cooper. He was rocking back and forth. I didn't think I was going to be able to get him back into the kitchen."

"He's been treated and released to his parents. I spoke to them briefly and they thanked you for being there. He's pretty shaken up. Everyone is."

"The mother and young girl?"

"Treated and released. The mother had a few scratches on her arm from broken glass. Nothing that even required stitches." Cooper stood from the chair. He tugged the covers up and brushed strands of my hair away from my eyes. "Come on, now. Get some rest. You can worry about everyone later."

"Did you call my mom?"

Cooper nodded. "I told her I'd call her when you woke up. She wanted to fly down but I told her you needed rest and it's not safe here. She wants you to go back to New York and recover at her house.

She knows you won't. She wanted you to know the offer stands."

The weight of whatever pain medicine they had given me started pulling me under. "I'm going to sleep," I mumbled as my eyes closed.

"It's the best thing for you right now."

I wanted to ask Cooper if he was going to stay there beside my bed. I fell asleep before I could ask.

When I woke again, the room was bathed in darkness. I heard Luke somewhere off in the distance. He was speaking to a nurse or doctor about my arm. He thanked them over and over again.

"I'm awake," I said softly as he came back into the room. "Are you okay?"

He smiled at me but there was sadness in his eyes. "I should be asking you that. You scared me, Riley." Luke came over to the bed and kissed me gently. "I thought I'd lost you. I heard about the shooting when I was finishing up with Clayton. That was the longest drive of my life."

"I woke up earlier and Cooper was here. He said you were at the scene. Did you find anything?"

Luke winced. "You don't want to hear about this right now. You need to sleep. Do you want more pain medication?"

My arm throbbed but I wanted to feel it. I didn't want to numb myself and go back to sleep again. "I need to know. Cooper told me there were five dead."

"Six now. The guy in ICU passed about an hour ago." Luke blew out a frustrated sigh and sat next to the bed. He looped his hand through the rails and took mine in his. "It's total destruction. I've never seen anything like it. The sniper broke into a house a block away and shot from a second-floor window, across the backyard and street into the shops. He had a good deal of tree coverage. No one even knew what was happening or where the shots were coming from. The best I can tell from witnesses is the first shot was fired at 11:47 a.m."

That sounded about right to me. "I wanted a frozen mocha. I needed a break from reading all those emails from Harvey. I still think it's him."

"It might be because it's not Clayton."

"Cooper told me the tip was probably a distraction. Something to get you out of the city."

Luke nodded. "Retaliation for Cat leaving too. I don't know what to do."

"It's not her fault," I said weakly and reached for the cup of water on the tray table near the bed. Luke jumped up and refilled it for me. He held it while I sipped it slowly. "Cat didn't know he would do this, Luke. No one did."

"She's in as much danger as everyone else. It's not safe for her out there alone." His words had a hollow ring to them and I knew there was more. I could see it in his expression.

"What is it you're not saying? Has something happened to Cat?"

Luke sat back down in the chair. He ran a hand down his stubbled face. "By skipping town like that, Cat has put suspicion back on herself."

"What do you think, Luke? You're the best homicide detective that Little Rock has ever had. Do you think Cat could be involved in something like this? She's not the shooter..."

"How do we know that? We are assuming the sniper is a man. It could be a woman," he said, interrupting me. He started to say something else and thought better of it. "Riley, you need rest. I shouldn't be in here talking to you about this. Not right now anyway. You're too weak. You had surgery just a few hours ago. I'm being insensitive."

Luke had never been insensitive to me a day in his life. I pushed myself up straighter in bed. "I got shot in the arm. I'm going to be fine and can talk to you about the case. Did they say when they are releasing me?"

"They want to keep you overnight for observation." Luke adjusted my blankets and then asked if I was sure I wanted to talk about the case. When I assured him I *needed* to continue, he relented. "I don't believe Cat could be the shooter. It doesn't make any sense to me that it would be her. There is some niggling doubt she could be involved somehow. The sniper knew enough to send Adele a message. Cat has a connection to Cooper. Out of all the defense attorneys in Little Rock, why her?"

To me that was easily explained. "If he's walking to Cat's studio to leave a message, he would also be near Adele's office. Her sign is out front in the building. Her name was also in the newspaper and online about her pending case with Buster, which would also tip off the sniper that he was sitting in county lockup. I think the sniper is about ten steps ahead of all of us."

"The Son of Sam case?"

I had been giving that some consideration too. "Theatrical. I don't know that the sniper has any interest in that case other than it made the first note seem wild and scary. Because of the note, we thought he might follow along the same path as David Berkowitz, shooting dark-haired women at night. Berkowitz shot with a .44 caliber at close range. This sniper never started that way and I don't think that was his intent."

"The first shooting followed the Son of Sam case with victim selection. Teresa was shot in the leg and he killed Gemma."

"Then he went wildly off track and shot a man and a woman in the early morning."

Luke raised his eyes to me. "The victims were having an affair. I had to tell Kristy's husband when he got to Little Rock last night. He had no idea and was devastated by the news. He provided me an alibi for the time of the shooting and it checked out. He's not involved."

"I had no idea, Luke. I knew you went to speak to Raymond last night and that didn't pan out either. I didn't realize you had spoken to Kristy's husband too."

"I didn't feel like talking about it when I came home. It was heartbreaking news to deliver and I didn't want to dwell on it." Luke grew quiet and I could tell he was reliving delivering the news. I asked him to go back to talking about Cat. He shook his head. "I don't know what more to say about her. It's not implausible she could be behind this. She could have sent herself those flowers and written the note to make it seem like the sniper was after her. It gave her a chance to escape town. We don't even know where she is."

"Have you heard back from your tech team about tracing that IP address for the Harvey emails?"

"The emails are coming from all over the place. He's smart enough to redirect his IP address. One came from London. Another from Denver and two more from Seattle. All of the addresses were coffee shops too. We didn't get one solid hit on a home address. We don't even know if Harvey is local."

I might not have had any proof but I was sure he was. "He wanted to meet her for lunch and told her to pick a place."

"That doesn't mean he's local. It means he was willing to travel to see her." Luke rubbed his eyes. "Do you think you can reach out to her and try to get her to come back?"

Cat and I had developed a better rapport, but it wasn't as strong as her connection to Cooper. "I think that might be a job for Cooper. He might be willing to talk her into meeting him. I don't think she's going to allow you to put her in protective custody, Luke. She doesn't trust you because you initially suspected her. Check her out though and make yourself feel better. Dig into her background like you would any suspect." I didn't know what else to tell him other than the obvious.

Luke checked the time. "I hate to leave you. I have to get back to the scene. I have several more witnesses coming in. I'm going to need to interview you too."

"Can we wait until my head is less foggy?"

Luke stood and kissed me. "We can wait."

I didn't want to spend the night in the hospital but I felt safer there than if I'd been back home.

CHAPTER 24

After the shooting in the Heights, the whole city came to a screeching halt. A week had passed and people were rightly terrified. Schools that had only returned from vacation were locked up tight during the day while the students were there. Few children rode the bus and more parents dropped off their children and picked them up. Some children weren't attending school at all. Their parents chose to keep them at home until the sniper was caught.

Businesses were letting their employees stay at home if the job allowed for it. Other shops and restaurants remained fairly empty, frequented only by those who were brave enough to venture out. Between the blazing heat and the sniper's threats, people wanted to be at home.

Over the week, Cooper had spent time trying to connect with Cat, asking her to come back to Little Rock. He assumed by the little she had told him that she left the city completely. With the added national media attention and the few leads Luke had, she saw no reason to come back.

When Cooper asked if she was going to do any more podcast episodes on the sniper, she said she didn't know. Justice Exposed was badgering her to continue because the two sniper episodes already published were the highest in ratings. Her once-local crime podcast had garnered international fame because of the case.

It wasn't the kind of attention Cat had been seeking or so she claimed.

Cat explained Luke had contacted her a handful of times asking the same question as Cooper had about the podcast. Luke had left the decision up to her. He then asked her a series of questions that made her feel like she might be the only suspect he had. Cat assured Cooper she answered all of Luke's questions and provided him with as much information as she could.

It came down to the fact that she did not know the identity of the sniper and denied any involvement in the shooting. Later, when Cooper had asked Luke about the interview, he said there was nothing in Cat's background to indicate she might be a co-conspirator, and no evidence pointed in that direction. Still, Luke wanted her back in Little Rock in police protection.

There was only one question Cat had not been able to sufficiently answer – her alibi. She was home alone for the first shooting, received the note, and went directly to Luke's house. Then she was asleep in bed alone during the second shooting. The third she was gone. When Luke pressed her for an alibi on the third, she was hesitant to provide it because it would give away her location. Cat said she assured him she had never shot a gun in her life and certainly would not have been able to operate the AR-15 used in the Heights shooting.

No matter how much encouragement Cooper gave her to come forward and let the police protect her, Cat refused. She was convinced the sniper knew her and, if he found her, she was as good as dead. She trusted no one and Cooper couldn't blame her.

During that week, Cooper found three notes from the sniper at Cat's. A surveillance video set up across the street from her studio had caught a man dressed in black slipping mail through the door slot. His face was shielded from view each time. They were looking for a Caucasian man about five-foot-ten.

What Luke didn't know was if the sniper had paid someone to deliver the notes or if he was doing it himself. They had tried to stake out the studio but no note was ever left during that time. The city wasn't going to pay to have cops sit there around the clock after they had installed the surveillance.

Adele had been hoping that if the sniper left communication for Cat, he'd have left some for her. She was more determined now than ever to open a line of communication with him. But he hadn't left her anything.

Her client, Buster, refused to disclose who it was in county jail that had given him the tip about Clayton Dalton. He said it didn't matter if they gave him the full jail time for his robbery, he'd never give up the name. Buster stuck to the same story – he'd been provided the information and was doing what he had to do by coming forward and telling the cops. He was adamant he knew nothing about the shooting that took place in the Heights.

In the end, Luke said he was sure Buster had been used as a patsy.

Rolling blackouts plagued the city all week. Cooper had lost power for a few hours each afternoon. Riley often lost power first thing in the morning. Both of them were lucky that neither had been plunged into darkness at night the way some in the city had been.

Riley had been released from the hospital the morning after the shooting. Luke had been there to bring her home and made sure she relaxed. Cooper and Adele took turns stopping by to check on her all week, especially because Luke was working long hours and she was left alone.

All Riley wanted to do was get back to work. She couldn't type well one-handed. Cooper had to sit down with her while she dictated the final report she had been working on before the accident. She didn't seem too upset that she couldn't type it herself. She was frustrated having to do everything else one-handed. All Riley wanted to do was talk about the sniper case.

There wasn't much to tell her. Luke had few leads on the case. They had all dried up. Each avenue he tried, he hit a dead end. He had hoped the media would tire of no new information and leave. He wasn't so lucky. The national news remained camped out in downtown Little Rock but they never came back to their house.

Earlier that morning, Cooper and Riley attended the swearing-in ceremony for the newly promoted Captain Tyler. It was the first time she had left the house. The mood was somber and the weight of the case weighed on everyone. Captain Meadows gave a short statement at the ceremony that he had full faith in Tyler and the rest of the team. The mayor also expressed his support and shook Tyler's hand in front of the cameras. Cooper wondered if the mayor did support him or if it was only a political photo-op. There was a small reception held after the ceremony at a local restaurant and when it was over, Riley asked to go back to Cooper's loft with him.

Luke had looked at him with uncertainty when she made the request. Cooper assured him he'd get Riley back home safely. Although she had been cleared to drive and had stopped taking the pain medication, Luke was still protective.

"Is there something you wanted to discuss?" Cooper asked out of earshot from Luke, who had walked over to say goodbye to Tyler.

Riley gave a solemn nod. "I had a call about a case and I wanted to discuss it with you." She looked around them to see if anyone was listening. "Not here though. There's too many people."

Cooper raised an eyebrow. "The call came to you directly and not our main line?"

"He called me this morning and left a message. I haven't returned the call." It wasn't unusual as both their cell numbers had been used as business numbers before. It had just been a long time since anyone had called them like that. Most used the number on their website.

"What's the case?" Cooper asked, wanting to know right then. When Riley wouldn't answer him, he told her they could go back to his loft. They walked the few blocks together and when Cooper closed and locked the door behind him, he said, "Okay, you've been quiet the whole walk over. This must be serious."

"Hollis Hopkins called me. He lives in the Heights with his wife. Do you know him?"

Cooper hadn't heard the name before. "Should I know him?"

"He was a defense attorney." Riley went to the couch and sat down, cradling her sling on top of a pillow she pulled to her lap. "He said he had heard that I was shot in the Heights shooting and he wants to pay us to look into the case. He's lost faith in Luke and the police department."

"I assume you haven't told Luke about the call." Cooper sat on the other end of the couch from her and angled his body so he was looking at her.

"I didn't want to tell Luke anything until I spoke with you first. I'm not saying we should take the case, but if he's lost faith in the police, then we should assume many residents have. I don't know how I feel about taking money from him though. It doesn't seem right."

Cooper wasn't sure of her point. They had already been involved in the case and hadn't gotten any further than Luke. "I'm not sure what you expect us to do that Luke isn't doing."

"I want to go after Cat. I'm going to go to Chicago and speak to her family and see if she's there. I think she knows more than she's telling any of us."

Cooper wondered if Luke's suspicions had spilled over. "Luke has already questioned her at length, Riley. I'm not sure if there's more we can do. I don't think she's involved in the shooting. Unless you have actual evidence to show me, I think it's a dead end."

Riley was prepared for his resistance. She stood from the couch and paced in front of him as she listed off the reasons – most Luke had already presented to him, except for the final one. She turned to face him to make her point. "Cat didn't stick around to find out who sent the flowers. That didn't bother me at first. I figured she assumed it was the sniper and it spooked her. But of all the things to spook her, that was strange to me. I've had a whole week of sitting around doing nothing. I'm convinced Harvey is the sniper. I'm sure it's him as sure as I'm standing here. I think Cat knows him, and I believe he's tied to her past. I think she's gotten flowers like that before and when she saw them, she knew without reading the card. That's why she left in such a hurry and won't tell anyone where she is, even in the face of the cops suspecting her."

Cooper absorbed the information. "Are you saying you think Cat is hiding him and purposefully not telling the cops?"

"I don't know," Riley said evenly. "I'm worried she may not be connecting the two things. She may know without fully knowing. Something about those flowers spooked her though. After everything she'd been through with the threats and even those few men seemingly obsessed with her and then the sniper's notes, nothing spooked her like those flowers."

Cooper thought he understood then. "Are you saying you think she's afraid of the person who sent the flowers and she might not be connecting it to the sniper?"

"Correct. I also think if she finally connected this person to the sniper, she might be afraid to come forward with the information for some reason."

"That's a big stretch, Riley. All based on something you're not even sure about. Cat was shaken up earlier in the day. The flowers might have been the breaking point. You're making some huge leaps in logic."

"I know." Riley sat back down on the couch, tipped her head back, and closed her eyes. "I've been thinking about it all week and can't explain it better than I am right now. Cat went from being fully cooperative to fleeing in the middle of a conversation. Something spooked her. It wasn't even a rational decision."

The more Riley talked, the more Cooper agreed with her logic. "What do you think it is?"

"Maybe she was in a violent relationship and was hiding out here in Little Rock," she suggested and then thought better of it. "That can't be it. She wouldn't have had a public podcast with the name of the city in it if she were hiding from someone."

Cooper agreed with that. "She could have received some earlier threats she didn't tell law enforcement about. She didn't seem to take any of the threats or the messages from men seriously. She could have called the police when she first got them. Instead, she printed them and shoved them in a file."

"The first message she got from the sniper was sent to her a day before the shooting. She didn't bring it to Luke until after the first shooting. She claimed she hadn't checked her mail. It's possible she had checked and didn't take it seriously. If she didn't take the threats seriously, Cat might assume she's an accessory to the crime."

"If she knows who the killer is and isn't telling law enforcement, she might be an accessory." Cooper felt the weight of the implication. "Maybe she didn't connect all the pieces until the flowers and then she was too scared to stay and face the truth."

"Maybe she's so afraid of whoever it is that she'd rather be an accessory than turn him over to the cops," Riley said. "People do stranger things when they are afraid, even things that don't make much sense."

"What do you want to do then about Hollis?"

"I say we meet with him and see what he's offering."

Cooper couldn't disagree with the logic – even if he knew Luke was going to be steaming angry.

CHAPTER 25

After convincing Cooper we should take Hollis up on his offer to officially hire us for the investigation, we made our way to his house. He lived in one of the mini-mansions in the Heights. I thought his house was garish and out of place next to the smaller Craftsmen-style homes on the same street. This, unfortunately, was the direction the neighborhood was going.

Cooper and I had a brief conversation about the ethics of taking money for the case. If we were going to trek up to Chicago to look for Cat, we decided that having the trip funded wasn't that much of an ethical dilemma. Getting Luke to agree would be another conversation.

I knocked on the front door. Cooper stood a few feet behind me on the porch steps. We waited and then I knocked again. Hollis had told me he was coming home from the office to meet with us. He didn't want the other lawyers at his law firm to know he was hiring a private investigator.

A white BMW pulled to a screeching halt in the driveway, making us both turn to look. He threw open the door, shoved sunglasses up from his eyes, and rested them on the top of his head. He was tall with a thick mane of blond hair. "A meeting ran late."

Hollis brushed past us and unlocked the door. He had an arrogant air about him I wasn't expecting. "Will your wife be joining us?" I asked as we followed him into the house.

"No. I want to keep her out of this." Hollis directed us through the ornate foyer into the formal living room. There were large windows that looked out to the side yard and deep comfortable tan couches facing each other. "We can talk in here."

"Is there a reason you don't want your wife to know?" Cooper asked as he sat. When Hollis didn't respond, he said, "We won't tell her. I'm curious about your interest in the case and why you wouldn't want your wife to know you were doing this great thing for the community."

Hollis splayed his knees wide and dropped his wallet and keys on the coffee table. He sat kind of hunched over staring at us. The silence went on far longer than I was comfortable. When he spoke again, he clicked his tongue. "Here's the thing. I might know who the sniper is and I don't want to give the tip to law enforcement until I know for sure. It's a delicate situation."

I looked at Cooper and couldn't read his expression. While I had convinced him to be here, neither of us was expecting this. I turned back to Hollis. "What do you mean delicate? Is he a client?" Attorney-client privilege only went so far. An attorney couldn't keep secret a crime he knew was about to be committed.

Hollis made a dismissing waving gesture to brush off my question. "Let's get the paperwork and money out of the way first. Once I know this is confidential, we can proceed." He raised his eyes to me. "You are Det. Luke Morgan's wife after all. I'm taking a risk coming to you, but you're the best private investigators in the city. Some would argue the best in the whole south."

"We can't do any paperwork until you explain the situation to us and we decide to take the case," Cooper informed him. It wasn't what we had planned. Given the new information though, Cooper was making the right decision.

"How can I be sure you will keep this confidential?"

"You can't," Cooper said with emphasis. "We can assure you that we'll take the information seriously and investigate it. If it comes down to collecting any evidence we believe will be critical to a court case, we are going to take this over to law enforcement."

"I don't want to do it that way."

"Okay, then. We can go. You can hire one of the other private investigators in the city who don't do things the right and legal way." Cooper stood to leave. He wasn't playing around with Hollis and I appreciated that.

"I'll tell you," Hollis relented, realizing Cooper wasn't going to budge. "I believe it's my wife's brother, Len Woltman."

Cooper eased back to the couch. "Why do you think it's Len?"

"He's a quirky guy and loves guns. He's an angry guy too and frustrated with life. He's awkward around women, threatening almost, so he's never married. I don't even know if he dates much, to be honest with you. The few dates I knew he went on in the past ended in disaster. One woman even called the police because he started emailing and threatening her."

I thought back to Cat's emails. "Threatening her how?"

"It wasn't direct. It was covert, stalking-like. He'd mention seeing her places and knew the names of her friends. He kept asking her to meet him for dinner or lunch. Len wasn't asking though. He was demanding and it scared her. Real controlling stalker behavior."

Cooper said he understood. "There has to be more than that to accuse him of such a thing. When did you first start to suspect him?"

"It was after the second shooting – the two lawyers. Len had talked about them two weeks before the shooting. He said the government shouldn't be bringing a case against Ezo Technologies. He was angry with the government and had been asking around about the attorneys involved. Len used to work for the company."

I tried not to show a reaction. "How long ago?"

"He left a few years ago because of a disagreement with his boss. Len is a brilliant man. As I said, he can be difficult to be around. I thought he might have been fired. It turns out he left on his own accord. But I have a feeling that shooting was personal for Len."

I couldn't remember how much information had been made available to the media about the letters. I knew Cat had covered a little of the sniper's Son of Sam reference in the podcast. I asked Hollis if he had listened. When he said he had, I asked, "Did Len ever talk about the Son of Sam case or any other serial killer cases?"

"It was an unhealthy obsession of his. My wife, Evelyn, has tried to get him to speak to a psychiatrist several times over the years. It's only gotten worse as he's aged. Evelyn would never say this about her brother, but I think she's afraid of him. I don't like him coming here to the house much. Mostly, we meet him out for dinner if we need to see him."

"Has he spoken about the Son of Sam specifically?"

Hollis nodded. "It was a while ago. We were out to dinner and he was talking about a documentary he had watched on one of the streaming channels about the case. He was obsessed and said that David Berkowitz had created the perfect storm. Len said he would have gotten away with it for much longer had he not made a few mistakes."

That was interesting to me. "Did he tell you the mistakes?"

"No," Hollis said with emphasis. "Evelyn stopped the conversation. She told him it was sick and she didn't want to discuss it further. Len loves his sister and didn't want to upset her."

"What about Cat and the *Rock City Killers* podcast?" Cooper asked the obvious question. "Has Len listened to that?"

"Since the very first episode. He's the one who called us and told us about it. I wasn't interested and my wife doesn't want anything to do with killers or murder. She's never listened. I only caught the most recent episodes about the sniper because the whole city is involved and the cops haven't been saying much."

"What about Cat O'Conner? Did Len ever talk about her?"

"He said that he's been communicating with her, helping her on the cases. I didn't believe that, but I knew he had been posting on social media. Len acted like he had a real bond with her. I can't imagine Cat was interested in him."

I was having a hard time figuring out Hollis's age. "How old is Len?"

"Forty-eight last month. He's my wife's younger brother. Their parents have passed on. Len has always been the baby and his quirks were always passed off as nothing more than that. It's because he's so smart, everyone said. He's misunderstood." Hollis cursed under his breath. "I hated that they dismissed him so easily. I've had concerns about him for a while now. You can't say a bad word about Len though. Evelyn defends him and it blows up into a huge argument. That's why I'm sitting here and she's not. It's also why I want the investigation to be done discreetly. I don't want to end my marriage over this."

Cooper and I took turns asking a few more questions. Hollis was forthcoming with the information we needed without hesitation.

When we were done, Hollis grew quiet, sat back on the couch, and stared over at us. "What do you think? Do you think it could be him?"

I didn't need Cooper to say it. There wasn't a lot to go on. "There must be something else for you to think he's responsible for something so heinous." I raised my arm in the sling slightly. "I was shot during the shooting in the Heights. The person who did this is depraved and has no concern for human life. He's a psychopath. If we are going to take this case and investigate your brother-in-law, we need something more than this."

"What I said isn't enough to concern you?" Hollis asked, surprised. His voice grew louder and his face more animated as he laid out his case. "Len has a connection to the podcast. He has a connection to the two lawyers who were murdered and he's local to Little Rock. In addition, he has guns and is obsessed with serial killers, particularly the Son of Sam. I don't know what more I can give you without investigating the case myself – which is why I'm coming to you."

I was feeling jaded given how many dead ends the case had already encountered. "What do you think?" I asked Cooper. I assumed he might want to go outside to talk.

He surprised me though. "We'll take the case. First, though, you said something to Riley about wanting to find Cat. Is there a reason for that?"

Hollis blinked rapidly as if he didn't understand the question. "I'd assume like the second shooting was about retaliation for the podcast, he's angry Cat is gone. You need to find her and bring her back. She could help us bring him in. If Len is right and they had a special connection, then she might be the only one that can appeal to him to stop."

There had been rumors going around the city that Cat was gone. It didn't surprise me Hollis knew even though it hadn't been made public. "How do you know Cat is gone?"

"Len told me. He speculated Cat left because the sniper scared her off."

More than anything else Hollis said, that alone caused the hair on the back of my neck to stand on end. "When did Len tell you this?"

"A few days ago when I saw him for lunch. He knew I'd been listening to the podcast. After the Heights shooting, he expressed concern and wanted to meet. I already had my suspicions about him and thought sitting down to lunch with him, I might be able to figure it out. It only increased my suspicions."

"Why is that?" Cooper asked.

"Len said he didn't think the sniper was ever going to be caught. He said the sniper was too smart for the cops and he was doing things exactly as Len would have done if he were the sniper." Hollis swallowed hard and appealed to us with a look. "Who says something like that? It may seem like an innocuous statement, but he seemed gleeful that the cops were being outsmarted. Len acted in awe of the sniper and nearly praised him. Len's main concern was finding Cat. He said he was going to track her down. I think the two of you should get to her first."

"We'll find her," I said, barely finding the words. I remained quiet the rest of the time while Cooper went through the usual paperwork and accepted payment from Hollis.

When we were outside the house, Cooper turned to me. "Are you sure you feel up to going to Chicago?"

"I'm ready to get out of Little Rock for a bit." I wasn't sure if that was true. The one thing I knew was that we had to find Cat.

CHAPTER 26

After the official ceremony, Luke went back to the police station to go through the evidence again. He'd been working on the case for close to two weeks and he didn't feel any closer to a suspect than he had after the first shooting.

The evidence also didn't tell him much. The same weapon was used in the first two shootings and then an AR-15 was used in the Heights shooting. One of the houses had been broken into while the couple was at work. The sniper had taken a position in their son's bedroom window that faced the backyard and the shops along Kavanaugh Boulevard. He had the perfect position to shoot at those on the sidewalk, cars driving by, and the front of the shops.

Six people were dead and more than a dozen including Riley were injured. Now that it was personal for Luke, he didn't think people could say that he wasn't trying his best to solve the case.

Luke flipped through the evidence but there still wasn't anything for him to go on. There were no prints in the house or on the shell casings. There were no witnesses who saw anyone. The neighbors hadn't been home at the time and didn't see anyone break into the house. In all the confusion after the shooting, no one saw him leave either.

"Luke," a male voice called from across the office. He raised his head to see Granger walking toward the desk. "Are you okay, Luke?

I wrapped up those other cases and spoke to Captain Tyler this afternoon. He's officially assigned me as your partner. What do you need from me?" He sat down at Tyler's old desk and turned the chair to face Luke.

Luke hated that he felt relief to share the workload, not that there was much to be done. There were no more leads to run down. "I don't know where to tell you to start. We don't have much to go on."

"Have you found Cat?"

Luke shook his head. "I tried her family back in Chicago but they claim they haven't heard from her. If she wants to hide out, there's not a lot I can do to stop her. I have no witnesses, leads, or suspects."

Tyson reached his hand out to take the files. "You head home for the night and let me go through these. Maybe I'll see something with fresh eyes."

Luke didn't want to leave. He wasn't going to stop Granger from going through the files though. He closed it and slid it over to him. "I have boxes of other evidence in the conference room. We mostly have bullets and shell casings but not a print on any of them. No prints on the letters or envelopes either. He's wearing gloves."

"How did he get into the house in the Heights?"

"He broke the flimsy lock on the back door and walked right in. I suspect he had been staking out the place for a while and knew no one would be at home. I even questioned if he'd been in the house before because the window in the back was the perfect vantage point. There was a little tree coverage so that someone might not have seen him from the street but he'd be able to get a clear enough look at the shops. He shot indiscriminately at whoever was out there. There was no precision to it."

Granger tapped his finger on the desk for emphasis. "You've made progress then. You figured out a lot about him. He's a meticulous planner. He didn't need sniper skills and he's blending into environments enough to go unnoticed."

Put like that, Luke had made some progress. "Why do you think he's blending in?"

"We both live in the Heights. People are friendly but the community is small. They question when someone is an outsider, especially loitering around their neighbor's house. He also got into that apartment building in North Little Rock and shot Todd Hall without leaving evidence behind or anyone seeing him. He's a ghost, Luke. He's someone who walks among us. I don't think he's an outsider coming in to destroy the city. He's doing it from the inside."

It was an insightful statement and one with which Luke couldn't disagree. He wasn't too proud to ask, "What would you do next?"

"Have you run down previous shooting cases to see if the ballistics match?"

Luke had done that first thing. "There were no matches."

"Have you searched for where he could have bought the guns and the ammo?"

"I tried a few places and no one would talk without a warrant. You know how it goes."

Granger thought for a moment. "This might be a long shot but have you talked to any gun ranges to see if there's been anyone suspicious hanging around?"

Luke hadn't done that. It was a scatter-shot approach but with no other leads, it couldn't hurt. He knew from another recent case that there were five gun ranges within a thirty-mile radius. "I'll take three of them if you take the other two."

"I'll take three of them and you take the two. You look like you could use some sleep. After you do that, go home and rest. You're no good to anyone completely exhausted."

Luke couldn't disagree with him. This was the part of having a partner that he needed the most – someone to give it to him straight when he worked himself beyond what he should. Riley tried to take care of him in that way but he fought her on it. He never fought Tyler when he tried.

"I appreciate it," Luke said and shook his hand. He shared with Granger the names and addresses of the three ranges he should visit. When he was done, Luke admitted, "I think we are going to work well as partners."

Granger agreed with him. "We already are. If you find anything, call me and I'll do the same." As Granger walked off, Luke stood from his desk and stretched his arms overhead. The tension was starting to set into his muscles and make him feel stiff. He was headed toward the stairs when his desk phone rang. Luke looked back at it knowing he could check his voicemail remotely. He debated for only a moment and decided to jog back to his desk.

"Det. Luke Morgan," he said as he answered.

"Are you the detective in charge of the sniper investigation?" a woman with a soft voice asked.

"I am. Can I help you with something?" Luke sat down at his desk and waited. When she didn't say anything, he tried again. "I can meet you in person if that's easier."

There were a few moments of silence before the woman explained, "I believe my son saw the sniper break into our neighbor's house in the Heights. You spoke to us once already and he lied to you, Det. Morgan. I'm sorry but he's a teenage boy who was skipping school and didn't want us to know. I know lying to the police is a crime. I don't want to see him get into trouble for that. He was afraid he'd be grounded and didn't understand how serious it is to lie to the police."

Luke didn't care the kid had lied. All he cared about was that he was coming forward now and might have a description of the elusive sniper. "I was a kid once and skipped school from time to time. I'm sure I lied to avoid my mother's wrath. Are you home now? Can I come and speak to your son?"

"We don't want this on the podcast, Det. Morgan. I'm concerned for our family's safety once he comes forward."

"This won't be on the podcast," Luke assured her and appealed to her sense of responsibility. "We don't have many leads on this guy. Your son would be doing the whole city a favor by coming forward with this information. I know it's scary."

"Will you come to the house so we don't have to be seen at the police station?"

"Certainly." Luke grabbed a pen from the holder on the desk and jotted down her street address and the family name – Sheffield. Luke knew it sounded familiar even though he couldn't quite place it. "I'll be there within fifteen minutes." He hung up the phone more than a little excited to finally have what could be a real lead instead of the runaround he had faced.

When he pulled his SUV to the side of the road in front of the house, he recognized it and realized why the name sounded familiar. Edward Sheffield was a local orthopedic surgeon and his son had been in some minor trouble last year. He had been with a group of boys late at night and they had caused some property damage a few streets over. The boys had been fined and had done some community service, and once it was completed, their records had been expunged. That might have been why Trevor's mother had been so hesitant to call law enforcement. He'd already had one run-in with the law.

Luke cut the engine and got out of his SUV. By the time he reached the driveway, the front door opened and a woman with short curly blonde hair stepped outside and waved to him. "He's inside, Det. Morgan."

Luke greeted the woman who told him her name was Mary. She hadn't provided it on the phone and he hadn't pushed for it. She had told him their last name and that was enough. Luke followed her into the house and found a sullen-looking teenage boy sitting on the couch. He had a tee-shirt on and a pair of blue basketball shorts. Luke remembered speaking to him right after the shooting. He hadn't said much of anything and only shook his head when asked if he'd seen anything. At the time, Luke chalked it up to typical teenage behavior.

"Trevor. I'm Det. Luke Morgan. Your mother called me and told me you might have seen something the day of the shooting." Luke sat down on the chair across from him as Mary left them alone to talk.

When his mother was gone, Trevor asked, "Am I in trouble for lying to you?"

"No. But don't do it again," Luke cautioned him. "You're the first person who has come forward that might have seen him. Could you tell me what you saw that day?"

Trevor took a breath and sat up a little straighter. "I skipped school, which is why I didn't want to say anything in front of my parents. They told me if I skipped again, they wouldn't let me play football. We've only been back to school a few weeks and I hate my math class, so I skipped with a few friends. We came back here to the house and were home about thirty minutes when a car pulled up in front. I got nervous thinking my mom or dad was home. When I looked out, it was just an old truck."

"What kind of truck?" Luke asked, not meaning to interrupt.

"I'm not sure. Ford maybe. It was blue but faded and there was rust on the bumper. I didn't get a tag number because when I saw it wasn't my parents, I stopped looking."

"Did you see who was inside the truck?"

"Not at first. I had been coming downstairs when I heard it first pull up but my friends were in the kitchen so I walked to the back of the house. Then we heard some noise like someone hammering something. We walked out to the back deck and saw the guy in the backyard next door. He had a bag with him and was doing something with the back door. He glanced up at us and waved. He said the Smiths hired him to do some work and he was having trouble getting the back door open."

Luke inched to the front of the chair, excited to hear the information. "You spoke to him?"

"Yeah," Trevor said. "It wasn't a long conversation or anything. After he told us he was there to do work, we went back inside the house. About twenty minutes later, the shooting started. We were upstairs in my bedroom at the time. When we looked out my bedroom window, we saw what was happening. We got down on the floor. I didn't know where the shooting was coming from until later. I didn't even realize I had seen the guy who was the shooter until we saw it on the news that night. That's when I figured out it was probably the guy we saw. I asked Mr. Smith if he had hired someone to do work on the house and he said no. I was sure then but I didn't know what to tell my parents. We left when the shooting stopped and the cops showed up. We almost didn't get past the barricade. I told them I was trying to get to my parents. The cops cleared us to leave. Then I came home when school let out."

Luke was sure in the confusion on the street he was able to pull that off. "What did the man look like?"

"He had on a blue ballcap without any writing on it. He was about my dad's height but bigger in the arms and stomach. He had kind of a pointy nose."

"How tall is your dad?"

"About five-foot-ten. The guy had dark hair too and it kind of poked out the sides. One of my friends wondered if he was wearing a wig because it didn't look like real hair. He was wearing jeans and a white shirt. Thinking back now, I should have known he wasn't there to do work."

"Why is that?"

Trevor furrowed his brow. "His jeans were too clean. They looked new. It's too hot out to be wearing jeans and who does work in new clothes? It was kind of weird. I didn't think about it then."

That was a solid observation. Luke asked Trevor for the names of his two friends. He hesitated to provide it but Luke urged him on. Then he told Trevor he was going to send a sketch artist to the house. "Hopefully, once you do that, we'll have our first sketch of the sniper." Luke stood and crossed the room to shake Trevor's hand. "I know it was hard to tell the truth. You've done a real service to your community."

CHAPTER 27

"I don't understand what you're telling me?" Luke asked as we sat down at the table to eat dinner together for the first night in weeks. He took a bite of the lasagna and looked over at me while he waited for an answer.

Cooper and I had decided it was better to tell Luke about our meeting with Hollis Hopkins. I had saved it for an in-person conversation when we were both relaxed. Luke had come home from work hyped up about the young witness who saw the sniper break into the house in the Heights.

He was waiting for an artist to provide him with the sketch of the sniper.

Luke visited gun ranges after but found nothing suspicious. Det. Granger had called him a few minutes after he arrived home to tell him he didn't get much either.

He stared at me expectantly. "I want to understand your reasoning, Riley. I'm not saying don't do it. I just don't like that this guy called you and Cooper instead of me."

"I don't like it either, Luke. You know how some people are though. He said he doesn't want to accuse his brother-in-law until he is sure. I figured we could find more evidence, locate Cat, and bring everything to you."

"How are you going to find Cat and investigate Len?"

This was the part I hadn't wanted to tell him. I forked the piece of lasagna that he had cut for me. "I'm going to Chicago alone to speak to Cat's family while Cooper stays here and investigates Len. I'll take the train up and go to her family's house. We have the address, but her mother won't speak to us on the phone. I have a feeling Cat is hiding out there or at the home of another family member. It makes sense she'd go back to Chicago."

"I spoke to her mother and she told me Cat wasn't there."

I knew that. "That's the point, Luke. I think she's lying to protect Cat. In person, it's harder to lie."

"How are you going to get around with one arm?" He pointed his fork toward my plate. "You can barely eat by yourself. You're not going to be able to drive."

"That's why I'm taking the train and I can do a rideshare the rest of the time. I can make it work."

Luke knew better than to argue with me about that. "You don't even know for sure she's there or if her family will let you speak to her if she is."

That was the risk we were taking. "We have to find her, Luke. This Len guy seems like he could be a danger to her. Something spooked her about those flowers. Even if Len isn't a viable suspect, I believe Cat knows something she isn't telling us. It's better to have the confrontation in person." I raised my slinged arm. "I'm also hoping if she sees I've been shot, she might have a little more sympathy and help us out."

Luke took a sip of his tea and then took a big mouthful of his salad. He chewed and considered what I was saying. He had an expression on his face that told me he was thinking it over. "I'm not saying don't go. I think Cooper is right to focus on Len. We already wasted enough time on Clayton Dalton and Raymond Bollin. Neither of them amounted to anything other than wasted time."

"Clayton Dalton was a distraction to get you out of Little Rock. If Buster was willing to tell you who gave him the information, you'd be one step closer."

Luke shook his head. "It's a no-go. I tried a few different ways. He wasn't giving up the information. If I didn't believe he was terrified of whoever told him, I might have charged him. As it is, Buster is a patsy. He had to deliver a message. He didn't know if it was true or not."

"Someone got to him in prison. Who had access?" I had changed the subject on him to give him more time to mull over my going to Chicago. I was sure I could handle it alone. Luke didn't look convinced. "Who had access to Buster?" I repeated.

"It could be anyone. We weren't able to narrow it down. It could have been a guard or one of the other prisoners. We checked out his cellmate thoroughly. He was cleared. Buster was in the showers and the yard. It could have been anyone. Someone got information inside and passed it to Buster. I spent too much time as it is going down that dead end. Adele is still working on him for me." He popped another bite of lasagna in his mouth and grinned. "You're trying to distract me. Don't think I don't know your tricks by now."

"Guilty as charged. I know you're worried about me going alone."

"I think you can handle it," Luke said, surprising me. He took a sip of his drink and considered what he was going to say. In the end, it was practical. "It might be a waste of time or it could prove beneficial. I have no authority to hunt Cat down. If you did it and let us know where she is, that would be helpful. She refuses to answer my calls. She declined another interview and I have no reason to hold her. She'd been cooperative right up to the point she took off."

I still sensed an undercurrent he wasn't saying. "What's your hesitation then?"

"It's not a hesitation. I'm concerned about this guy following you right to Cat. He might not even know the Chicago connection. Given we have no idea what he looks like and we know he's been watching Cat and Adele, he might know you. Who's to say he won't follow you right to Cat? There was a good reason she went into hiding."

I hadn't thought of that at all. Luke was a little all over the place with his thoughts on the trip. We hadn't told anyone, not even Hollis, that I was going to Chicago. "Do you want Cat found or not?"

"Of course, I want her found. I just don't want her killed in the process." Luke ate more of his dinner while I picked at mine trying to decide how much merit to give what he said. When we were done, he cleared the table and started the dishes.

I sat at the table and watched him, wondering if I was going to put Cat at risk. "I have a photo of Len, so I'll be able to watch out for him. If you show me the sketch, I can watch out for that guy too. I need to go."

Luke looked over his shoulder at me. "You should go. I didn't mean to suggest otherwise. I was only thinking through what could happen. I want you to remain aware, which I know you always do. It will be a relief for me to have you out of Little Rock."

I knew what he meant but still hearing that my husband was glad I was going wasn't the best feeling. "Trying to get me out of the house, I see. Throwing a big party in my absence."

Luke dried the last of the dishes and then his hands. He turned and leaned on the counter. He had a mischievous grin on his face. "Do you think I want you out of here for any other reason than your safety? It's been lonely living without you all the times you travel up to New York." He took a few steps toward me and stopped. "We need to make up for some lost time. That is, if you can with your arm."

His expression told me everything. "I think I can manage it. Aren't you supposed to be home from work tonight to rest? Isn't that what Det. Granger told you – come home and rest. That wouldn't be resting."

Luke laughed and gave me a big smile. "I always get the best night of sleep after. You'd be helping me rest." He closed the distance between us and gently pulled me up by my good hand. He kissed me on the lips and then left a trail of kisses down to my neck, nuzzling my ear and telling me how much he wanted me.

His breath on my ear and the things he was saying made me shiver. I didn't know how exactly we were going to manage it with my arm but we were going to give it a go. It had been far too long and we needed to reconnect.

Luke broke the kiss and guided me up the stairs to our bedroom.

Nothing was going to interrupt us this time.

Later, when Luke was snoring softly beside me, I reached for my phone on the bedside table. I texted Cooper that I'd be leaving for Chicago in the morning. I hadn't told Luke or Cooper but I had already bought my train ticket and reserved a hotel room a few blocks away from Cat's mother's house.

Hollis had texted a photo of Len after our meeting. He looked like an average guy to me. Len had a soft jawline, deep-set dark eyes and brown hair that looked to be thinning on the sides and top. He wasn't a bad-looking guy. If I passed him on the street, I wouldn't have thought twice about it.

Cooper had done some early research on him after the meeting. Len would be welcomed back at Ezo Technologies. Cooper pretended to be doing an employment check and Len's old supervisor had nothing but glowing things to say. The man did admit Len had some quirks but most highly intelligent people did. There were no other big red flags though. Cooper had Len's address as well as some contacts with friends and such. He couldn't find any social media accounts for him, which struck me as odd. I was still thinking about Harvey and wondering if Len might have been him. He might have a fake account even if he had no real one.

Cooper texted me back quickly and asked if there was anything I needed. He hadn't said anything to Cat about Len or my trip to Chicago. He had texted her to check in but otherwise acted like this was status quo. He didn't want to spook her into running again.

I settled back into bed and closed my eyes. I was hoping to get a little sleep before leaving in the morning. I must have been tired because I was fast asleep before I even knew it.

The next morning while sitting at the kitchen table over coffee and bacon and eggs, Luke showed me the sketch from the witness account. "The artist did a pretty good job. Tyler wants to put this out to the media today. I'm on the fence about it. Grady Cullen has been giving interviews to the news and told us he'd speak for the victims if we released the sketch. He didn't know the man though. I want to check a few places first to see if he looks familiar to anyone before he knows we have the jump on him."

"Did the other boys confirm the description?"

Luke nodded. "Trevor was the one who had the best look at him. The other boys didn't have as many details as him. The descriptions were similar enough. Do you think we should go to the media right away with it?"

"What's your hesitancy? You don't have other leads."

Luke had a blank expression on his face. "I don't know. Call it a weird gut feeling. I think once this is out there, we are going to get a lot of media traction and possibly a lot of false leads to follow. I'm also worried that once we have a description of him, he might ramp up the violence. Whenever things don't go his way, he acts out with another shooting."

"You're worried the quiet of the last week isn't going to last."

"That's exactly it." He drank the last of his coffee. "I'm worried about what he's planning and also hoping he isn't planning anything and that he has stopped."

I rubbed his arm. "We both know he didn't stop. He might be distracted with Cat gone. Maybe he's trying to find her. If he was doing all of this for attention and that source of attention is gone, he might change up what he's doing."

"You think he's going to reach out to more traditional media instead?"

I had considered it. "That's what David Berkowitz did."

"I'm not even sure how all of that fits into this case anymore," Luke said and sat back. "He might have just said it initially to get our attention, which it certainly did. It could have just been an initial scare tactic."

I looked back down at the sketch again and studied it longer than I did the first time. "This doesn't look anything like Len." I pulled out my phone and showed Luke the photo Hollis had given me. "Even with a wig on, it doesn't look like Len. There is something familiar about his face though."

Luke looked at the photo of Len and then the sketch. He agreed the two looked nothing alike. "Is it possible you saw the sniper the day of the shooting? Maybe you saw him on the walk over to the coffee shop that morning."

I wasn't sure where I had seen him. I wasn't able to place the face. "I don't know. Can you text me a photo of the sketch so I can look at it later? It might come to me."

Luke texted a photo of the sketch and then kissed me goodbye. He had a morning meeting with Det. Granger and Cooper was driving me to the train station. There were a few things we needed to go over before I left.

"Call me the minute you get in," Luke said and waved from the door as he left.

I opened my texts and saved the photo of the sketch. I couldn't look away from it and knew it would bother me until I figured it out.

CHAPTER 28

Cooper had made it a habit to walk Adele to her office each morning, wait to see if she had any communication from the sniper, and then walk the two blocks to Cat's studio and check her mail. The last message sent had been a couple of days prior when he told Cat she needed to come back and finish what they had started. Cooper assumed the sniper knew he was checking her mail. Why else keep sending them?

The tone of the message was stern and commanding. He was also angry Cat never acknowledged the flowers he had sent her. Riley figured out the flowers were from a local shop. When she went there to inquire, she was told they had been ordered online and without a warrant, they weren't able to provide credit card information. She had passed the information to Luke and he was running down that lead. Cooper didn't assume the sniper would be dumb enough to leave a trail that easily followed though.

Cooper turned each new message over to Luke and they were put into the case file. The media didn't know about them and neither did Cat. He had told her about the first one before the shooting in the Heights. After that, Cat asked him to stop telling her about it. She said she felt safer and was better off not knowing. Cooper didn't think that was true but he abided by her wishes.

Cat had also told her assistant to work from home and not to come to the studio, so Cooper was surprised that morning to find her at her desk.

"Can I help you?" the young woman asked when Cooper entered the front office.

He held up the key and introduced himself. "I've been checking the mail for Cat while she's away. Are you Angela?"

"I am. I know Cat told me not to come into the office but she's starting research for her next podcast and I had a bit of work to do." Angela stood, smoothed down her skirt, and tucked blonde strands behind her ears. "Cat told me the sniper has been sending her messages. I checked the mail and didn't see anything."

Cooper held out his hand. "Do you mind if I go through it?"

Angela hesitated. "I'm not sure I should allow that. Without Cat being here, I think you better go."

"You don't understand. Cat asked me to check in on her studio and check the mail. I've been turning everything over to law enforcement." He stepped back but wasn't going to leave. "Call Cat if you need to check me out. I can't leave without checking the mail myself. You're also not supposed to be here."

Angela drew back and bit her lip. "I can't work at home. Everything I need is here in the studio. I know Cat told me not to come. I'm not sure what else I'm supposed to do though. Please don't tell her I'm here."

Cooper felt for the young woman who was only trying to do her job. "I won't tell her but you can't stay here. It's not safe for you. The sniper or someone he sends drops off messages to Cat. I don't know what he'd do if he found you here." Cooper decided to take the opportunity to learn more about Cat. He sat down in one of the chairs without being asked and changed the subject. Casually, he asked, "How long have you worked for Cat?"

"Since the start of the podcast. Cat put out an ad that she needed an assistant, someone who could help her research, keep track of information, help with the recording technology, and work with the advertisers. I was interested and she's flexible with my college schedule. It worked out for both of us."

Cooper had assumed she was young. "What year are you in at college?"

"I'm a junior now but started working with Cat the summer after my freshman year. She's a great boss." Angela sat down at her desk, seeming to forget about calling Cat or kicking Cooper out. "How did you meet her?"

"She profiled one of my cases and then she followed me down the street one day and staged a meeting at a coffee shop. It was soon after that she got the first note about the sniper. You weren't here when all this started."

Angela confirmed what Cooper already knew – she had been out on vacation. "It was my first week of classes. She let me take the time off to get adjusted to the new schedule. Cat wasn't sure what her next podcast episodes would be. She didn't have a lot of work for me. We talked by text and a few phone calls during that time and she told me about what was happening. Of course, I watched the news and knew about the shooting."

"You were local this whole time?" Cooper asked, not hiding his surprise. He didn't know why but he had assumed Angela was out of the area. It had been a poor assumption on his part.

Angela confirmed she was still local and lived in West Little Rock. "I'm not downtown much other than for work. I go to the University of Arkansas here in Little Rock."

"Cat shared with me some of the threats she had been getting as well as the few men who were obsessed with her. Did she tell you much about that?" Angela grew quiet and Cooper assumed she didn't want to say anything bad about her boss. Cooper pressed her. "I know you feel loyalty to Cat. I can appreciate that. We are in a tough spot here trying to track down this guy. He seems to have a connection to Cat and we are trying to figure that out. I won't tell Cat you spoke to me. I can keep it confidential."

Angela relaxed back in her chair and folded her hands on the desk. She stared over at Cooper. "I'm not sure what to say. I didn't agree with Cat on how she handled it. I thought she should have gone to the police when the threats started. She had me print them and keep them in a file in her office. I thought it was more serious than that."

"What about the men who seemed obsessed with her?"

"I didn't like it. It didn't seem as serious though, except for the time she got flowers."

"Flowers?" Cooper asked, sitting up a little straighter.

"She got a bouquet of white lilies, which are her favorite. She didn't say who they were from, but I assumed it was one of the men who had been sending her emails. She threw them away and told me to never accept a flower delivery again."

Cooper didn't understand. "Do you know why she was so upset? The studio address is on the website. It stands to reason if one of the men was obsessed with her he'd know the address. She might have assumed one of them would send her something."

"I don't know. She refused to discuss it further."

Cooper started to believe Riley had been right about the flower connection. "There was a man named Harvey who was emailing her. Did Cat ever express any concern about him?"

"She had been trying to figure out who he was but she didn't know for sure."

Cooper raised his eyebrows in a question. "Of all the men who emailed her did she seem most interested in figuring out who he was?"

"I'd say that's true," Angela said after considering it. "After Cat first moved here, she and her boyfriend broke up. She told me once she had a short fling after that and the guy ended up being married. Cat broke it off when she learned that but he'd gotten a little obsessive with her. She suspected that he was posing as Harvey. She was never able to confirm it though."

Cooper had seen obsessive men do similar things before so it didn't surprise him. It was dangerous behavior and he wished Cat had taken it more seriously. "Did she ever confront this other man, the one she had been seeing?"

"Cat didn't say. She told me she did make it clear to him again that they were never getting back together. He said he understood. The emails from Harvey continued though."

Cooper wanted to make sure she was telling him the whole story. "Angela, I know this might seem like an invasion of privacy. Do you know the name of the man she was seeing? If you don't want to let me know, then you should tell Det. Luke Morgan who is investigating the sniper case. This killer also is obsessed with Cat and we believe it's someone close to her. I don't know if she told you but she left after she got a flower delivery of white lilies. It was from the sniper."

Angela's hand went to her chest. "I didn't know that. She didn't say anything to me about flowers being delivered. I'm sure the whole thing is terrifying for her." It took her a moment to put two and two together. "Wait," she said slowly. "Are you suggesting that the sniper might be this Harvey person and also possibly the man Cat had been involved with?"

"That's exactly what I'm saying. If the boyfriend knew Cat liked white lilies and she ended the relationship because he was married, he could have started to communicate with her as Harvey. I've seen men do things like that. If Harvey sent similar flowers to Cat that the sniper sent, it stands to reason they might be the same person. My partner, Riley, had already suspected that. Why did Cat tell you she left?"

Angela's jaw tensed. "She said she was afraid of the sniper and needed to be someplace safe. He knew where to find her in the studio and she didn't like being here alone."

"Did she tell you where she was going?"

"No," Angela said with a shake of her head. "When we talked on the phone the other day, it was noisy like a big city wherever she was. There was a lot of street traffic and people talking. It was hard to hear her and people kept bumping into her. She had me hold on while she walked to a bench and sat down."

That sounded like it could be Chicago. "Was there anything else you heard on the call that could help us find the location?"

Angela sighed and closed her eyes. "I'm not sure."

"Think about the call and what you heard in the background. Take your time."

Angela recounted the call for Cooper. Cat had been telling her about some research she was doing about a case out of Missouri. She didn't have enough to pursue any interviews yet. It was all researched online. Angela snapped her fingers. "I remember something. At one point, after the guy bumped into her on the street, I heard someone shout that they were going into Big Lou's for pizza. Does that help?"

Cooper pulled out his phone and searched for Big Lou's Pizza in Chicago and found one location on Lake Shore Drive. He noted the address and sent a quick text to Riley saying he'd explain more when he called her later. He looked back up at Angela. "This is helpful. Did Cat say anything to you about going home to Chicago?"

"No. It's not surprising that she'd go there. I figured she'd head back to her mom's or her brother's house. If she wanted to feel safe that's where I assumed she'd go."

Cooper realized he had never asked Cat about her family. "What's her brother's name?"

"Brian," Angela said then winced. "I feel bad telling you this. She's going to be angry that I told you. She doesn't want to be found."

"It's okay. It's important we know where she is. She's in danger, maybe even more than we realize if the sniper is someone she knows. Do you know if the man she was seeing knew about her family?"

"I have no idea. I don't see why she'd hide it. They were seeing each other for a couple of months before Cat found out about his wife. That's when the whole thing blew up."

Cooper felt an urgency to get the information to Riley. There might be no shootings right now because the sniper was in Chicago searching for Cat. He stood from the chair and held his hand out. "I need to see the mail."

This time she didn't hesitate. She handed over the stack of it. "I was serious before that nothing looks out of the ordinary."

Cooper flipped through it and realized Angela had been telling him the truth. He put it back on her desk and explained, "I need to make sure Cat doesn't know we had this conversation. If she does, she might leave the safety of wherever she's hiding in Chicago and try to go somewhere else. In the process, the sniper might find her. My only goal is to keep her safe."

"I believe you," Angela said. "I don't want to tell her I was here so there's no way I'm telling her we spoke. I want to keep my job."

"We have a deal then." Cooper thanked her for the information and headed to the street. As soon as he was down the block, he called Riley. She answered from the train and he gave her the rundown of the conversation with Angela. "You were right about the flowers," he started and then went on with the rest of the information. When he was done, he asked, "Didn't you get the impression from Cat that her assistant was out of the area and couldn't be reached?"

"That's what I assumed. I don't know if that was just my assumption when she said her assistant was on vacation or if Cat said something to make me think that. Do you think she lied to us to keep anyone from talking to her?"

"I don't think Cat wanted anyone talking to Angela. She knows too much. I think Cat is afraid the sniper is her ex. I don't think she wants to admit the affair." Cooper finished with the call and headed back to his office to focus on Len. There was nothing more he could do about finding the ex. Riley would have to make some headway with Cat. Maybe Riley would have better luck in person. It was clear Cat wasn't going to be straight with him.

CHAPTER 29

Luke met with Granger first thing that morning and discovered that one of the gun ranges on Highway 10 west of the Heights might have some information for them. Granger had gone there the previous day as planned but wasn't able to speak to the owner. The young man on duty had told Granger there was a guy not that long ago who had been asking all sorts of strange questions about firing from a building and had made a few threats. A couple of the regulars had brought the concerns to the owner but the young man wasn't sure what became of it.

Granger was scheduled to speak with Rick Watts later that morning. He asked Luke if he wanted to go with him. Luke had a meeting with Tyler and then a press announcement to make. He'd have to skip the meeting with Granger but had provided him with a copy of the sketch to take with him. Granger was also hoping to find out the names of the men who had witnessed the guy making threats and interview them. He assured Luke he'd show them the sketch.

Before leaving, Granger asked, "Is there anything about this guy that looks odd to you?"

"There's a lot odd about him," Luke said, staring back down at the sketch. He had been looking at it on and off since it had been provided to him by the sketch artist. "The hair looks like it's a wig and he looks like he's wearing makeup of some kind. He's also not dressed like a workman."

"I know this is only a sketch and this is going to sound crazy."

"Nothing sounds crazy at this point."

Granger narrowed his eyes and pointed to the man's nose. "Doesn't it look like his nose could be fake? It's out of normal proportions like the bridge of his nose is too narrow for his nostrils. I've never seen a nose look like that. He could have broken it a few times and had it repaired or maybe he's had plastic surgery."

Luke leaned down and looked closer at the photo. The bridge was one skinny line and the nostrils flared to two wide bumps that looked uneven and out of sync with the rest of the man's face.

"It could be a prosthetic," Luke suggested, studying it. "He might be concealing his appearance or he might have been punched one too many times and broke the heck out of it."

Granger pulled back from the sketch. "Either way, it's a distinctive feature. We should caution people about his nose when they are looking at the sketch. We should mention the wig too because I don't know anyone that has straw hair like that. He almost looks like a poorly drawn cartoon villain."

Luke appreciated the insight and he'd mention it at the press conference. He wanted Granger's opinion on something. "What do you think about releasing this so soon?"

Granger leaned back on the edge of his desk. "It's a risk but one we have to take. It might generate leads. The community is more than ready to help us out."

"How's your wife doing after the shooting?" Granger's wife, Sarah, worked at a shop in the Heights that had been impacted by the shooting. No one inside the shop had been injured. The front glass had been blown out and there was a mess to clean. Customers had hidden in the back with Sarah and Hattie, the owner. Luke had spoken to them at the scene but had forgotten to ask Granger how she was doing, which he felt terrible about now.

"She's about as good as can be expected. Luckily, no one was injured in the shop. How's Riley doing?"

Luke hadn't mentioned to him about her trip to Chicago. He was trying to keep that as low profile as possible but there was no reason not to share it with his partner. "She's well enough that she's going up to Chicago to look for Cat. She got a lead and she's following it."

Granger chuckled. "These women are tenacious. If I got shot, I'd be babying myself on the couch for as long as I could get away with it."

"Same," Luke said with a laugh. "I hope she finds Cat. Riley is convinced she is the key to this whole thing. She's speculating that it might be someone Cat knows, even if she's not connecting all the pieces yet."

"That would certainly make sense."

As Granger headed out of the office and Luke gathered his files for the meeting, his desk phone rang. Before he could even get out his greeting, the woman on the other end of the phone was insistent that he meet with her. He couldn't understand what she was saying. "Miss, please slow down. I can't understand you."

The woman slowed and spoke loudly. "This is Janelle Brady with Channel 5 news, Det. Morgan. The sniper has sent a letter to our office that he is going to start shooting someone every night until Cat O'Conner returns. He threatened to start here in the newsroom. You need to get over here."

Luke's stomach dropped because he was sure the sniper would carry out any threat he made. "Okay," he said calmly, trying to get the situation under control. "I'll head over there right now. As you know we had a press conference scheduled in an hour."

"Cancel it!" she shouted and ended the call before Luke could say anything else.

Luke had met Janelle before on a couple of cases. He knew her to be pushy and overly dramatic. She almost cost him finding the suspect in a previous case by going public with evidence before they were ready to release it. While Luke was concerned about the sniper's threats, he was more concerned if he didn't get over to the news station immediately, she'd release the letter and cause even more city-wide panic.

Luke rushed to Tyler's office and shoved open the door. "I'm sorry to disturb you but I just got word the sniper sent a message to Channel 5. He's threatening to shoot someone every night until Cat O'Conner comes back. He said he's going to start with the news station."

Tyler's eyes opened wide. "Who got the letter?"

"Janelle Brady," Luke said, letting her name linger in the room while Tyler grimaced. No one liked Janelle. "I know why it was sent to her. Everyone knows she doesn't hold back anything. I'm afraid if I don't get over there she's going to release it on their website or make a breaking news announcement on the station."

"Did you ask her to hold off?"

"She didn't give me a chance. She demanded I get over there and immediately ended the call. We are going to put our press conference on hold."

Tyler stood. "It's fine. I'll handle that. You focus on the new letter and Janelle. What about Cat? What are we going to do about finding her?"

Luke had not wanted to add more to Tyler's plate so he hadn't told him about Riley's trip. He stepped into the office, closing the door behind him. He explained about the client who had hired Cooper and Riley to find Cat and explore Len Woltman's involvement. "Riley is on her way to Chicago right now. It's where Cat is from and Riley thinks there's a good possibility she's hiding out there with family. I tried speaking to her mother but she denied Cat was there. We've had no reason to pursue her."

"Until now," Tyler said with emphasis. "Let me know what Riley finds. If we have to send over a Chicago PD officer that's what we'll do. I'd rather she be willing to come back to Little Rock on her own though."

"We don't have a reason to bring her back. We can't force her."

Tyler took a deep breath expanding his chest. He knew Luke was right. "Let's hope Riley can convince her."

"Should I tell Riley about the new threat?"

"Let her know and leave it up to her discretion if she tells Cat. She might be able to get her back here without it. I have a feeling that would make anyone keep running."

Luke agreed with him there. "Granger is running down a potential lead at a gun range. Hopefully, by the time we have the press conference, we'll have some solid information for the public."

Luke rushed out of Tyler's office, stopped at his desk long enough to grab his keys, headed for the back door of the station, and sprinted across the parking lot. It was only three blocks to the Channel 5 office but the heat slowed him to what felt like a crawl. He had sweated through the back of his shirt by the time he was a block away from the police station. He slowed to a brisk walk.

The rush of cool air hit him as he entered the building. He flashed his badge to the man at the desk and made his way to the elevator. The doors opened to a flurry of newsroom activity. There were open desks in the middle of the space with closed offices around the perimeter, much like at the police station.

Luke could see the hair sprayed poof of blonde hair from across the newsroom. Janelle stood in a doorway in her bright pink suit shouting at someone Luke couldn't see. As he made his way over, he realized it was the office of Dave Brockton, the news director. Luke had previous dealings with him too. He was more calm and level-headed than Janelle but could be just as pushy and fierce if he wanted the story. They made a great news team but a terrible adversary to criminal investigations.

"Janelle," Luke said as he approached. "I made it as quickly as I could."

She spun on her three-inch stilettos. "It wasn't fast enough." She moved into Dave's office in front of Luke then slammed the door behind them. "What is the meaning of involving us in this investigation."

Luke's defensiveness rose. "We didn't involve you in anything. The sniper did."

She folded her arms across her chest. "Right because you couldn't keep an eye on Cat O'Conner and she bailed on the whole thing. If she was still here and doing the podcast then he wouldn't have sent a letter to me. I'm not dealing with this psycho."

"I've got news for you, Janelle…" Luke let the first part of his sentence linger and he took slight joy in delivering the rest. "You've got no choice. The sniper has set his sights on you and now you're involved. We are doing the best we can to find him. I need to see the letter."

"Det. Morgan, what do you expect us to do?" Dave asked as he stood from his desk and handed over the bagged letter in what looked like a used freezer bag. "It's the best we could do. My prints and Janelle's are on the letter. I know you have our prints already to run the comparison."

Luke pulled gloves from his pocket and slipped the letter out of the bag. He didn't have an answer for Dave. Channel 5 was going to do whatever they were going to do. He hoped they wouldn't run anything yet without discussion. "I need to read this letter before I do or say anything. When did you receive it?"

"It was in this morning's mail. There's no postmark. I assume someone hand delivered it, which means that psycho was in this office."

Luke raised his eyes long enough to explain, "We don't know if he's delivering them or paying someone to do it for him. I need to see your surveillance footage. If the letter was hand delivered, where did it end up? Who was the first to receive it?"

Dave sat back down at his desk and looked up at Luke. "It went to the guy sitting at the front desk. He brought it to the administrative assistant and she brought it to Janelle. She didn't open the letter. Their prints will be on the envelope but not the letter." Dave told Janelle to go get security and bring the downstairs surveillance footage from this morning.

Luke smoothed out the letter and read it over. *Everyone will be punished until Cat returns. One person will be shot dead each night until she's back in her studio telling my story. All focus should be on me. I might even start in the Channel 5 newsroom if this is not made public by five tonight. No one is safe. Fear me.*

It was the longest letter to date. It was typed though and couldn't be used for handwriting comparison. Given the destruction he'd already caused, Luke had every reason to believe the sniper meant what he said. "Have you beefed up security here since getting the threat?"

Dave shook his head. "I wasn't sure whether to believe him or not. Isn't that what they try to do, just instill fear? We want to share this threat with the public. They need to be aware."

"You need to focus on making sure your team is safe first. Then we can discuss what we are going to do with his demands."

"We are going live with the letter within the hour, Det. Morgan. There's no debate about that. I know you've got a press conference pending and we want to be out in front of that. It's not up for debate."

"This is evidence, Dave," Luke said, trying to control his temper. It wouldn't help the situation if he went off. He'd been down this road before with them. If Luke got angry and demanded things, they only dug into their position more. "We have to come up with a rational plan that works for everyone. I have someone looking for Cat right now. If you make this public, she's going to go further underground and then we might never find her."

Dave bit the inside of his cheek. He didn't look pleased with what Luke said. It was clear though he was considering the implications of going public. "What do you suggest?"

"When Janelle gets back, we can discuss it." Luke was stalling for time and Dave knew it.

CHAPTER 30

Luke put the letter in an official evidence bag he had brought with him and then paced around Dave's office waiting for Janelle to return with security. "Before we can do anything," he said finally after Dave pressured him for the plan, "I need to see the surveillance video and check in with my partner who is running down a potential lead right now."

"You have a plan though?" Dave asked with skepticism in his voice. "Janelle is not going to budge on her position of airing this in an hour unless you come up with something better. You know how she is."

"You're her boss," Luke countered, looking over at the man.

Dave threw his hands in the air. "She doesn't listen to a word I say. Janelle is going to do what she wants to do. She brings in the ratings and that's all that matters around here some days." There was frustration in his voice that hinted that not all was well in the newsroom.

Luke knew Janelle had a contentious relationship with her boss and many others. He also knew the public loved her frank style. She didn't pull any punches, often scooped other reporters, and was ruthless with getting to the heart of the story. She was a terrific journalist, sometimes at the cost of being a good person.

Before Luke could continue his discussion with Dave, Janelle returned with a thumb drive. "Security is too busy to join us but

I have the whole download from the front lobby this morning."

Luke took the drive from her. He didn't want to sit there and watch the footage. "Janelle, I know you want to go live with a broadcast about the letter in an hour."

"Forty-nine minutes to be exact," Janelle said, interrupting him in a tone that told him she wasn't going to waver.

"I need to review this footage first and we need to make a plan for what you're going to say." Luke wasn't going to be able to stop her but he could minimize the damage. He explained to her about Cat. "I'm concerned airing this letter in its entirety is going to have the opposite effect about bringing Cat back here. If that's the goal, we need to consider what you say about it."

"He said to go public with the letter and that's what I'm going to do," she insisted. "Do you think I'm going to defy him and have him come in here and shoot up the newsroom? I'm not going to have that on my hands if I even live through it."

Luke didn't know how to get through to her. He sat down in one of the chairs and took a few breaths to consider. "Janelle," he said calmly, "I don't want to scare you. The reality is the sniper is going to do whatever he wants when he wants to do it. We've found no matter what we do in response, he does whatever he wants. We had a letter after the first shooting that Cat needed to do a podcast, so she did it. He committed the second shooting a few hours later because he didn't like what she had to say. If you go on a broadcast and talk about this letter and he doesn't like how you talk about it, you're going to be a target. If you don't do a broadcast about the letter, you'll be a target. All I'm asking is that we strategize the best thing to say to accomplish all our goals."

Janelle swallowed hard and looked over at Dave who offered the same words as Luke. "How long do we wait?"

Luke held up the drive. "As long as it takes me to go through this footage and reach my partner. Once I know a little more, then we can craft something for you to say that will appeal to Cat while also meeting the sniper's request. I think we can do both."

"There's still a chance I'll anger him."

"As I said, you're in this now." Luke wanted to say welcome to the party but he figured that wouldn't go over well. "Where can I watch this?"

Dave carried his laptop over to a small table pushed up against the wall. Janelle and Dave sat on one side and Luke on the other. They allowed him to go through the footage without peering over his shoulder.

"What time did you get this letter?"

"Around ten in the morning. Right before I called you."

"What time does the building open?"

"Seven."

Luke started the footage at the beginning and played it on fast forward, watching a wave of people coming into the building for work. For the first hour, no one handed anything to the man sitting at the security desk. Some passed without acknowledging him while others said good morning and waved to him as they passed. A few people flashed their badges while most were probably known to him and no longer needed to.

It wasn't until five minutes after nine that a man approached the desk and handed him a white envelope with no writing on the front. It matched what Janelle had given him. He had a dark long-sleeve shirt, jeans, and dark shoes. He also had a hat pulled low on his head with the same straw-looking strands that had been under the hat of the man Trevor had seen breaking into his neighbor's house. The man seemed to know how to shield his face from the view of the cameras. He walked to the desk and back out the door while obstructing everything but a side view of his face.

"I'll be right back," Luke said, getting up from the desk and racing into the hall to the elevator. He was glad to see neither Janelle nor Dave followed him. He went back to the ground floor to the guard at the desk. Luke showed him a photo of the sketch. "Have you seen this man?"

The guard leaned forward and took a good look at it. "He was in here this morning. He handed me an envelope for Janelle Brady and I brought it up to her." He jabbed his finger at Luke's phone. "There was something odd about his face. His nose looked like it was falling off."

"Falling off?" Luke wasn't sure he'd heard the man correctly.

"Like it was peeling at the sides. I think he was wearing makeup too." The guard sat back. "I don't know, man. People are strange. We get all kinds in here but his face was something else."

"Did he look like he was trying to conceal his identity?"

"He looked like a clown with that ridiculous hair. If anything he was trying to draw more attention to himself. If you ask me, he's begging for people to stare at him. That hair couldn't have been real. I've never seen anything like it."

Luke had all the information he wanted. He thanked him and made his way up to Dave's office. Before he went inside, he placed a call to Granger.

"We have a confirmation on the sketch, Luke," Granger said after they exchanged greetings. "I have four men here who can confirm the man in the sketch was the man here asking questions about firing from different shooting positions. He asked if shooting from the ground in the weeds was better than high up in a building. He was asking about trajectory and so forth. A few of the men thought he was being disingenuous though because he was a great shot. They weren't sure why he was asking questions he already knew the answers to. It was an odd exchange. They took their concerns to Rick who didn't do anything with them. He planned to call the cops if the guy showed up again but he never did."

Luke knew the man would have to show some identification at the range. "Do you have the name of the suspect?"

"I don't," Granger said with frustration. "Rick isn't good at book-keeping and doesn't make a note of who is in there. He confirmed the guy's not a regular member and was only there three or four times. Rick thought his name was Peter or Paul or something like that. The guy used a range of other names with the other members. He's trying to hide his real identity."

"What about his appearance?"

"The hair and nose?" Granger asked and Luke confirmed. "One of the guys said his nose looked normal and said it wasn't like in the sketch. Another guy said the day he saw the guy, the hair wasn't like in the sketch. Seems like the guy keeps changing it up. They are sure though the man is the same as the one in the sketch."

Luke caught Granger up to speed about the new message sent to Channel 5. "I'm here now and Janelle is going to go live on a broadcast soon. I need to check in with Tyler. I'm on board with an interview before our press conference. We'll give Janelle the exclusive and then show the sketch."

"The city is going to be sheer panic."

"We don't have much of a choice. The sniper has us in a stranglehold. Now that we have multiple confirmations on the sketch, I'm more comfortable releasing this to the public. Hopefully, we'll have more leads. I'm going to discuss how I think the hair and nose aren't real."

"I took formal statements and I'll be back to the station soon and we can catch up then."

Luke ended the call and went to the bathroom. He looked himself over in the mirror and made sure he was presentable for television. When he was done, he called Tyler and prepped him for what was to come.

"Are you sure this is the way you want to do this?" Tyler asked after Luke explained everything.

"We don't have a choice. Either we try to work with Janelle or she's going public without us. I'd rather be in the mix and try to control the message. Set the press conference for one. I should be done with the interview by then." Luke realized he was giving orders to his boss and backtracked. "That's if this is all okay with you."

"You're fine, Luke. You have a handle on this case and finally seem to be making progress. I'm not going to slow that down now."

When the call ended, Luke took one last look at himself in the mirror. He was quickly approaching forty – two more months to go. Fine lines had already started to show themselves in the corners of his eyes and his beard had speckles of gray. He had been shaving his head for years and wondered if he let it go whether the hair would grow back. The job was aging him.

By the time Luke made it back to the office, Dave and Janelle were already crafting a statement. She looked over at him when he entered. "I assume you have a positive confirmation."

Luke pulled out his phone and showed her a photo of the sketch. "I can get our public affairs office to send you a file for the news broadcast and the website. This is the guy. We've confirmed it now several times including your security officer downstairs."

Janelle eyed him suspiciously. "You're willing to be interviewed?"

"I need to see your statement if you want the exclusive." It was the only bartering chip Luke had and he never knew Janelle to turn down an exclusive.

Janelle paused for a few beats before she stuck out her hand. "You have a deal."

Forty minutes later, Luke sat under hot lights with Janelle to his left. Their chairs were positioned at an angle so they were toward the camera but they could still turn their bodies and have a conversation. He had gone over her statement removing things he felt might trigger Cat to go further into hiding.

The news producer counted down to the live broadcast.

Janelle put on her game face. She had her legs crossed and a stern smile on her face. She spoke directly to the camera and informed the public about the sniper's communication to Channel 5, how worried she was for everyone's safety, and then introduced Luke. "Det. Morgan, would you say that you have a better handle on the investigation now?"

Luke hated how she phrased the question. He turned toward the camera instead of looking directly at Janelle. He wanted to speak directly to the public too. "I know this has been a challenging time for our city. This is a case that has affected me personally. My wife was shot during the Heights shooting. We all know someone who has been impacted. Thanks to concerned citizens who were willing to come forward, we have a sketch of the sniper. It's been confirmed by several people. Let me be clear that we do not believe this is what he always looks like. The hair is a wig and his nose is a prosthetic. It's not a great disguise by any means and it makes him appear clownish. He stands out, which isn't what you'd think a killer like this would do since he's hiding in a perch above the city streets shooting people. Look at his eyes, the shape of his face, and other features. Remember him because he walks among us." Luke paused and then with more emotion said, "He is one of us and it's going to take the whole community staying vigilant to stop him."

Janelle drew his attention with another question. "What do you plan to do about this recent threat from the sniper?"

She hadn't explained the threat. It was up to Luke to deliver that news. "The sniper has indicated that unless his demands are met he will shoot someone every night." He looked directly into the camera again. "I'm sure you all know his demands were met in the beginning and he still shot people. We have done everything we can short of catching him to get the sniper to stop these actions. He is playing a dangerous and deadly game and no matter what we do, he does not intend to stop. If you know the man in the photo, please contact the tipline. In the meantime, there will be increased patrols, the city is issuing a curfew, and we are calling in extra police support until he is caught."

"Do you have any message for Cat O'Conner?"

Luke spoke directly to her. "Cat, we need you to come back to Little Rock. We have information from the sniper we believe only you can decipher. We believe this is someone you know and we need your help. The city of Little Rock needs your help."

Janelle wrapped up the newscast and showed the sketch of the sniper again. She read the tipline number twice and encouraged people to call in. When she was done, she tugged off her mic. "Do you think she'll call you?"

"I don't know," Luke said with doubt in his voice. "The sniper heard us ask though and that's all we can do."

CHAPTER 31

The train pulled into the Chicago station just as the sun set. Given my injured arm, the train porter helped me with my bag and I found a taxi right outside the station to my hotel. I needed a shower and some food before I hit the street in search of Cat.

On the train ride, Cooper provided me with the information about Brian, Cat's brother, as well as all the information about the relationship she had and broke off. I didn't know if it was a potential lead. All I knew was Cat was running from something and she needed to come back to Little Rock with me.

Luke had called me after his press conference to let me know about the specific threat made to the city and Channel 5. I didn't like Janelle Brady any more than she liked me. That said, I didn't want her to be shot.

Nothing about the case made any sense from the initial focus on the Son of Sam to the myriad of suspects that didn't pan out. Cat seemed to be at the center of it all. Now, the whole city depended on me convincing Cat to come back.

After a refreshing shower and hot meal in the hotel restaurant, I stopped at the front desk and asked the concierge the best way to get to the address I had for Cat's mother. He gave me directions on the L and then as he appraised my arm and tired face, he thought better of it and suggested a taxi. He escorted me outside, flagged one down for me, and sent me on my way.

The taxi driver was affable enough, giving me pointers about sightseeing in the city. I had only been to Chicago twice and didn't know my way around. Luke and I had talked about a weekend trip but we hadn't made it yet. I noted everything he said, thanked him, paid, and got out on a tree-lined suburban street in Oak Park about fifteen minutes outside of Chicago.

Cat's mother lived in a Craftsman-style brick Foursquare on a massive corner lot. There were two cars in the driveway and lights on in the house. I stood on the tree-lined sidewalk and let my eyes roam over the house watching the windows. I could see a woman moving around the dining room.

I made my way up the walkway to the front porch and rang the bell. A dog barked and someone told him to be quiet. It didn't sound like Cat to me. I stepped back from the door as someone approached. I tried to psych myself up to be smiley. The truth was I was too tired.

A woman, not much shorter than Cat, pulled open the door. "Can I help you, dear?" She had warm dark eyes and short gray hair. She was a little soft in the middle and had a warmth about her I immediately liked.

"Is Cat here?"

"No," the woman said a little too quickly.

I introduced myself and explained how I knew Cat. "I understand why Cat left. I might have done the same in her position. I need to speak with her. I believe she's in real danger. I also think she might know the sniper and is worried she might get in trouble. I'm here to tell her that Det. Morgan doesn't care about any of that. He just wants to know the sniper's identity. She won't return any of my calls."

"I'm Irene O'Conner, Cat's mother." She stuck her head out the front door and looked to the curb and then to each side. "Come on in. After I spoke to Det. Morgan, I figured someone would be here looking for her eventually."

"Is she here?" I asked again.

"She's not and I'm afraid I can't tell you where she is. We can chat and maybe figure it out. I'm worried about her too." She led me down a long hallway past a living room and dining room to a large eat-in kitchen in the back of the house. Irene gestured toward a four-seater table against the back wall. "Can I get you something to drink?"

"I'm okay, thank you." I winced though as I sat and adjusted my arm.

Irene got me a glass of water anyway and then sat down. "What did you do?"

"I was shot in one of the sniper shootings. I was at a coffee shop and he shot up the entire street."

Irene pursed her lips. "It's personal then. That's why you're here."

I suppose maybe it was personal. I hadn't considered that before now. Irene had a way of looking into my eyes that saw past the investigator in me. "I didn't like Cat when I first met her," I admitted, although I wasn't sure why. "She had covered a murder investigation related to my husband's sister and the sister of a friend of mine. Cat didn't do a bad job on the podcast but it felt like an invasion of privacy given she didn't ask to speak to any of us or interview my husband who was the lead detective on the case. Cat said she didn't think she'd get any of us to participate. It felt like a violation and so did her taking off in the middle of this case. Cat received flowers and immediately left without even telling us. She snuck out of her apartment and hasn't been seen since."

"I see." Irene sat for a moment with her hand folded on the tabletop. "Did Cat tell you about her ex-boyfriend?"

I shook my head. "Cat didn't tell us much of anything. She told Cooper, my investigative partner and friend, that she went to Little Rock with a boyfriend but they broke up. She chose to stay in Little

Rock and ended up starting the podcast as a way to get over her broken heart. She never told us anything about the boyfriend though."

"They were childhood sweethearts. They had been together since they were in eighth grade." Irene laughed gently. "I was surprised it lasted as long as it did. They made it work through high school and long distance in college. He asked her to move to Little Rock with him. Soon after though, he broke it off with her. Cat uprooted her entire life for that relationship and he ended it within a few months. Cat has a lot of stubborn pride. I told her to come back home. She could have moved back in here with me. She wanted to stick it out there. I suspect that she hoped he'd change his mind and she wanted to be there when he did. He never changed his mind."

I wasn't sure where this was going. "I'm sure it must have been difficult for her."

"It shook her confidence more than anything. I don't think Cat knew who she was without that relationship. They were so young when they got together, she didn't have a sense of identity. I think the podcast was a part of figuring it out. I say that so you understand that she was telling you the truth when she said she didn't think you'd all respond to an interview request. I knew she regretted how she went about the earlier episodes but live and learn."

When I said I understood, Irene went on. "Cat was vulnerable and shortly after she realized he was never coming back, she met a man she called Elliott. I never got a last name and Cat never shared it with me or many details about his life. What she did share made me suspicious. I told her I suspected he was married about a month before she confirmed it. She was vulnerable though and wanted so badly to distract herself from heartbreak. I don't think she cared much for Elliott other than the distraction he provided. When she broke it off, he got downright obsessive."

"Did you have contact with him?"

"No. Cat never told him where she was from," Irene said, her voice hinting at relief. "Cat has good instincts and it wouldn't surprise me if she suspected there was something odd about him from the start. She either didn't tell him things or outright lied about her past to keep it private. When I asked her why she was doing that, Cat said she wasn't sure. I think she knew without really knowing. Does that make sense?"

Women's intuition. We all had it, some of us used it more frequently than others. "Was Elliott dangerous?"

"I was concerned he was." Irene took a sip of water and looked right at me. "He came by her apartment and studio long after Cat ended things. She decided not to tell the man's wife as she didn't want to get caught up in more drama than necessary. He was also a bit older than Cat."

I didn't have any idea how old Cat was. "How old was he?"

"Late forties. I know age doesn't matter at that point but he had more life experience. He had the upper hand in every regard in that relationship. All Cat wanted to do was break free from it." Irene frowned and looked away. "I wasn't sure how much more I could help her, especially being so far away."

"I'm sure you did everything you could." She still hadn't told me why she thought Elliott might be dangerous. I reminded her she had said that. "Is there anything specific he said or did? I know he harassed her and stalked her after the relationship ended. I need to know if he made any specific threats?"

"Nothing specific. It was the way Cat spoke about him. I had never heard her sound afraid of anyone. He didn't like her podcast and said she was inviting all kinds of trouble. He didn't like her living downtown. He said it wasn't safe for a young woman." Irene raised her voice then and red flamed up her neck. "Elliott was the only trouble she had."

I knew from the threats and the men who seemed enamored with her that wasn't true. "Do you believe Elliott could be the sniper?"

Irene pulled back then and a look of horror came over her face. "Is that what you think?"

"I don't know what to think. I want to know if Cat thinks Elliott could be the sniper. That's why I'm here. The sniper is connected to her. He wanted to toy with her about the podcast." I didn't want to disclose information to Irene that Cat hadn't but I didn't feel like I had a choice. "Did Cat ever tell you about the threats she was receiving on social media and her email?"

"There were threats?"

I explained some of the emails and messages I had read. "There was one man in particular – Todd Hall. He sent many harassing messages to her. The sniper killed him as a favor to Cat."

Irene's eyes got so wide they appeared to bulge out of her head. "I had no idea. She never told me about that."

"There was also a man named Harvey. Did she tell you about him?"

Irene swallowed hard. "I'm afraid my daughter didn't tell me many things."

I told her about Harvey and his enamored emails. "He wasn't threatening her outright. He was obsessed with her and wanted to spend time with her. I suspect he thought they had a special relationship. Harvey used language in his communication with her that the sniper used in his messages. I firmly believe they are the same person."

"Do the police believe this?"

Luke was still a skeptic and had followed other evidence. "There isn't a lot for them to go on. They tried tracing the emails Harvey sent but he blocked his location. What I'm trying to figure out is if this person posing as Harvey could be Elliott. If he was that obsessed with her, it stands to reason that he'd do anything to get her attention."

"Including shooting up a city?"

I gestured with my hand to indicate I wasn't sure. "The sniper has a lot of rage. All of his interactions seem to hinge on what Cat does or doesn't do. His most recent communication to Channel 5 news indicated he'd be shooting one person every night until Cat returns."

Irene gasped and she said something under her breath I couldn't hear. "Is that why you want to bring her back? Can you keep her safe there?"

I avoided giving a direct answer. "She isn't safe here. You have no idea what the sniper knows about Cat's background. He could find her here. At least back in Little Rock, law enforcement will put her in protective custody and keep her safe."

"I don't think he will find her here. I'm not even sure where she is."

"You don't know?" I asked, not hiding my surprise.

Irene shook her head. "Cat didn't tell me, to keep me safe. She figured if someone came here looking for her, I wouldn't have to lie. I don't think she was expecting you though."

"We didn't tell her we were going to come looking for her." I sat back then and expelled a frustrated breath. If Cat's mother didn't know where she was, did anyone? "Does Cat have other family or friends she'd stay with here? What about her brother?"

"Brian? I don't know if Cat would go there. He's not the most responsible person."

"Could you make some calls and try to find her? It's really important that even if she doesn't come back with me, I see her face-to-face." When Irene didn't look convinced, I pushed harder. "I'm not a cop. I don't have any powers to arrest her and the Little Rock police have no reason to bring her in. I just need to sit down and have a proper conversation with her."

Irene understood. "Let me make some calls. I don't know that anyone will tell me when Cat refused to tell me herself. I don't think she would put the burden on her family. She has a few aunts, uncles, and cousins here. She's not particularly close to any. Her friends are loyal to the core."

Irene excused herself from the table and came back carrying a small brown book and her cellphone. She laughed lightly. "I don't trust my cellphone enough to keep my contacts." She tapped the book. "I have everything I need right here."

For the next hour, Irene called friends of Cat's and family. I stopped counting after the eighth call. Irene stressed how important it was that Cat come home. Everyone denied Cat was with them including her brother. She wasn't anywhere and Irene was growing as frustrated as I was. She put the phone on the table. "I don't know. If she's with any of them, they are lying for her. What do we do?"

I remembered what Cooper had told me about Cat's call with her assistant. Cat had mentioned the name of a restaurant and it pinned down her location while she was on the call. I recounted what Cat's assistant had told us. "Is there anyone that lives near Big Lou's?"

Recognition came over Irene's face. "I know where she might be." She stood from the table and went into the living room. She came back carrying her purse and her keys. "I'll take you there. If Cat's in as much danger as you say, she chose the perfect person to protect her. I don't know why I didn't think of it sooner."

CHAPTER 32

Cooper took the last bite of pork chop Adele had cooked in a cast iron pan and savored it. She had paired it with fresh asparagus and a small salad. She was trying to stay away from carbs and had skipped the potatoes, which was fine with Cooper. He had gained a little weight around the middle after his injury a few months back and he was working to get in shape again. Not that there was anything wrong with carbs. He ate his fair share but didn't miss them with this dinner.

"I have another in the pan if you want it," Adele said as she smiled over at him. The light caught her eyes just right and made them sparkle.

Cooper didn't think he'd ever seen prettier brown eyes before. They were dark but rimmed in flecks of what he considered gold. "This was more than enough. How was work today?"

Adele started to answer but a knock on the door interrupted her. She stood to answer but Cooper gestured for her to sit. They were still on edge, particularly as night fell. Cooper knew the sniper was out there searching for his next victim since Cat had not returned to the city.

He had been hoping to hear from Riley soon. To be fair, she'd only been in Chicago a couple of hours and he didn't think it was going to be that easy to find Cat. He crossed the room, went to the door, and peered through the peephole. Luke leaned against the far wall looking frustrated and defeated.

"Has there been another shooting?" Cooper asked as he unlocked and opened the door.

Luke shook his head. "There will be though, tonight. I'm powerless to stop him. I have patrols out all over the city. Our undercover detectives are everywhere. Tyler is even taking a shift. He sent me home to sleep and eat so I'd be fresh for tomorrow. I want to be out there with the rest of them."

Cooper waved him in and locked the door behind him.

"I'm sorry. I didn't mean to interrupt dinner," Luke said, stopping in the middle of the room when he saw the plates on the table. "I can go."

"Don't be ridiculous." Adele went to the cabinet in the kitchen and pulled out another plate. "I have another pork chop in the pan and some vegetables. There's salad too. There's more than enough. Sit and eat, Luke. Tyler is right that you need to keep your strength up. There are more than enough other officers out there tonight. Let someone else take some of the burden. You've been doing this on your own since the start."

He didn't decline or protest the offer. "I appreciate it. I keep forgetting to eat and forget about sleep," Luke said as he sat at the table. "Riley told me the same. I feel like if I'm not out there every second trying to catch this guy more people will die. Every second not out there is wasted."

"That's a good way to run yourself right into the ground." Adele set the plate in front of him then sat back down at her place setting. Cooper joined them at the table too.

Luke cut a piece of pork chop and put it in his mouth. "This is incredible," he said as his body relaxed into the chair. He raised his eyes to Cooper. "Any luck with your investigation?"

"No work talk at the table," Adele scolded him with a grin. "Eat and relax. You have all evening to discuss the case."

"Yes, ma'am." Luke smiled back at her and did as he was told. He finished off the meal with praises of appreciation. When he was done with that and the tea Adele had poured him, he sighed. "Have either of you heard from Riley? I talked to her while she was on the train and updated her about the sniper's letter to Channel 5. I haven't heard from her since, not that I'm worried."

Adele tsked at him. "Of course, you're worried. I'm worried about her. She should be home on the couch relaxing. You can't talk any sense into her sometimes."

Cooper side-eyed her and tried not to laugh. He shared a knowing look with Luke. Adele was the same way, possibly even more stubborn than Riley. He wanted to ask her if she was kidding but thought better of it. "Riley was heading to see Cat's mom. It was first on her list. We didn't think she was there though. Riley hoped she could talk some sense into the mother who might be willing to reveal where we could find Cat."

"Why would she come back to only be at more risk?" Adele asked as she began to clear the table. Cooper and Luke started to stand to help and she told them to sit. "Let me handle this while you talk about the case." She posed her questions again to them.

Luke disagreed with her. "I think Cat's more at risk there in Chicago. She may think the sniper doesn't know where she is, but he's been a step ahead this whole time. There's no telling if he has eyes on her."

"You don't even know if she is in Chicago," Adele countered as she carried the plates to the sink.

That was true. It had only been a guess on Riley's part. Cooper didn't know why Cat would come back. "We don't know where Cat is. Chicago was the only other place we knew she lived. She could be anywhere. I'm hoping Riley can convince her to come back. If not, what's the plan, Luke?"

"The plan is always what it's been regardless of where Cat might be – I need to find the sniper and bring him in. That is proving to be a more difficult task." Luke stretched his arms over his head and yawned. "Did you have any luck on your research?"

"About Len Woltman?" When Luke confirmed that's what he meant, Cooper explained what he did earlier in the day. "His brother-in-law said he was a professional guy, so I started with LinkedIn, which provided Len's photo, educational background, and a list of his employment record as well as a section at the top where Len filled in a narrative about his current business. He's working as an engineering consultant for energy and gas companies."

Most of what Len wrote Cooper didn't understand. It was filled with industry jargon that didn't make much sense to him. If Len wrote it himself, then he was articulate, well-versed in his field, and a decent writer. Nothing written there matched in tone or language to the sniper's letters though. Cooper told Adele and Luke that.

"After I looked at that, I called Ezo Technologies, where he had been previously employed, and checked him out. I pretended I was doing an employment verification, so I don't think I raised any alarms. I've spoken to more than one person there and they have all been fruitful conversations. They missed Len and the expertise he brought to the table." Cooper shrugged, not sure how much the guy's work mattered. "If he was still working for the company, I could understand why he might want to kill the lawyers involved in the federal case against them. As it stands, it doesn't seem like Len wants anything to do with them. He doesn't seem like he has much motive."

"We don't know that the sniper targeted them knowing who they were. It could be a coincidence that he targeted them."

Adele walked back to the table with a dishtowel in her hand. "There's something that's been bothering me about the first two cases."

"What's that?" Luke asked.

Adele stood with her hand on her hip and her head cocked to the side. Cooper knew that was a look of deep thought, putting pieces together she hadn't before. "The sniper targeted a defense attorney's daughter and then two federal attorneys in the middle of a big case. Then the sniper comes to me and drops me a message while also getting to my client in prison. Have you considered this guy might be a lawyer? He seems connected and in the know for an outsider."

Cooper hadn't put those pieces together before now. "You think he's someone currently working as a lawyer?"

"Why not? If he has a client in prison right now, he'd be in and out of that county jail. He'd also know the guards and at least one inmate. He'd easily be able to get a message to Buster right under everyone's nose. Those conference rooms are secure and private for attorney-client privilege. He could have met with his client, passed the message for Buster along, and his client delivered it. No one would be the wiser that it went down."

"You get anywhere with him today?" Luke asked, taking a sip of tea.

"No," Adele said the word in a breath of frustration. "Someone scary got to him. He'd rather rot in prison right now than give up the name. He knows there is no deal on the table and he's looking at potentially more time for lying to the cops. He insists he didn't know it was a lie. He's not giving up his source though. I went round and round with him today."

"What do you think, Luke?" Cooper asked, considering Adele's theory.

"It's too wide a suspect pool." Luke had his mouth set in a firm line and seemed to be mulling over something. Finally, he spoke, "Isn't the guy that came to you and Riley also an attorney?"

"Corporate. He had concerns about Len for a long time though."

"One more attorney involved," Luke said without any real meaning behind it.

Adele raised her eyebrows and asked him a question she had never asked before about a case. "Cooper, who is your client?"

Cooper hesitated to share the information. He didn't normally share his client information, just like Adele didn't share the things she discussed with her clients. There was a line of confidentiality in their work they didn't cross often. Cooper had already shared about Len though. "Hollis Hopkins," he said after losing the argument with himself.

Adele tossed the dishtowel toward the counter, missing by a wide mark. It fell to the floor and remained there as she sat down at the table. "Hollis isn't *just* a corporate attorney, Cooper. He used to be a prosecutor and then he became a defense attorney. He got a corporate offer about three months ago. He hasn't been doing corporate law for that long. He still has deep connections into criminal law here in Little Rock."

Cooper hadn't dug into the man's background. "I only know he said he was a corporate lawyer and his house and the money he was flashing around certainly matches that." He pinched the bridge of his nose. "Do you know him?"

"Not well but you hear things at bar meetings and such," Adele said, giving them a knowing look. "He's an arrogant guy and a bit of a blowhard know-it-all. He was let go at the prosecutor's office. They didn't outright fire him but they pushed him out. The same thing happened at the defense firm. Hollis is hard to get along with and he hasn't won many cases recently because he doesn't make the best decisions for his clients. I wouldn't be surprised if some of his defense case convictions were overturned on appeal for ineffective counsel. He's kind of an odd duck. Many attorneys are arrogant and full of themselves. Heck, people could say that about me in the courtroom when I'm fighting for a client. After, the gloves come off. With Hollis, that was his personality, but most of what he said didn't hold water.

Nothing to back it up."

Cooper understood what she was saying. He had seen glimpses of those personality traits when he had met with Hollis. "What about his brother-in-law? Do you know his wife or her family?"

Adele shook her head. "Hollis doesn't bring her around. I've never met her, even at events where spouses are welcome. He's one of those guys who either avoids talking about his wife or when he is talking about her, he's talking her down. I got the impression she wasn't smart but that may be what he wants us to think. He sounds like he runs his family like he runs his law practice."

Cooper had gotten that impression too. "What do you suggest I do?"

Luke had been quiet that whole time, so what he asked next surprised them both. "Does he have any clients in jail?"

Adele dismissed him outright. "I wouldn't think so. He would have finished his cases or passed them to another attorney when he left the defense firm."

Luke made a dismissive gesture. "I'm grasping at straws here and looking at everyone as a potential suspect because he's left us with little to go on."

"I don't think it's the craziest thing you've said," Cooper acknowledged, although he was having trouble seeing Hollis as the sniper. "I was more suspicious of Hollis's actions than Riley. He came out of nowhere and wanted us to find Cat and investigate his brother-in-law. We have no intention of telling him Cat's location and we didn't tell him Riley was heading to Chicago. As far as he knows, she's still here in Little Rock. I can start digging into his background if you like. He's a client so he's fair game as far as I'm concerned."

"I don't have any evidence tying anything to him. If you want to investigate him, I can't stop you but tread carefully."

"I'll bring any evidence to you," Cooper assured him.

"That's not what I mean." Luke leaned into the table. He started to speak but his words were overshadowed by a distinctive sound – *pop pop*.

Cooper and Luke were on their feet racing to the front door with Adele right behind them. The sniper had made good on his threat.

CHAPTER 33

Irene drove through the city streets like a woman who knew exactly where she was going and didn't have time to waste getting there. She took one side street after another, barely stopping at stop signs and then accelerating when she had a break in traffic. She hadn't told me anything since we left the house even when I tried to ask her what she suspected.

As soon as I mentioned the restaurant Big Lou's, it was like a light went on and she needed to get to her daughter as quickly as possible. I wasn't sure if Irene felt Cat was more in danger with the person who was hiding her or if Irene was so filled with relief that she knew where Cat might be there was no time to waste.

Even when I tried to ask a question, Irene drove like a woman on a mission. She didn't turn or acknowledge me at all. I was starting to wonder if she remembered I was beside her. After a few more turns, we were on downtown Chicago streets. "It's up here," she said without offering more.

After four more blocks, she pulled over to the curb a few businesses down from Big Lou's. Its neon flashing red sign lit up the whole block. Irene got out of the car and I followed right behind her. She walked as she drove.

When I thought we might walk into Big Lou's, she walked beyond it and crossed the block to the high-rise building that looked newer than the whole neighborhood by about fifty years. Its glass and metal structure looked out of place against the old Chicago feel of the rest of the buildings.

Irene marched up to the desk and spoke to the man standing behind it. "I need to see Angelo Martello right now."

The man didn't look in a hurry. "Do you have a meeting with him?"

"No. I believe my daughter is up in his penthouse with him and I need to speak to her immediately. It's an emergency."

"Then you can call him," the man said and went to handle another task.

"I don't have his number," Irene insisted, trying to remain calm. Her hand balled to a fist and for a moment I thought she might pound it down on the counter. Instead, she steadied herself. "Call him for me and tell him that Irene O'Conner is down in the lobby and needs to speak to him. Please, I need your help."

He raised his eyes to her and they stared at each other, locked in a stalemate for several moments. His hand hovered over the phone but he didn't pick it up. "I'm not supposed to disturb him."

Irene wasn't backing down. "I'm not leaving here until I speak to him."

There was a part of me that wanted to tell her we could call Cat and let her know we were there. I thought better of it because Irene could have done that herself. She knew better than me what was going on.

"Please," Irene said one more time.

The man relented and reached for the phone. "If he says you need to go, you need to leave or I'll call the police."

Irene stepped back from the desk and simply nodded. "He'll speak to me." There was confidence in her voice that reassured me.

The man spoke to someone I assumed was Angelo and then hung up the phone. He gestured toward the white couches in front of a simple metallic fireplace. "Have a seat and he'll be right down."

Satisfied, Irene went to the couch and sat. I eased myself down next to her. "Can you tell me what's going on? Who is Angelo?"

Irene shifted her eyes to me. "Cat's father."

It occurred to me then that I had never heard Cat mention her father. She didn't share his last name. "Have you been divorced long?"

"Since Cat was a baby and he's only been sporadically in her life." She turned to me then. "He's not a good man, Riley. He's involved in a lot of criminal activity. I didn't know that when I married him but learned soon after. I divorced him and raised my kids myself. Angelo is powerful though and he can keep Cat safe from the sniper. I'm not sure he can keep her safe from himself though. I don't want him mixing her up into his world."

She told me that with an edge of concern as if I might judge her. "Something similar happened with my parents. It's a long story. I don't judge you for any decisions you make. My only goal is finding Cat."

"Angelo is not going to be easy, Riley. Let me handle him when he comes down. We haven't spoken in a long time."

"What's a long time?"

Irene looked over at me with her eyes wide. "A decade or more. That's why I didn't think Cat would be here. They have a strained relationship. It's also why I knew he'd speak with me. He knew I had to be desperate if I was willing to come here to his building and speak to him."

"His building?" There was an undercurrent in the way she said it that caught my attention.

"He owns this whole monstrosity as well as several others in the city. His family is in construction. He's lived on the penthouse floor since it was built."

"That's why you knew when I said Big Lou's." It was more a statement than a question, and I hoped he'd be amenable to helping.

We waited for roughly fifteen minutes until the elevator doors opened and a short man with dark slicked back hair and a swagger in his gait exited the elevator. He had on pressed blue pants, an open-collar linen white shirt, and shoes that cost more than three months of my salary.

"Irene," he said, beaming a warm smile. She stood to greet him and he took her in his arms and kissed both of her cheeks. He extended his hand to me and introduced himself. "You must be Riley."

I stepped back unsure of how he'd know that.

Angelo laughed and gestured up toward the ceiling. "I have cameras everywhere."

"Cat is here then. There's no way you'd figure out my identity that quickly."

"You'd be surprised," he said, offering no confirmation. "Let's sit and talk."

"No." Irene's tone was firm. "I want to see Cat and I'm not leaving until I do. We need to speak to her. She's not in any legal trouble, not yet anyway. I'm trying to prevent that, not that you'd care about that."

"Let's not start all that, Irene. I care about our daughter and don't want to see her in any trouble." He let those words sink in and then delivered a blow. "I'm afraid you can't speak with her though."

"Why is that?" Irene asked not missing a beat.

"She's not here."

"I don't believe you. We were involved long enough, Angelo, that I know when you're lying." She leaned toward him and stared right into his eyes. "I know you're lying. Cat didn't tell me where she went to keep me safe. It's the only reason and I'm not scared. I need to see her and you're going to bring us upstairs to your penthouse now." It was clear she wasn't going to take no for an answer. When Angelo made no move, she snarled. "Take us there. I know where all the bodies are buried. I can make a lot of trouble for you, so…" She didn't finish the sentence and didn't need to.

Whatever power Angelo thought he had in the situation dissipated. "She's going to be angry with me."

"Then she can be angry," Irene snipped, marching toward the elevator.

This was a side to her I didn't know existed in the short time I knew her. I also wondered what she meant by the bodies – was it literal or figurative? I didn't want to ask. I followed Angelo and didn't say a word as he punched in a code to access the penthouse and the elevator ascended to the top. The tension remained thick between us and Irene barely even looked at him. Her anger only rose as the elevator reached its peak. She was breathing short loud breaths through her nose like a bull ready to fight.

The doors slid open and I came face-to-face with two beefy armed men standing guard at the door. Angelo ushered us past them into his residence. "Cat, your mother and Riley are here," he called as he entered the space. When there was no response back, he stood looking at us like he told us so.

My breath caught in my throat as I stared past him at the massive windows that went from his fifteen-foot ceilings to the marble floors. It looked out over the Chicago skyline to Lake Michigan. I didn't get to enjoy the view too much because Irene shouted for her daughter.

Met with no response, she set off to check the rooms. "Cat, please. Riley and I are here to talk to you."

Angelo started to tell me we were wasting our time when my cellphone buzzed in my pocket. I tugged it out and clicked my texts. There was one from Cooper. My heart sank as I read his words, letting me know there had been a shooting. He didn't have much to share only that one person was dead about a block from his condo. He told me he'd share more details when he could.

I looked up at Angelo barely keeping it together. "You need to convince Cat to speak to us. There's been another shooting and I think she might know the identity of the shooter. I'm not saying she's purposefully holding back on the police. Please convince her to speak to me so we can stop innocent people from dying."

Angelo gestured toward my arm. "What happened to you?"

"I was shot by the sniper." I told him the whole story about being shot and the impact it had on me and the community. "This has been devastating for everyone. We need Cat's help. I wouldn't be here if it wasn't that important."

"I don't think that's who Cat is hiding from," Angelo said, raising his thick dark eyebrows in a question. "I'd think coming all the way here, especially so soon after getting shot, you'd know why she ran."

He made me feel slightly silly for not having all the facts. "Angelo, she took off after flowers arrived at her place. She left without warning – went upstairs, threw things in a suitcase, and climbed out an upstairs window and down a fire escape. I didn't think her actions were that of a person thinking rationally. We assumed Cat was hiding from the sniper, which is perfectly understandable. If you know something different, please tell me."

"Cat has barely mentioned the sniper to me since she arrived." Angelo took a few steps toward me and spoke with his hands. "She's afraid of her ex and rightly so. Set aside Cat's tough girl exterior, she's quite sensitive and kind. She was devastated when she realized her ex was married and even more devastated when she realized that he had a family. She was embarrassed and humiliated that he had lied to her for so long and she felt even worse for his wife and daughter. She debated whether or not she should tell them. He started trying to get her back and keep her quiet. Once he realized the gifts, flowers, and sweet words weren't going to work, he started with threats."

"Do you know who he is?" I hoped Cat had confided in her father.

"No. When she talked to her family and friends she called him Elliott but admitted that wasn't his real name. It was something she had made up to conceal his identity because she always felt odd about the relationship, even when she didn't know why. I demanded to know the truth, but Cat said she couldn't tell me. It would only make it worse. He finally stopped and Cat had close to three months of quiet before the sniper started this nonsense. She's been through a great ordeal and she came to me because I can keep her safe. Now you're asking her to put herself in danger again. It's too much to ask."

"I'm not. I swear that to you. I only need to know who she was involved with because I think he might be the sniper. I think he might have assumed some other identities to keep tabs on Cat and keep in contact with her." I locked my gaze on him. "She can't hide out with you here forever."

Something I said finally sunk in. He resigned himself to the situation. "Let me speak to her."

"Angelo," I called after him. "Please tell her this isn't going to stop until she tells us what she knows. There was another shooting tonight. I don't want to put her at risk. I want all of this to end."

He nodded in understanding and retreated from the room, leaving me alone to stare at the view out the window. I didn't know where Irene had gone but I hoped one of them would convince Cat to speak to me. I watched the lights of the city sparkle as I stood perched above the city. There was a certain power that surged in me and a feeling of being removed from it all. I wondered if this was what the sniper felt when he was looking down at people before shooting them.

"Cooper didn't tell me you'd been shot," Cat said from behind me.

I turned and took her in. She had dyed her hair brown, getting rid of the purple streaks, and she had cut it shorter. The bob was a few inches off her shoulders now. She had removed the row of earrings in her ears and had on pink pajama bottoms and a tee-shirt.

"It happened during the Kavanaugh shooting. There's been another tonight, Cat. The sniper has made a threat to shoot someone every night until you return."

Cat winced. "That's not fair to lay that at my feet, Riley. I played his game long enough and no matter what I did, he shot someone. It won't matter if I go back."

"I don't need you to come back with me," I assured her. I hitched my chin toward the couch. "There might be another way for you to help me. All I need is a conversation."

CHAPTER 34

Luke had raced out of Cooper's building and hit the sidewalk in a sprint, running in one direction and then back down the other end of the street when onlookers pointed him in the right direction. He skidded around the side of the building and came right to the feet of a woman shot twice – once in the abdomen and once in the head.

Luke didn't need to drop down and check her pulse to see if she was dead but he did just that. He cursed when he confirmed what he already knew. Luke pulled his cellphone from his pocket and called for backup. It was already on the way as many bystanders had already called 911.

"Move back," Luke yelled to the crowd that had already started to gather. "Back up, please." He directed two men to push the crowd back and divert the traffic coming down the street. He wanted a wide berth to assess the crime scene.

"I saw the shooter," one woman yelled as men nudged her back like Luke had asked. "I saw the shooter!" she yelled again.

"Wait. Wait." Luke moved past the men into the crowd as sirens wailed in the distance. He grabbed the woman's arm and tugged her free of the people who had started to swarm her, demanding to know what she knew.

Luke had her firmly by his side when the first officers arrived on the scene. He shouted instructions to them as he moved the woman to safety across the street and down two blocks away from the crowd. He introduced himself, feeling rushed and out of breath. "You said you saw the shooter. What's your name?"

"Marcy Quinn." The woman appeared shaken now and the confidence she had drained from her. "I was a block behind the victim. We were all rushing home because of the curfew. I had seen her earlier in the evening with friends in the Flying Saucer. We left about the same time. It could have been me who was shot." Her eyes glazed over in shock.

"It's okay. You're safe now." Luke didn't have time to wait because if she saw him he was still in the area or could be. Each passing minute gave him time to escape. "Please tell me what you saw. We need to catch him. Which direction did he go?"

Marcy pointed down the road in the opposite direction of them. "He was on foot. He walked right up to her and shot her in the stomach and then when she was on the ground he stood over her and shot her in the head. I froze, not sure I was seeing it correctly. I don't even know if he saw me. Then he ran in the other direction."

"He was close. He didn't shoot from somewhere above?" Luke's questions came in rapid succession, barely giving her a chance to respond. He wanted to shake the information out of her. When he realized that she wasn't going to respond to that kind of questioning and the shooter had probably already gotten away, he backed off. "Can you tell me what he was wearing or anything you remember about him?"

Marcy stared off into the distance. "He was wearing clothes too warm for this heat. He had a long-sleeve shirt on and tan cargo pants and sneakers. He was white and had a ballcap on his head pulled low. It was a red Razorback hat. It stood out from everything else he was wearing. His hair looked wild under the hat."

That was enough for Luke to radio in an all-point bulletin for patrol to be on the lookout for the suspect. "How tall would you say he is?"

"A little shorter than you."

Luke radioed the information to other officers. He cautioned all that he was to be considered armed and dangerous. "What more can you tell me?" he asked her, knowing she'd have to give a formal statement later. He didn't want too much time to pass between what she saw and getting the information. He knew witnesses were often unreliable particularly when in shock.

"As I said, I noticed the Razorback cap before I saw anything. The whole city has been on edge and people haven't been doing much of anything. The River Market was empty tonight, which is the only reason I noticed her with her friends. I was there with a friend. We didn't want to give this guy any more power than he has, so we met for dinner." Marcy shook her head as if she were rethinking that decision. "It was dumb. I should have stayed in."

"If you weren't there, you might not have seen him," Luke said, hoping she realized how vital the information was she provided. "Is there anything distinguishing about the guy?"

"Besides the crazy hair, I don't know. I saw him approach her as if he knew her but then he pulled a gun."

"Where did he pull it from?" When she blanked on the response, Luke said, "Take your time. Think back to what you saw."

Marcy nervously licked her lips. "When he was walking toward her he had both hands down at his side. He might have had the gun in his hand and I didn't notice it because he was wearing dark clothes and the light was good but not great. When he raised his hand toward her, he had the gun in his hand. I don't remember him going under his shirt now that I think about it. It possibly came from his pocket and I missed it."

"Okay. Do you remember him getting out of a car?"

Marcy shook her head. "Definitely no. He was walking and came around the corner. But he ran in the opposite direction."

Luke needed to make sense of that. He pointed down the block toward Cooper's building. "He came from that direction and turned the corner walking toward you down the street. Then he turned back and ran away in the opposite direction away from where he came from. Is that correct?"

"Yeah, that's it." Marcy wrapped her arms around her. "I didn't get a good look at his face."

"Did it seem like the woman knew him?"

"It happened too fast to know. I never saw her face and as I said, he didn't seem to say anything to her." Marcy looked away from Luke. "Can I go home now?"

"I'm afraid not. You're going to have to come to the police station and give a formal statement." Luke gestured to one of the uniformed cops. "He'll take you down to the station. I'll call and ask someone to meet with you. It shouldn't take long."

Luke called Tyler and was glad he was still at his desk. He gave him a brief update. "I don't know much about the victim. I have a witness who saw the shooter. He walked right up to the victim and shot her. He's changing the game on us."

"I'll take the witness statement when she gets here," Tyler assured him and noted that crime scene techs and the medical examiner were already on the way. "Let me know when you have information about the victim."

Luke promised to call when he knew more. He thanked Marcy for coming forward with the information and then headed back to the scene. He arrived to find Granger.

"You got down here quickly," Luke said, grateful to see him there.

"I was at the station when the call came in." Granger lowered his large body to a crouch over the victim and tugged the sheet that had been put over her in Luke's absence from her face. "I know her, Luke. She's Sandy Dumont and she is an assistant prosecutor. She's only worked there for about a year. It was her first job out of law school. I had a case with her a few months back."

Luke knew then that Adele's theory about the sniper's legal connection had to hold some water. When Granger stood to his full height, Luke gestured toward the building moving them farther away from the crowd and the growing media. He lowered his voice and told him Adele's theory. "With every shooting except for the one on Kavanaugh, we have some legal connection. I don't get it but I'm starting to think this guy might be a lawyer or have some legal connection."

Granger cursed softly under his breath. "Do you have any ideas?"

"Cooper has a client who came to him and said his brother-in-law could be a suspect. I'm starting to wonder about him. He wants to find Cat and is willing to pay for it. That sounds a little suspect to me."

"That's not a lot to go on."

"We aren't going to be able to do much until Cooper gets something for us. It's the only thing I have right now. Even the tipline hasn't produced much."

"Det. Morgan," a female voice shouted from the crowd. "Do you have any statement for us?"

Luke turned to see Janelle shoving her way toward the crime scene tape that had been set up around the perimeter. He looked back at Granger and rolled his eyes. "I was hoping to get a handle on this before the media showed up."

"You know we are never that lucky. Do you want me to handle it?"

Luke would have gladly handed it off, but he needed to remain the face of the case. He wouldn't pass off that responsibility to anyone else. If the public was going to hate someone, it was going to be him. "I got it. Could you find me Sandy's next of kin? Then if you can call the prosecutor and let him know and find out what Sandy has been working on. I think we need to start exploring their connections to their cases and other attorneys. We might find that there's something that connects all of them. This might not be as random as we initially thought."

"Doesn't sound like it's random at all," Granger said and agreed with Luke's plan. "I'll call you when I have the details." He left Luke standing there staring out at the crowd that had gathered.

Luke sighed and waved to Janelle as she called his name again. He might as well get this over with. "I don't have much of a statement to make right now, Janelle. We have to notify the victim's family first before we can release any information."

Janelle wasn't deterred. She stuck the microphone in his face as he turned his head slightly to the side to avoid the brightness of the lights from the cameraman standing behind her. "What can you tell us about the shooting, Det. Morgan? Is it the work of the sniper who made good on his earlier threat?"

"We can't conclusively say this is the work of the same shooter. However, we are exploring all possibilities. We believe it might be connected but until we know more, we just don't know. The shooting only happened about forty minutes ago."

"Can you confirm the victim is a young assistant prosecutor?"

Luke kept his face passive and unresponsive. "We aren't releasing any information about the victim right now. We know the victim is a woman who was leaving the River Market before she was shot. That's all we know right now."

"But you're not ruling out she's from the prosecutor's office?"

"I'm neither confirming nor denying that information, Janelle." Luke's tone was enough for her to back off. She asked if there was any other information he could share at this time and Luke gave a general description that had been provided by the witness, who he didn't name. "We are asking the public if they see an individual who matches the description of the sketch we put out earlier to call 911 immediately. Do not approach this person. He is armed, dangerous, and has shown us he is willing to kill."

As Luke stepped back from the camera thinking he was done, Janelle shouted one last question. "What can you tell us about this sniper's connection to Little Rock's legal community?"

Luke was taken off guard by that and his expression momentarily gave him away. "We don't have any information to share about that," was all he could say before turning and walking away. He made it back to the body as Purvis and his team at the medical examiner's office showed up. He burned with anger at the question, mostly because he didn't know how Janelle had the information so quickly.

Luke spoke briefly to Purvis. "The victim is Sandy Dumont with the prosecutor's office."

Purvis glanced over at the media and back at Luke. "The media has her name already?"

"Det. Granger has worked with her. He made the identification." Luke glanced back at the media. "If Janelle knows it, she has the good sense not to say it. They know where she works, which is just as bad."

"Anything is possible," Purvis said and then got down to work with his team.

Luke spent time discussing what he wanted from the crime scene techs based on the witness statement. As he was wrapping that up , Granger called him with the next of kin information for Sandy Dumont. She and her husband Sean lived only a few blocks from Luke. He canvassed the scene one more time, checked in with Tyler, and then headed back to his neighborhood. He parked in his driveway, sitting there for a moment trying desperately to summon the emotional fortitude it took to tell one more person their loved one was dead from a killer he couldn't seem to stop.

The emotion in him bubbled over. Luke slammed the palm of his hand into the steering wheel until it hurt and released a guttural groan of frustration. Pulling down the visor, he stared at his reflection in the mirror and cursed himself. Then he took a few deep breaths and got it together.

Luke walked the short distance to the Dumont's house. There were lights on and one car in the driveway. He hesitated before he knocked.

A moment later, a man with dark hair and glasses pulled open the door. He got one look at Luke's badge and said, "It's about Sandy, isn't it? She should have been home hours ago and I can't reach her. The news said a young prosecutor was killed. Tell me it's not her."

Luke could barely get out the words as he delivered the news. When he was done, he said, "I have a few questions."

Sean let Luke in the house but before they got started, he raked his hand through his hair. "It's Hollis Hopkins. He threatened her more than a week ago. I knew I should have confronted him."

Luke wasn't sure he heard him right. "How does Hollis know your wife?"

"He came to talk to her about one of his past clients. When Sandy wouldn't give him any information and kicked him out of her office after he got loud and aggressive, he threatened to end her career."

Luke felt in his gut they were onto something. "Tell me everything you know."

CHAPTER 35

Cat followed me to the couch and sat down on the edge as if she was ready to jump up and run away at any moment. "How can I help?" she asked in a tone that said she didn't want to.

I laid out my case for her, including everything I knew about her ex and how I thought he might be Harvey and the sniper. "The flowers spooked you and that's why you took off. I got the sense that you knew who they were from without seeing the card."

Cat shifted her eyes away from me. "I didn't know he was married."

"I'm not judging you, Cat. That's not why I'm here. I'm here because you're afraid of him. I believe you've already suspected that your ex might be Harvey and the sniper."

Cat turned and looked at me then. "I have no evidence of that."

"The flowers. The white lilies. He sent you flowers just like the ones you received when you left. Those flowers weren't from your ex or Harvey. They were from the sniper."

Cat nodded slowly with confusion on her face "Those flowers were from the sniper?"

"That's what the note said. Why did you run?"

"I didn't even consider the flowers were from the sniper. I thought they were from my ex, and it all got too much for me, Riley. Between the men from the podcast threatening and harassing me, to the sniper forcing me to do a podcast about him and killing people in my neighborhood, the idea that my ex was trying to get me back again was too much." Cat tucked her hair behind her ears and fell into silence.

I wanted to say I understood but it felt fake. I remained quiet and waited for her.

When she spoke again, I felt her exhaustion. "It was hard for me to break it off with him and he kept trying to get me back. Then he started to threaten to ruin my podcast by telling people that I was a whore, sleeping with married men. I'm sure he wasn't going to mention I was sleeping with him. He tried all different ways to get me back. Once I found out he was married and lying to me the whole time, I was never going back, Riley."

"Believe it or not, I understand that, Cat. I had a similar relationship years ago. He wasn't married at the time but was involved with someone he eventually married. It caused all sorts of chaos in my life when she found out. She fought for the cheater and I walked away."

"How did it turn out for you?"

I thought back to the situation and didn't want to share what a nightmare it ended up, much like Cat's situation. "I was glad when it was all over and he was out of my life for good. Trust me, that time will come. I need to know though if you think he is capable of this kind of violence."

"I can't say no. I feel like I don't know anyone anymore and I don't trust my judgment."

It was like that with abusive relationships. "Cat, you've been through a great deal of mental trauma. You are great at examining cold cases and being objective. I need you to step outside of yourself right now and tell me what you think of your ex." I wanted a name but didn't want to push too hard.

Cat stared out the window and considered the question. "He was controlling in little ways I didn't see early on. Part of it I think was keeping me a secret from his wife. We went out for dinner but he took me to restaurants in other towns. I realize now that was to keep me hidden. At the time, I thought he was finding unique places for us. He always came to my apartment but again, he worked downtown so I figured it was easier. He was always jealous though. If I interviewed a man, I'd get the third degree if we flirted. He never hit me or raised a hand to me. He did yell a lot though."

I didn't say anything when she became quiet. I knew there was more to come.

Cat took a deep breath and sighed. "Do I think he's capable of pretending to be a podcast listener and sending me emails as someone else? Yes. Do I think he's capable of committing violence against people?" She turned her face to look at me. "When I allow myself to mentally go there, I think he's capable of tremendous violence. But, Riley, I still don't think he's the sniper."

"How can you say that, Cat? All of the evidence points to him. You just said he's capable of tremendous violence."

"The circumstances," she said without explaining more. Cat retreated to the impact on herself to avoid what she needed to tell me. "If I give you his name, it's going to make life a lot worse for me. I'll have to publicly admit to the affair. My reputation will be destroyed."

I wanted to shake her and tell her that in the context of what was going on, her affair with a married man was barely going to be a blip. "Cat, there's so much more at stake. There was another shooting tonight. He said if you don't come back, he's going to kill someone every night and he's already made good on that threat."

"I'm not going back. I don't care what he threatens or what he does, I'm safer here than I am in Little Rock." There was resolve in her tone.

I couldn't argue with that. She was safer in Chicago with Angelo. The sniper would surely kill her if he had the opportunity. I was sure of that. It didn't mean I was going to leave without getting a name. "I need a name, Cat. I need to know who he is so we can stop all of this. Let us investigate him. If it's not him, the evidence will show us that. If it is, we can make sure he never bothers you again."

"I'm telling you, Riley. It's not him. There's no way he would have shot Gemma Cullen if he was the sniper."

That piqued my interest. "Why, Cat? Why wouldn't your ex have shot Gemma Cullen?"

Cat leaned forward and put her head in her hands. "Please don't make me say it."

My heart raced at what I thought she was about to tell me. "Cat, were you having a relationship with Grady Cullen?" I didn't know the man but Luke had spoken highly of him. He'd become a media darling in the case, speaking so eloquently about his daughter and the trauma his wife was going through with the loss. I remembered back to Cat not wanting to interview him and the resistance she gave us about doing that. I remembered the tension and weird looks between them that I didn't fully pick up on then.

I touched her shoulder. "Please tell me. I'm not judging you."

She gave the slightest nod of her head in confirmation. "I'm so ashamed. His daughter was such a sweet girl. I felt awful about it." She raised her head to me. "I think Gemma might have found out about the affair. She came to my studio one day shortly after I ended the relationship and she asked me if I was involved with her father. I didn't even know who she was at first. I found out Grady had a daughter but I didn't know anything about her. When she told me her name, I knew then. I tried to deny it, but I don't think she believed me. She said she saw me with him. I acted like it was about the podcast and said I didn't know Grady was married, which probably wasn't the best thing to say. I don't know if I convinced her or not."

Cooper had texted me about Adele's suspicions about the legal connection and Grady fit that perfectly. He even pointed Luke in the direction of his client and had been the public face of the victim impact of the case. It was sociopathic if he was the sniper. "Is that why you haven't connected the cases to him sooner?"

"I'm not saying I didn't consider it, Riley. But who would shoot their daughter in cold blood in the street like that? I couldn't fathom it was him. Then when I had to sit in the studio and interview him about it, he seemed so broken up. I kept going back to that moment every time I started to question if it was him. I still can't believe it."

"What was he like when you interviewed him? Did he readily agree to the interview?"

"I don't know. Luke spoke to him about doing it and then he showed up at the studio at the appointed time. You were there. Grady acted like we hadn't met. We played it off for the podcast well, but I was shaking inside the entire time."

I had a few thoughts in my head but wasn't sure what I wanted to share. The sniper killed Gemma Cullen and then insisted on a podcast. It would have only been natural for Cat to reach out to the parents to be interviewed. I wondered if Grady was delusional enough to shoot his daughter to garner Cat's sympathy and speak to her again – the ultimate manipulation tactic. It was also possible he shot his daughter to protect his secret about the affair. It might have been a combination of both.

"What are you thinking?" Cat asked me.

I didn't want to pile on any more guilt than she might be feeling. "Has Grady been in contact since you interviewed him?"

"A few times," Cat admitted. "I didn't take his calls. His messages and texts have been trying to commiserate with me – like how sad we are both stuck in this horrible situation. That's why I thought the flowers were from him. That's why I didn't suspect him. He seemed so sincere, but I also knew I couldn't trust him. I've been struggling to make sense of the situation and my feelings. I didn't want to blame someone for something horrific with no evidence. What was I going to say to Luke? I had an affair with the man whose daughter was shot. I think he killed her. I'd sound like a vengeful, horrible person. There was no evidence to support it. I kept my mouth shut and when it got too much for me again, I ran."

It all made so much more sense to me now. "Do you still have those texts and voicemails?"

"I saved them. Do you think Luke would want them?"

I didn't know if Luke would believe anything I was saying given how much he seemed to have rallied around Grady. "I think it's best if you keep them. I don't know where things are going. It's best to hold onto them. Do you have any other evidence it could be him?"

Cat surprised me with her answer. "The language Harvey used in his emails and the sniper used is also language Grady used in texts with me. It was all familiar."

I had noted the similarities before between Harvey and the sniper. I had no idea Cat had noticed or had connected it to her ex. "Did you think Harvey was Grady?"

"I suspected but I had no proof. It's part of the reason why I kept my interactions with him so limited." Cat sat back on the couch and stared up at the ceiling. "What am I going to do now?"

"You're going to go back to Little Rock and face this mess," Angelo said from behind us. We both turned to see him and Irene standing together. They had been listening this whole time. When Cat protested, Angelo persisted. "I'll go back with you. You cannot hide out here any longer. You are stronger than this. You have to face it head-on. No one is going to judge you for being duped by a married man, and if they do, then that is their problem. You're going to use your voice to draw out the sniper. You are strong enough to do this, Cat. I'm going to be with you the whole time." He raised his eyes to me. "It sounds like you've got some other people who will be there with you too."

I laid my hand on her arm. "We will, Cat. We'll all be there for you."

She still didn't look convinced. "What do you expect me to do? I can't call him out over the podcast. I can't blame this on someone with no evidence. I'll get sued for defamation if I'm wrong."

"I don't think you're wrong, honey," Irene said, moving around the couch and sitting down next to Cat. "Can't you figure out a way to address it all in the podcast without naming him? Send a message directly to him and let him know you suspect him?"

I didn't want them to get ahead of themselves. "Let me speak to Luke first and see what he wants you to do. I don't want us to overstep in the podcast and send Grady running if it is him. We want to de-escalate the violence not increase it."

"Of course," Angelo said. "I already gave my driver the night off but I can drive us to Little Rock tonight. We can meet with Luke in the morning and decide the best plan of action." He zeroed in on Cat. "You have to tell him everything, even if you think it doesn't matter. You're not accusing Grady but you are saying you suspect him. It's up to the police to prove it but the whole community deserves the truth."

I appreciated Angelo and Irene's support on this because there was no way I was going to get Cat back to Little Rock on my own.

"Okay," she said slowly. "Let's go back to Little Rock and stop this sniper – no matter who it is."

I knew that was easier said than done. I felt a sense of relief and accomplishment for the first time in the case.

CHAPTER 36

"Sit down, Hollis. I'll be right back," Luke said to the man he had pulled from his home and brought to the station. Given he was a lawyer, Hollis knew the drill. Luke was surprised the man didn't lawyer up immediately. Even though Hollis and his wife were confused by Luke's late interruption while they watched television together, he came willingly.

Luke walked back to the conference room at the police station and gestured toward Granger, Tyler, and Cooper. "I've got him in the room if you want to observe the interview." After hearing Sean Dumont say Hollis Hopkins had threatened Sandy, Luke wanted to interview him.

Hollis had inserted himself into the investigation by pointing the finger at his brother-in-law and had the kind of reputation that fit with the overview psychological profile of the sniper – it fit in a lot of ways for Luke. Not to mention, he was desperate for a suspect.

Luke wasn't so desperate as to arrest or make a spectacle of bringing the man in for questioning. The evidence wasn't *that* good. As they walked down the hall toward the interview and observation rooms, Luke pulled Cooper back. "Is there anything with him you think I should know?"

Cooper turned his head toward the interview room. "Nothing I haven't already mentioned. As I said at dinner, I was just getting into the investigation with his brother-in-law, Len. I'm not sure based on what I'm hearing that Len is even a viable suspect and it doesn't sound to me like Hollis has the same impression of him as other people. He is cocky, like Adele said."

It wasn't much to go on. He thanked Cooper and then waited for him to enter and closed the door to the observation room before entering the interview room. "I appreciate you coming down to the station with me tonight. I have a few questions for you."

Hollis raised his eyes to Luke. "This is about Len, isn't it? I hired a private investigator and he told me once he got evidence, he'd hand it over to the cops. I didn't know Len was involved. I suspected but didn't know for sure."

Luke realized then Hollis had no idea that he was the suspect instead of Len. "You're not here about Len."

"Then why am I here?" Hollis asked sharply, cutting Luke off before he could finish.

"How do you know Cat O'Conner?" Luke wasn't even going to give him the option of denying he knew her. He didn't have that kind of time to waste.

Hollis leaned forward on the table. "I know her from the podcast."

"And?"

Hollis raised his hand off the table as if to gesture as he spoke but it hung there in the air while he seemed to reconsider what he was going to say. "I've met her a few times at the coffee shop downtown. She's been there a handful of times. I struck up a conversation."

"About?"

Hollis seemed flustered by the question. "Her podcast, mostly. I had started listening to it like a lot of people in Little Rock – nationally even. The first time I spoke to her, I said I was a fan. After that, we chatted when we saw each other. Nothing serious though. I'd tell her good job on an episode or comment something about her evidence. She knew I had been a prosecutor and defense attorney. It was chit-chat with a colleague."

It sounded plausible but he had lied to Cooper and said he had only recently started listening to the podcast when the sniper case started. He hadn't mentioned anything about knowing Cat. Luke wasn't willing to let up. "When did you become obsessed with her?"

Hollis caught on then. "I was never obsessed with Cat. That was my brother-in-law to an unhealthy degree. That's why I called the private investigator. I thought there might be something there."

"Where were you earlier tonight?" Luke asked, allowing his tone to grow angrier and stern.

"I worked until six and then went straight home and had dinner with my wife. I was in my study while she did a few things and then she and I sat down to watch television together at nine, which is where you found us."

There was a window. "It's fair to say then your wife didn't see you for a time?"

"I was in my study and she was in another part of the house. I guess that's a fair statement. What are you trying to ask me, Det. Morgan? I'd rather you get to the point."

Luke wasn't going to follow his orders. "What time did you go to your study?"

"After dinner," Hollis said with a shrug. "I'd say seven or so. I wasn't paying attention to the time."

There was enough time for him to drive down to Little Rock, shoot Sandy, and retreat home. He had two hours to do whatever he wanted. "Can your wife say with certainty that you didn't leave the house during that two-hour window?"

"I didn't leave the house," Hollis stressed but his face showed concern as his forehead wrinkled. "I don't know if she saw me or heard me during that time. She was upstairs and my office is on the first floor in the back of the house. I'm sure she'll tell you about dinner and after.

What is the point of this?"

Luke asked about where he was during the time of the Kavanaugh shooting. When Hollis hesitated, Luke pushed. "You're a busy lawyer, Hollis. You must have an administrative assistant who handles your calendar. I'm sure it's on your phone. Let's see it."

Hollis hesitated far too long for Luke's liking and then said, "I wasn't in the office that day."

Luke raised his eyebrows. "Where were you?"

"I was driving around. I fought with my wife that morning and there was nothing on my calendar for the day, so I took a drive to clear my head."

"Can anyone corroborate that?"

Hollis expelled a breath and shook his head. "I told my assistant I was working from home."

Luke went through the other shootings and found that Hollis was only claiming an alibi for the first one. He claimed to have been meeting with a client at the county jail, which raised another question. "I wouldn't think you'd still have clients in jail given your career change."

"He's an old client and he got in trouble again. I'm not representing him but I said I'd meet with him to discuss his case and help him find a new attorney."

"That's nice of you," Luke said with a hint of sarcasm. "How many times have you visited him?"

"Just the once." Hollis showed no reaction to the question.

"You didn't happen to pass your client a message to pass on to another inmate did you?"

Hollis squinted his eyes in confusion. "I don't understand what you mean. I don't know of another inmate in the jail. It was only that old client and I met him briefly that evening."

"Is there a reason you went so late?"

"My schedule is hectic, Det. Morgan. He had been arrested earlier in the evening and called me. He didn't want to talk to the cops and they threw him in a cell to wait for the hearing in the morning. I wanted to get in there right away to speak to him to find him the right attorney."

"Did you?"

Hollis confirmed he did.

"Do you know the exact time you were there?" Luke knew he could easily confirm this at the jail.

"I can't recall now."

"When did you hear about the shooting that night?"

"Late," Hollis said and then added, "I think it was on the news later that evening."

Luke wasn't going to give up that easily. "Do you own any guns?"

Hollis shook his head. "I used to be a hunter but my wife doesn't like guns in the house. I didn't have much time for my hobby with work and I gave it up. I never saw a reason to have a gun in the house."

"Protection," Luke suggested and watched for a reaction. Hollis gave none. "I'm sure you've had some difficult clients as a prosecutor and defense attorney. I'd think you'd want to ensure your protection at home. It's not uncommon for personal addresses to get out."

"My wife doesn't like them. It wasn't worth the argument. You're married so you know how it goes." When Luke didn't say anything, Hollis added, "We all do things to keep the peace, and no guns in our house was one of them."

No guns in the house. Luke wondered if choosing those words was purposeful and if Hollis was keeping the guns someplace else. He'd have to do a property search after the interview. He had other things to focus on. "Have you ever contacted Cat by email or her social media pages?"

"There was no need to. We weren't friends, Det. Morgan. I'd see her in the coffee shop and we'd chat for a few minutes and that's it. No more, no less."

Luke recalled what Riley said about the flowers. "Were you having an affair with her?"

"Of course not," Hollis responded, not hiding the shock at the question. "What am I doing here?"

"Do you know Sandy Dumont?"

"She's an attorney with the prosecutor's office. I don't know her well."

Luke knew he was lying then. "It seems you knew her well enough to try to speak to her about your former client and his new pending charges."

Hollis sat back in the chair and folded his hands on the desk. His fingers drained of blood from squeezing them so tightly. "There might have been a conversation."

"My understanding is there was a conversation in which you threatened her. Told her you'd ruin her career if she didn't drop the charges against your former client." Luke didn't even wait for him to respond. He could see by the expression on Hollis's face that it was true. "Why would you threaten a prosecutor over a *former* client."

"I was angry and lost my temper. I wasn't going to do anything to her. Things are said in the heat of the moment sometimes. I regret it." Hollis stared at Luke across the table. "Do you want me to apologize to her? I can do that if you want."

"She's dead, Hollis. The sniper shot her tonight." Luke said the words and watched as recognition took hold. "Yes, Hollis. That's why you're here. You seem to be connected to this case in ways that don't make a lot of sense to me – unless you're the sniper."

Hollis furiously shook his head. "I swear to you, I didn't do this. Please, check out my brother-in-law. If things are coming back to me, then he's setting me up."

"I think you're having everyone focus on Len to keep the focus off you." Luke pushed his chair out so hard it scraped on the floor. He stood to his full height. "I think you're obsessed with Cat and you were doing this to get close to her. When she rebuffed you, you snapped. You created fake accounts to email her and harass her. When she didn't give in you lost it and used this case as a way to bump off some people you don't like."

Hollis furrowed his brow. "What are you talking about? None of this is true."

"The ties between this case and the legal community are undeniable. I didn't see it at first but now that I do, it's obvious."

Hollis opened his mouth to speak but only partial words escaped. "Ties to the legal community?"

Luke explained all the connections to him. "We have three attorneys dead, one daughter of an attorney, there was a note provided to another attorney asking for representation, and then someone sneaked a message into the jail so law enforcement would be out of town for the Kavanaugh shooting. There is someone heavily connected to the legal community here in Little Rock that's committing these crimes."

"It's not me. I swear it." Hollis turned his head and raised a finger to point at the door. "Polygraph me right now. You'll see I'm not lying."

"You know as well as I do that they aren't admissible in court."

"I don't care about court. I care about you knowing that I had nothing to do with this."

Luke could see the fear in his eyes. He didn't have enough to hold Hollis and the polygraph examiner wasn't in the office. He settled on a compromise. "Come back tomorrow morning and I'll see that you have a polygraph. In the meantime, I'll check your alibis. Are you willing to take a gunshot residue test?" Luke had to ask because he didn't have enough evidence to compel him to take it.

"I'll take it."

Luke was glad that wasn't a fight. He left the room and called for a tech. When he returned, the tech administered the test and then left him alone with Luke. He pushed a pad of paper in front of him. "Write down your wife's contact information for me."

Hollis swallowed hard. "You're going to speak to my wife."

"I don't have a choice. I have to check your alibi. Is there a problem?"

"Please don't tell her I said anything about her brother."

Luke slowly sat back down in the chair. "Are you afraid of your wife?" Hollis shook his head but Luke persisted. "If you are, I want to know why. Every time you speak of her, you seem to go out of your way to make sure you don't anger her."

"It's not like that."

"Then tell me what it's like."

Hollis shifted his eyes toward the door and then at the mirror behind Luke. He had been a defense attorney, so he had to know people were watching. He cocked his head to the side and sighed in defeat. "My wife has a trust fund. We have everything we have because of her. I've not had the success as an attorney that I would have hoped. I try to keep the peace."

Luke had nothing to say to that. "Can you be here tomorrow?"

"I'll be here." He looked over at the door. "Am I free to go?"

Luke stood. "I'll see you tomorrow." When Hollis was gone, Luke met everyone back in the conference room. "That went nowhere. I'm not sure what we can do."

"I'll check the jail," Granger offered. "It will have the times he was there."

Tyler agreed with that. "I want to know who the client is that he's willing to threaten a prosecutor. Did you believe him, Luke?"

"We'll see what happens at the polygraph tomorrow."

"I might have something," Cooper said, holding up his phone. "Riley is on her way back with Cat and her parents. She said she has some information about the case but needs to tell us in person. She said they'd be here by morning. They are going to drive all night."

"Tomorrow it is then," Luke said, wishing he could have accomplished more. He hoped that if the sniper was Hollis he'd be scared enough of getting caught that he wouldn't do anything else that night.

CHAPTER 37

Cooper woke the next morning and immediately put on the local news to see if any progress had been made in the case. He had been there for Hollis's interview and felt the man was even more suspicious than he had already thought.

Before the shooting last night, Cooper had planned to go to Len's house after dinner and speak with the man directly. Luke and Adele had warned him that it wasn't a good idea before zeroing in on Hollis as a potential suspect.

Cooper didn't see anything in Len's background that would give him cause for alarm – then again, the sniper walked among them. He also considered this an opportunity to learn more about Hollis. He'd interview Len, even if no one else thought it was a good idea.

Adele had left more than an hour ago, stopping in the bedroom briefly to say goodbye. She was preparing for another court date and had a mound of research to go through. It was just as well because Cooper didn't want her filling his head with all the reasons he shouldn't go see Len alone. She had a way of convincing him of things.

It was only a conversation, Cooper told himself more than once as he prepared for the day. He sipped his coffee while leaning against the kitchen counter and checked his phone. There was still no word from Riley or Cat. They planned to get in that morning and go directly to the police station.

Riley had told him that Cat's father was a powerful man with illegal connections. She stopped short of calling him a mob boss. That's what it sounded like to him. They were protected was all that mattered. Still, Cooper was itching to know what Riley knew. She insisted it was better to wait until morning and let Cat tell him herself. She also wanted Luke to hear the information first. Cooper assumed Riley had a conversation with Luke sometime in the early hours of the morning.

Cooper made his way to the parking garage, and as he slid into the driver's seat, noticed a tall man with a messy mane of dark hair leaning against an older model Honda looking directly at him. Cooper kept his eyes on the man as he pulled his seatbelt around him and clicked it into place.

The man didn't move. He leaned back against the car with his back end perched on the hood and his long legs crossed at the ankles. His posture said he didn't have a care in the world. His expression though said something else.

Cooper had never seen the man before. That wasn't unusual. However, he knew most people who parked on this floor because it was reserved for his building. The man could have been a guest of someone, but Cooper didn't think so.

He reached to start his ignition and then thought better of it. He unbuckled the seatbelt and slowly opened his car door, waiting to see if the man would move or stop looking at him. Cooper put a foot on the pavement. "Can I help you with something?" he called across the garage.

That was all the invitation the man needed. He advanced on Cooper and stopped at the hood of his SUV. "I'm Len Woltman. I want to know why you're calling around about me."

Cooper put his hand on the gun attached to his hip. The mere motion caused Len to step back.

"I'm not going to hurt you," Len assured him. "I only want to know why you're stalking me. Did Hollis put you up to this? I know you're a private investigator."

"How do you know that?"

"My sister, Evelyn, told me. She knew Hollis hired someone and she gave me your name. She said I needed to watch my back. Then two days later my old job called me and said someone was asking about my employment with them." He stepped toward Cooper again. "I want to know what you want."

Cooper closed the car door and walked to the front of his car without drawing his gun. He extended his hand to Len and introduced himself. "Believe it or not but I was on my way to see you."

Len reciprocated the handshake. His light blue eyes lit up in confusion. "Why would you be investigating me? I know Hollis hired you, but I still don't understand."

"There's a coffee shop around the corner. Would you like to sit down and chat for a bit? It might be more comfortable than this garage."

Len shook his head. "We're safer here. I didn't want to come downtown given the shootings that have been happening." There was a flicker of recognition in Cooper's face that Len picked up on. His facial features grew stiff. "Is that why I'm here? You think I had something to do with that?"

Cooper didn't want to tell him everything Hollis had said. "There's been a concern. Do you have an alibi for last night's shooting?"

"I was home working. One of my neighbors saw me earlier in the evening. I didn't go anywhere all night. I was on a video conference with a client until about eight."

That was right around the shooting if Len was telling the truth. "What about the others?"

"I was in Seattle during the shooting that happened in the Heights." Len stared at Cooper as the shock of the accusations settled in. "I wouldn't shoot anyone. I don't own any guns and…"

Whatever Len was about to say, he didn't finish his sentence. "Do you listen to the *Rock City Killers* podcast?"

"No," Len said with a shake of his head. Then he held his hand out to stop Cooper from speaking. "I listened to it once when all of this started. I didn't hear the first in the series but the second with the sniper telling his story."

This was in direct opposition to what Hollis had told him. "What are your feelings about Cat O'Conner, the podcast host?"

"Feelings?" Len paused and furrowed his brow. "I don't have any feelings about her. She seems like a nice enough girl but has a morbid curiosity about all the murder stuff. There's not much more that I can say. I don't know her other than listening to her that one time."

It was Cooper's turn to feel confused because he believed Len. "If I were to tell you that I was told you were obsessed with Cat and that you listened to her podcast nonstop and even contacted her on more than one occasion – what would you say?"

Len stood upright, his posture rigid. "I'd say you were completely misinformed. I don't have time to listen to podcasts and I have no interest in murder." He crinkled up his features in disgust. "It's bad enough what's happening in this city right now. I don't need to be inundated with murder around the country. I have more important things to focus on. Who told you that?"

Cooper raised an eyebrow. "Who do you think told me that?"

"Hollis," Len said with a frustrated sigh. "That man has hated me since he started dating my sister. He's all arrogance and bluster with nothing to back it up. I told my sister early on not to marry him."

"Why?"

"When our parents died, they left us wealthy. My sister has never worked and she's involved in a lot of charity work and sits on several boards. Hollis is a user. I was concerned he was with my sister for the money and prestige she brought him. I figured once he got his hands on the money, he'd be controlling and more insufferable. It's why I insisted she put her money in a trust. We both have our names on it and Hollis can't touch a cent without both of our authorizations. If something happens to my sister, the bulk of her estate goes to me."

This gave Hollis motive to blame the shooting on Len. Cooper thought back to Hollis's interview with Luke. "Do you think Hollis is capable of violence?"

When Len realized Cooper might believe him, he relaxed his shoulders. "I think Hollis is capable of greater manipulation than any of us knows. He's also one of the most vindictive people I've ever met. He can hold a grudge forever. It's why he hates me so much. He wants control over everything and I wouldn't give him that."

"Tell me about the manipulation you've witnessed?"

"Evelyn never had children because Hollis didn't want any. He told her that after promising her children and then flipping the script after they married. I never trusted the man. In addition to the trust, I also insisted she protect her assets with a prenuptial agreement. Luckily, my sister listened to me even though she stayed with him. I don't understand the appeal and never will."

"Has he ever been violent towards her?"

"Not that she has told me." Len looked over his shoulder and then back at Cooper. "I assume you're wondering if I think Hollis is capable of this sniper shooting. Yes, I do. I think that's why I listened to the podcast. I wanted to see if the sniper's story sounded familiar and it did."

Cooper thought back on the interview the night before and wondered if Luke was able to confirm the alibi Hollis provided. "What parts sounded familiar?"

"The whole victim mentality. Not the juvenile delinquency part of it but the poor childhood and not succeeding at work. Everything is everyone else's fault. Hollis wants money and power and control and he doesn't have any of it, no matter how hard he's tried." Len wiped the hair from his forehead. "I don't know if you know his work history but he hasn't been able to keep a job. He keeps getting fired and no one likes working with him. He only has the corporate law job because Evelyn used her connections and got it for him. He's walking on thin ice and the partners have had enough of him. I wouldn't be surprised if he's fired soon."

That was not how Hollis made it seem. Cooper believed Len over Hollis. Even Luke didn't trust what Hollis had told him in the interview last night. "What about access to guns?"

"I don't know about that. I've never seen him shoot and my sister doesn't like guns, so I know there aren't any in the house." Len considered what he said and then amended it. "He talked about guns early on though. He said he hunted a lot when he was younger. I also believe he has property in his mother's last name. Evelyn found documents about a company tied to Hollis's mother's last name, Brimmer. It was called Brimmer Inc. and there was property down by Hot Springs. When Evelyn asked about it, he told her that it wasn't property he owned anymore and that the company went bankrupt. Evelyn didn't necessarily believe that to be true, but she let it go."

Cooper pulled out his phone and typed in the note for later. "You think he might still have that property?"

"I do."

"Do you have the address?"

Len gave a curt nod. "I wrote it down in case Evelyn ever went missing or got into trouble." When Len saw the look of concern on Cooper's face, he said, "I told you I didn't trust him. It's just me and Evelyn and we don't have any other family. I felt a need to watch out for her. I never trusted him and you investigating me for these heinous crimes proves my point. He's not a good man. I don't think he's sane or stable."

It was the same thing Hollis had said about Len. He gave Cooper the address. There was something more he wanted to cover. "If Hollis were to take a polygraph, do you think he'd pass even if he was lying?"

Len let out a chuckle. "He'd like to think he would. He might even be arrogant and manipulative enough to do it. I wouldn't put anything past him. Plus, he was a prosecutor and defense attorney. He knows the ins and outs of a criminal case. He knows what cops are thinking and the kinds of questions he'd be asked. If he wants to get away with this, Hollis will have a plan and stick to it."

That's what Cooper feared. He had one last question. "I know you said you didn't listen to the podcast but what about Hollis?"

"He's listened to it. He's the one who told me about it. I don't know how much he's listened though. That we haven't discussed."

"Anything about the podcast host?"

"Not to me," Len said with a shrug. "Then again, we didn't talk much. I try to avoid him."

"Did he ever have a fascination with the Son of Sam or other serial killers?"

There was a flicker of confusion in Len's eyes. "You don't know?"

"Know what?"

"Hollis failed out of the FBI academy. He fancied himself a profiler but never had the education or willingness to get the training to match. He said he was naturally gifted and was better off without the FBI. He's had a fascination with serial killers for as long as I have known him. Hollis said that's why he became a prosecutor. When he wasn't given big, complex cases, he thought he was better than the rest and decided to go the criminal defense route. He's mentioned Son of Sam several times and pointed out how David Berkowitz could have easily gotten away with the shootings."

Cooper allowed that information to sink into his gut, stirring a feeling of unease. He took the information to confirm Len's alibi and said he'd be calling those contacts later today and would be in touch.

As Len walked back to his car, he turned back to Cooper. "Be safe out there."

Cooper almost forgot to ask one pressing question. "How'd you know where to find me?"

"My sister told me Hollis had your address written on a slip of paper in his office. I thought your office was here but then I didn't see a sign. I was waiting to see if you'd show up in the garage this morning and you did."

Cooper felt his throat tighten. He didn't know what to say other than wishing Len well and telling him he'd be in touch.

As Cooper headed back inside his building, his phone chimed with a text from Riley. It was simple and to the point: *Come to the police station. We know who the sniper is.*

CHAPTER 38

My arm had started to throb about three hours into the car ride back to Little Rock from Chicago, preventing me from getting any sleep. I hadn't wanted to take any pain medication because I wanted to be clear-headed when I met with Luke. We had pulled into the city about two hours ago and I went straight home to shower and prepare for the meeting I had arranged. By the time I made it back to the house, Luke had already left for the day. I found a note that said he was glad I was home.

I had mentioned the information about Grady Cullen over the phone sometime around one in the morning when he wrapped up his night. Luke had a hard time believing the information and questioned Cat's credibility given how she behaved during the case. He doubted Cat would be honest and forthcoming with the information and wondered if it was just another distraction.

I believed her wholeheartedly. The longer I spoke to Cat about her relationship with Grady, the more convinced I was that he had to be the sniper. All the evidence fit perfectly together. Angelo and Irene were convinced as well, which is why they thought it was so important Cat come back to Little Rock and help the police. Cat still wasn't convinced Grady would kill his daughter to keep the affair a secret, but she was going to follow through with the plan we conceived on the ride back.

Now that I was sitting in the conference room of the police station with Cat and her parents while we waited for Luke, I regretted not taking another pain pill. I adjusted my arm in the sling, hoping for relief that didn't come.

Irene looked over at me with sympathy on her face. She knew I had been in pain and had been pushing myself too hard. "You should have stayed home and rested," she scolded me.

"I wanted to be here for Cat."

Luke chose that moment to come through the door. He had heard the exchange and focused his stare on me. "Are you okay?" he asked as he slapped a file on the table and sat. He was in no mood for games and had had enough dancing around with Cat. His whole posture was rigid and annoyed. I also knew Luke would have preferred a one-on-one with Cat but neither Angelo nor I were going to allow it.

I raised my eyes to him. "I'm fine, just a little uncomfortable."

"Let's get started then." He turned his attention next to Cat. "I need you to tell me what you told Riley."

Cat glanced over at me and I could tell her confidence was already starting to shake. I shifted my eyes back to Luke so she'd do the same. After a beat too long, she looked at him and cleared her throat. "As I told Riley, I can't be sure the sniper is Grady Cullen. I didn't want to believe it and there's a part of me that still doesn't want to believe it. I had a previous relationship with him. I didn't know he was married, and once I found out, I ended it. That's when things took a turn."

"How?" Luke asked in a clipped tone.

"He didn't want the relationship to end. He texted me, stopped by the studio, and threatened to shut down the podcast. As you know, he's a powerful defense attorney in the city. He has far more connections than I have and I believe he might be able to do that. Still, I wasn't going to get back together with him."

Luke flipped open the file and jotted down a note. He asked Cat the dates of the relationship and she provided them. "Things like this happen all the time and it doesn't end in this kind of violence and bloodshed. What makes you think Grady is capable of something like this?"

Cat didn't look prepared for that question. "He's been controlling and manipulative and hasn't wanted to let the relationship go. Riley is convinced that the same person who is sending the emails from Harvey is the sniper. Grady used the same kind of language in those emails as he did with me in the messages he sent. There's also the white lilies."

Luke shifted his eyes ever so slightly over to me. I could tell that he was wondering if I had planted this idea in Cat's head. "What about the white lilies?" he asked Cat.

"Grady knew I liked white lilies. They were my favorite flower. He had sent them to me before. I ran because I received white lilies again and he had started texting me again after I interviewed him for the podcast. I assumed he had gotten the wrong idea. I didn't run from the sniper case, I ran because Grady scared me. That coupled with the sniper case was too much for me to handle." Cat looked over at her father. "I went where I thought I'd be the safest."

Angelo reached his hand over and squeezed hers. "Det. Morgan, I know this story might sound farfetched, but I listened to Cat and Riley talk about this and this man. There's merit to their concern, which is why I'm here. I'd never bring my daughter back to a place where her life could be at risk if I didn't think it was important."

"I'm not discounting there's merit," Luke said evenly. "If I'm going to go after a respected criminal defense attorney then I need some evidence to back it up. Has Grady ever threatened your life or caused you physical harm?"

Cat took a deep breath. "Never. He threatened my podcast but never my life. He was never violent with me. He was controlling and obviously he lied about his marriage. Once I got out of the relationship, I wondered if that was a precursor to physical violence. I see that often in some of the cases I've covered on the podcast. I was getting out of that relationship either way and never going back. I don't date married men." Her voice grew softer. "At least, I don't when I know they are married."

"There's no judgment, Cat," Luke said with his tone softer now. "I can understand getting involved with someone who is lying about being married and why this would all be too much for you. Is there any other reason you think the sniper might be Grady?"

"Grady knew Todd Hall was harassing me," she said, surprising me. It wasn't anything she had mentioned before now. "We had discussed it after we were dating but before Grady was the one harassing me. There were a few months where we thought we could be friends. I tried but he couldn't take no for an answer. During that time, I confided in him about the men who were harassing me, specifically Todd. I was hoping as a lawyer Grady might have some suggestions for me."

"Did he?"

Cat shook her head. "He only used it as another way to make the argument the podcast wasn't good for me. He said it attracted unwanted male attention." Cat rolled her eyes toward the ceiling. "It was never about attention for me. It was about bringing attention to these cold cases and finding justice for the victims. It became a passion of mine and wasn't something I was going to stop doing for anyone. No one was going to bully me into stopping."

There was something in what Cat said that struck a nerve with me. "If this is Grady, this might be why he involved the podcast. He wants to show you how scary it can get."

Cat lowered her eyes to the table. "I didn't even consider it that way."

I watched Luke's face as he processed the information. I knew he needed more, so I laid out all the facts from start to finish about Grady. "We don't have physical evidence tying him to the case yet. This sniper hasn't left you any physical evidence, Luke. You already said you thought it was someone connected to the legal community and Grady has access to the jail. He also sent you in the direction of his client. He's had this ongoing relationship with Cat." I sat back and cradled my arm. "The most compelling evidence is the flowers. I think Grady wants Cat to know it was him. Why else would he send such an obvious sign?"

"I don't know."

It was clear he was overwhelmed with the information. "We have a plan, Luke," I said with my voice clear and strong. "We are going to use the podcast to let the sniper know Cat is back in town and she's going to say things in the podcast that only Grady would know. She's going to ask him to meet."

Luke turned his head sharply to Cat. "I can't let you do that."

"I have to," Cat said weakly and then grew more confident. "I'm the reason for this whole thing and it needs to end with me. Whatever he wants, I need to address it head-on. I should have done this at the start. My father will be with me and you'll be listening in and watching. I don't think you're going to let anything happen to me. I'll be safe while I get him to confess. I'll make him believe we can get back together and that I need to know the truth if that's going to happen."

Luke had started to argue but then seemed to think better of it. He was out of options. He agreed with the plan and then called in for backup support. We decided to go to Cat's studio and air the podcast live instead of recording and uploading it. It was the first time Cat would ever go live. The plan was to stream it on her social media channels at the same time.

We left it up to Luke to alert the media it was happening so that word would get out and people would listen. I also urged Luke to call Grady directly and tell him Cat was back in town. Luke had let it slip the night before that Grady had called twice asking if Cat had returned. He hadn't thought anything about it given the whole city seemed to be waiting for her return because of the threat the sniper made.

We left the police station with confidence that we might have a shot at stopping him.

An hour later, Luke showed up at the studio while we were getting Cat ready to go live. "I told Grady and he played it off like he was relieved. He didn't show much emotion about it."

That didn't surprise me. "He wouldn't, Luke. He's done a good job of lying to you so far about Cat. Did he ever tell you he knew her?" I knew the answer because I had asked him that last night. "The sniper is a psychopath and he's not going to show you his true colors."

As Cat adjusted her headphones, Luke pulled me aside. "I don't want you here for this. I want you to go home and relax and let me take it from here."

"I promised Cat I'd be here for her."

Luke was adamant. "I can't have you here. If Grady shows up here, I can't have you in the mix of this. I'm not going to risk your life and we aren't arguing about this." Luke put his hand under my chin and kissed me on the lips. It wasn't something we ever did in front of other people during a case. "You're in pain. I can see it on your face, Riley. Go home, take some pain medication, and watch the news. You can listen from the safety of the house. You've done enough to get us here. Trust me enough to watch out for Cat."

I held firm and didn't want to leave. Irene saw the exchange and came over to us. "Go home, Riley. Your husband is right. We are all here for Cat and she will be fine. I promise you I'll call as soon as I know anything."

"Okay," I said, raising my eyes to Cat. She had overheard us and told me it was okay for me to go – that she'd be fine with everyone else there. She thanked me for coming to get her. I knew when I wasn't needed and Luke was right. I was tired and in pain. He called for a police escort to walk me to my car.

I made it back to the house in time to take a pain pill, down some water, and change into leggings and a tee-shirt. I parked myself in my favorite chair and linked to the podcast on my phone. I listened to the intro as Cat announced she was back in her studio in Little Rock. My eyes grew heavy as she continued with why she came back and what she wanted from the sniper. She thanked him for the white lilies and said she knew exactly who they were from. Cat told her listeners that she wanted to see the sniper face-to-face and it was time for them to speak. She invited him down to her studio and acknowledged that he must be in a lot of pain to have taken the actions he took. There was no judgment in her tone. She faked strength and sympathy so well that I wondered if she wasn't faking it at all. I was sure it was hard to have once cared for Grady knowing what he had become. Feelings had to linger.

As I closed my eyes to listen and finally rest, there was a knock at the door. I groaned as I pushed myself upright with one hand. I assumed it was Cooper as I pulled open the door and came face-to-face with a familiar man. I was about to ask him what he wanted when I looked down and saw the handgun pointed at me.

I stepped back instinctively and tried to close the door but he blocked it with his foot and advanced on me, rushing into the living room. He pointed the gun at my mid-section. "You were supposed to be dead. Killing the lead detective's wife was supposed to be one of my greatest achievements. It would have been what got me the most recognition. Get on your knees."

"Please don't kill me." I held my one hand up.

He laughed. "You're already dead."

The last thing I saw was the blur of the gun as it slammed into the side of my head.

CHAPTER 39

Luke was hoping Cat had been gone long enough that the sniper wasn't watching her office to know they were all inside. That was the only way this was going to work. The cops stationed around the perimeter were plainclothes officers and would blend into the downtown environment. SWAT had positioned themselves the same way.

Luke had been leaning against the wall watching Cat as she expertly baited Grady and proclaimed to anyone who was listening that she hadn't run away but had left for family reasons. She was back now to stay. She implored the sniper to speak to her and even thanked him for the beautiful white lilies. She included a few personal messages that only Grady should understand.

When Cat finished the podcast, she pulled off the headphones and looked up at Luke. "What do you think? Do you think if it's Grady he got the message?"

Luke didn't know how he could miss it. "Between my phone call earlier letting him know you were back in town and what you said, I'm sure he got the message."

"What do we do now?"

"Wait to see what he does. There's nothing more we can do." Luke hitched his chin in the direction of her office. "I know Cooper has been checking your regular mail but have you checked your email at all?"

"I've been checking it while I was away and didn't get anything suspicious. I've been watching social media too."

Luke didn't know what more she could do. Her parents were up in her apartment to give her space to do the podcast. "Was this theory about Grady Riley's idea?"

"Not quite," Cat said, wrinkling her nose. "Riley didn't know I was involved with Grady. She suspected I must know the sniper based on my reaction to the flowers. I gave myself away. I'm not sure how Riley came to learn there had been another man but she didn't know it was Grady. She had already surmised the sniper and Harvey was the same person. She connected all the dots long before she knew the man's identity."

"You never suspected Grady?" Luke knew Riley could be persuasive and he wanted to make sure they weren't barking up the wrong tree.

"I wondered but I dismissed it because his daughter was a victim." Cat stared off across the room and let out a breath. "I still have trouble believing he could kill his daughter like that. I can't make sense of it."

That was Luke's concern too. He knew people were capable of truly heinous things, but it took someone truly demented to shoot their daughter in the street. He admitted that to Cat. "In theory, Grady sounds like a good suspect but the reality is a little hard to wrap my head around."

They waited in the studio for nearly an hour after the podcast ended. Luke was about to give up when there was a knock at the front door. Luke jumped up and Cat lurched forward in her seat, the fear showing in her eyes.

Someone radioed to the small speaker tucked into Luke's ear that Grady Cullen was standing on the other side of the door. "It's him, Cat. They have eyes on him. Take him into the studio and close the door. I'll be right on the other side of the door." He hit the record button on the recording equipment they had set up earlier to record Grady's confession.

Luke had to back out of the studio through the secondary door in the back of the room as Grady entered. He had to time it perfectly or Grady would have been able to see him down the hallway.

Cat provided the perfect distraction as she greeted him and brought him into the studio.

"Are you alone?" Grady asked as he entered the space. He had his hand on her arm and stood close to her.

Luke watched through a crack in the doorway.

"My parents are upstairs," Cat said finally and looked over toward the door. "They won't come down. I'm fairly certain they are both taking a nap. It was a long drive overnight and none of us have gotten any sleep."

"Where did you go?"

Cat's back stiffened at the question. "I went to my father's."

"Where does he live?"

"That's not important now."

"It's important if we are going to be together." Grady wasn't going to let it go. He waited for her to answer. "Cat, we can't start this withholding information."

Cat stepped out of his grasp. "Grady, you have a wife and you just lost your daughter. Is this the best time for you to start a relationship?"

Grady stepped toward her and put his hands on her upper arms, trying to pull her close. Cat remained firm in her stance. "I'll figure it out, Cat. I was so happy when you said you wanted to see me. You don't seem happy."

Cat lowered her eyes to the floor. "It's been a long day, Grady, with the sniper and everything. I'm sure you can understand how scary it has been for me."

"I do understand and that's why I'm so glad you're back."

"It must have been hard for you when you found out about your daughter. Where were you when you got the news?" Cat and Luke had worked on how they'd try to get his alibi for the crimes.

Grady didn't seem phased by the question. "I worked late and then I was home with Rose."

Cat wrapped her arms around herself. "Were you at home for all of them?"

"Why does it matter, Cat?"

"I was only curious." She leaned her backside on the table. "I was here for all of the shootings, and as much as I love this studio and my apartment upstairs, it holds reminders now. I also know you sometimes have lunch in the Heights. I was worried you might have been hurt during that shooting."

"You were worried about me?" Grady's eyes lit up like a child's. Luke had to stop himself from groaning. But Cat nodded her head and Grady smiled. "I was at court when the shooting in the Heights happened. I don't want to talk about all this unpleasantness. How are we going to proceed from here?"

Cat didn't let it go. She pushed harder than she had discussed with Luke. "Grady, I have to know that you didn't have anything to do with these shootings."

If she had slapped him across the face it would have had less impact. Grady recoiled from her, releasing her arms and taking several steps back. "How could you think I had anything to do with the death of my daughter? That's what you're saying, right? I'm the sniper and I targeted my kid. How could you, Cat?"

The response while theatrical seemed genuine.

"The white lilies," Cat said calmly not losing her footing in the face of his response. "The sniper sent me white lilies like you sent me. The way he wrote is the same as you. Some commonalities can't be a coincidence."

When Grady made no effort to respond, Cat rushed toward him and kissed him on the lips. He stared blankly at her. "I can help you," she said softly almost reassuringly. "If you did this, we can cover it up and live our lives. I need to know the truth, Grady. No more lies. It's what hurt us the first time. If you want us to be together, you have to tell me the truth."

Grady remained quiet for several moments. Then finally, he released his feelings in a breath. "You're insane, Cat. You are insane if you think I had anything to do with this." He started shaking his head and backing up. "I might have cheated on my wife but I'd never kill anyone. I can't believe you'd want to cover up a murder. I don't even know you anymore. There's something seriously wrong with you."

Luke couldn't take any more of this. Cat was taking on a persona he couldn't stand seeing. He stepped through the door with his hand still on his gun. "Grady, I asked Cat to meet with you today. There have been some concerns. There are some questions you need to answer about your connection to these cases."

Grady's head snapped to attention when Luke walked into the room. The softer side he had shown to Cat was gone. "If you had questions, you should have come to me directly."

"Maybe so," Luke conceded as he walked toward them. He gestured for Cat to sit down. "I asked Cat and coached her to try to get a response from you. She doesn't want to cover up these crimes, she wants to find out who killed your daughter."

"It wasn't me," he insisted, looking between them. Grady went to grab something from his pocket and Luke advanced on him. "It's just my phone, Det. Morgan. I want you to call the court and confirm I was in the middle of a conference with a judge while the shooting in the Heights happened. You can speak to my wife about the others. I had nothing to do with this and the sooner I can prove my innocence the better."

Grady didn't wait for Luke to respond. He grabbed his phone and placed a call. He spoke to someone on the other end and then handed the phone over to Luke. "It's the judge's administrative assistant. She can confirm I was in the office for the meeting."

Luke spoke to her and confirmed the details. Next, Grady called his wife and again confirmed exactly what he had told Luke about his schedule. While he did that, Cat sat at the table with her eyes wide seeming to be in shock about who the sniper could be if it wasn't Grady.

"I don't understand how the sniper could know so much about my life," Cat said as Luke handed the phone back. She looked up at Grady and pleaded with him. "He knew everything, Grady. He knew about the lilies. He knew what you called me and he even knew about Todd Hall."

When Luke went to say something, Grady held up his hand for him to stop. He needed to think through what Cat had said. He sat down at the table across from the recording equipment. "Did you check the florist?"

"They were ordered online and paid with a prepaid credit card. The card had a fake name," Luke said, having checked that out earlier when Riley had told him. "This is someone who is covering their tracks well and isn't leaving any evidence behind. Do you have any idea who might have killed your daughter, other attorneys, and terrified Cat in this way? We believe there is a strong legal connection in these cases."

Before Grady had a chance to respond, an officer speaking through the ear pod in Luke's ear told him that Cooper was approaching the front door. "Let him through," he said and went to the door. Luke didn't know why Cooper was there. There was no reason for him to be there now. Luke pulled the door open to greet Cooper who was out of breath and had beads of perspiration beaded on his forehead.

"Where's Riley?" Cooper demanded.

"At home," Luke said and stood back so Cooper could enter. He stopped him in the hallway and explained what was going on. "It's not Grady, so we are back to square one."

Cooper had a hard time catching his breath. "It's Hollis Hopkins."

"He passed the polygraph this morning. It's not him." Luke had gone down so many dead ends that he wasn't taking anything at face value anymore. "Why are you looking for Riley?"

"I wanted to tell her to stay away from him." Cooper started to move down the hall and into the studio and then stopped. He turned back to Luke. "Did you say Riley was home?"

"I sent her home to take a pain pill and get some rest. She was awake all night."

"She's not home, Luke," Cooper said with a mix of confusion and concern. "I texted and called her and when there was no response, I went by the house. It's dark and her car is in the driveway. She's not there."

Luke didn't understand. "She has to be there, Cooper. Maybe she didn't hear you knock."

Cooper pulled a set of keys from his pocket. "You gave me your key, remember? I went inside and she was not there. I checked with the neighbors and no one has seen her. I was hoping she was down here with you."

Luke grabbed for his phone and realized his hand shook as he pulled up Riley's contact information and pushed send. The phone rang once then went directly to voicemail. "I don't understand," he said, trying not to panic. "Where is she?"

"I don't know."

"What's going on?" Cat called from the studio. She moved past Grady and came out into the hall. "Did you say Riley is missing?"

Luke tried the phone again and this time a man answered. He looked down at the phone to make sure he had called her. "Who is this?" he barked.

An artificial-sounding voice laughed on the other end of the phone. "I have your wife. Do you want to say goodbye? I'm going to kill her before you can find her."

"Riley!" Luke shouted and then the call ended. His head snapped up. "He has her. The sniper has her."

"It's Hollis Hopkins," Cooper said with confidence. "Trust me. It's him."

"Did you say the sniper is Hollis Hopkins?" Grady asked, joining them.

Cooper confirmed without getting into it.

"It makes sense it would be him," Grady said and Luke demanded an explanation. "He worked with me at my law firm. I thought we were friends and I confided in him about Cat. He was the only one I told. He knew about the white lilies, things I wrote to her, and about Todd Hall. He knew it all."

"Where would he have taken my wife?" Luke said, ready to grab Grady by the collar and shake the information out of him.

"I don't know."

Luke cursed. "I have to find her."

"I think I know, Luke," Cooper said and gave him the address Len had provided him. "I haven't checked it out yet but Len—"

Luke didn't wait for Cooper to finish. He was already walking out the front door and radioing to his team for backup.

CHAPTER 40

Hollis had forced me into his SUV and driven me about forty miles outside of the city to a rural part of Arkansas I had never visited. I hadn't even seen a sign telling me the name of the town. The only thing I saw was a small green population sign that said three-hundred-and-fifty.

We passed a small gas station that looked right out of the 1950s and a small grocery store across from it that looked like it had seen better days. Part of the wall slumped in as if it couldn't even hold itself upright anymore. Both the gas station and the grocery store were nameless. No signs hung out front giving me any clue as to their identity. I assumed people in the town simply said they were going to get gas or food and everyone knew what they meant.

After Hollis forced me into his SUV, he kept one hand on the wheel and the other hand on the handgun pointed at my side. I had already taken the pain pill and it was hard enough for me to concentrate let alone fight him. At least the pain in my arm had stopped throbbing, but where he clocked me on the head still ached. I had tried a few times to get him to talk to me. I couldn't get a word out of him though.

When he first dragged me from the house, I had assumed he'd take me downtown or to the middle of a populated neighborhood and execute me in the street to make a real show of it the way he did with his other crimes.

After driving past the gas station, we drove for probably another five miles and pulled off the main road onto a tree-lined dirt road. Hollis took that for about a mile and then took a right onto an even smaller path that only had tire grooves in the dirt and rock.

All I wanted to do was sleep and forget that this nightmare was happening. The attack had been so swift and precise that the house didn't even look like there had been a struggle.

He finally pulled up to an old house and cut the engine. I didn't even consider running. There was nowhere for me to go and I wasn't going to get far.

Hollis got out the driver's side door and kept the gun on me as he walked around the car and wrenched open mine. He grabbed me by the neck and pulled me out of the car. I hissed a curse at him. "I'm coming. There's nowhere for me to go. You don't have to grab me like that."

Hollis ignored my whining as he marched me to a small house that looked as dilapidated as the grocery store. He didn't need a key to open the door. His foot was all that was needed as he toed it open.

Stale air mixed with even more stale beer assaulted my nostrils as I entered. The place was smaller inside than I had assumed. It was only one room with a metal framed cot with a sagging mattress on one wall and a beat-up old threadbare brown two-seater couch and television along the other. The back had a kitchen with what looked like a brand-new stove and refrigerator. The appliances were in stark contrast to the rest of the place.

Hollis shoved me toward the square four-seater table, went to the fridge, and pulled out a bottle of water, which he unscrewed and almost finished in one gulp. He drank the rest and threw the plastic bottle in the bin. Then he leaned against the counter and eyed me. "How long do you think before they get here?"

I didn't know the answer to that. "You didn't tell Luke where you took me. How is he supposed to know? You could have just shot me downtown like you did all the others."

"I thought it would be more dramatic this way," Hollis said with a chuckle. "I'm going to get away with this, you know? No one has a clue it's me. Luke couldn't figure it out from the voice app I used. I showed up on time at the police station this morning, took that stupid polygraph test, and passed. That gun residue test Luke gave me last night isn't going to show anything. I wore gloves with every shooting. I even got the guard to fudge the record at the jail when I visited. He doesn't even have enough to get a warrant."

My focus on Grady wasn't going to help matters either. Hollis had created the ultimate distraction by sending us after his brother-in-law. "What's the plan, Hollis? Luke is going to know it's you as soon as he shows up if he can figure it out." I was stalling for time but hoped against hope that Luke or Cooper would find me. "You aren't going to answer my questions?"

"I'm in control here." He said that but his look told me he hadn't thought all of this through.

If I was going to be stuck here until he killed me, I wanted answers. "What's the deal with Cat? Why involve her?"

Hollis called her a vile name. "She rebuffed me several times but then had a relationship with Grady Cullen. Are you serious? Have you seen him?" He shook his head in disgust. "She could have gone so much better than that. Not to mention, he's married."

"You're married," I reminded him with too much sarcasm given the situation. "This whole thing was about you wanting a woman you couldn't have? Are you Harvey?"

His whole face lit up in a smile so broad it crinkled the corners of his eyes. "I knew you were smart. I assumed Cat would have figured it out but she never did. She didn't even respond to my emails."

"You scared her." When Hollis's face fell in confusion, I explained,

"Women don't like it when men they don't know start emailing them and insisting they meet up with them. Your emails came across as controlling. Most women don't like that."

"I wasn't going to get into another situation like I'm in now where I don't get to decide anything. I wanted a show of force right away."

He was a henpecked man who was trying to course correct. I'd say he swung the pendulum a little too far. "You thought going on a shooting rampage was the way to get her attention?"

Hollis said nothing for a moment then pushed himself off the counter and aimed the gun at my head. "It was a way to command everyone's attention and prove that I'm smarter than the rest. I pulled the strings just like the perfect puppet master. I watched you all dance. The whole city was at my mercy." He smiled again and laughed to himself. "The fear I instilled will probably never leave most people all while I got to take some revenge."

"That's what the murders were about then. Revenge?" His face contorted to sheer pleasure when I hit the nail on the head. "You're telling me that each murder was someone you had chosen purposefully and it wasn't at random."

"Never random, except for the shooting in the Heights. That was just to scare everyone when the city didn't seem to take me seriously."

"What did Gemma Cullen ever do to you? She was a kid and had barely started her life."

Hollis took a few steps toward me. "Her father fired me from his practice about a year ago. I was so tired of him talking about his precious daughter, how smart she was, and how one day she was going to take over his practice. When I learned he was having a relationship with Cat, I knew he didn't care about his family. It was just another way to cut me down, another way to brag about his life. So, I took it away."

"What about the two attorneys working on the Ezo Technologies case? What did they do to you?"

"I found out they were having an affair and were going to destroy their case. I tried to get them to go public, to admit their wrongdoing. They had to be exposed or die. They chose their fate." He dragged me up from the chair and shoved me to the cot. "Take a nap. I don't want to listen to your questions anymore."

I sat on the edge of the bed. There was no way I was lying down on the filthy comforter. "What's with the Son of Sam reference?"

"That was a clue for Cat that she missed." He let out a long breath. "I guess she's not as smart as I assumed."

I was starting to think Hollis wasn't all that smart either. "What's the plan? You've gotten away with this so just leave. I've already accused Grady Cullen and no one will believe me when I say it's you. As you said, there's no evidence."

He shook his head as if trying to shake lose a thought. "Right when they get here, I'm going to shoot you and then act like I was here trying to rescue you. I'll tell them I saw Len driving you out of town and I followed but I was too late to stop him. I'll send them off in the woods to try to find him. I'll testify against him in court. I'll be the hero."

"Luke is going to know, Hollis," I argued back to him, realizing that maybe that was the point.

He shook his head. "No. I'll get away."

Hollis had some magical thinking going on. It was the first time I questioned if he was in touch with reality. "Hollis, do you want to kill me or get away with these crimes? You can't do both. Leave and I won't tell anyone you took me. I'll lie and say it was someone else." He could technically kill me and get away with it if he killed me right there and fled. If he wasn't thinking right though, maybe I could convince him otherwise.

He touched the side of his head and stared past me. "Shut up! I need time to think."

I sat on the edge of the bed and closed my eyes. I don't know how much time had passed before Hollis scraped the legs of the chair across the floor. My eyes flew open as he pulled the curtain aside to look out the window.

"Who is out there?"

"Cooper. I don't know how he found me. It was supposed to be your husband." He turned and aimed the gun at me. "I have to kill you now for my plan to work."

"You don't! It's just Cooper." I said that but I knew if Cooper was out there, Luke wasn't far behind with a whole SWAT team of help. I was kicking myself for having taken the pain pill because I wasn't going to be doing much of anything including standing on my own.

There was a knock on the door before Hollis could pull the trigger. He hesitated and Cooper knocked again. He ripped open the door and pointed the gun at Cooper as he entered.

"What's up, Hollis?" he said casually with a slight raise of his hand like we weren't in the middle of a hostage situation. "You don't need to point the gun at me. I'm alone and we've arrested Len for the shooting." He glanced around Hollis to me. "You okay?"

I gave a slight nod to my head as a wave of nausea took hold. Even through my cloudy thoughts, I figured out what Cooper was doing. "We were chatting about the case. Hollis brought me up here to keep me safe from Len. It was a good thing too. I was home alone and at risk. He's a real *hero*." I stressed the word hoping Cooper would pick up the point.

"Right, I know," he said, catching on quick. He walked toward me.

Hollis kept the gun focused on Cooper who put his body between us.

"You are both safe now, Hollis," Cooper said slowly smiling at him. "You were right to suspect Len. The cops sent me up here to congratulate you. Det. Morgan wants to meet with you and they are going to give you a special commendation from the city for your heroism."

The gun shook in Hollis's hand as if he wasn't sure whether to believe what was being said. Cooper spoke so convincingly though. "Did Len confess to the crimes?"

"He didn't so they sent me up here because we think given your legal background, you might be able to get him to confess. We have a ton of evidence against Len and we wouldn't have been able to catch him without you. We don't have a lot of time, Hollis. We need to get back so you can help us." He said nothing about the call to Luke from a man who had taken me. Cooper acted like that hadn't even happened and he didn't explain how he found us.

"But I…" Hollis looked around Cooper over at me. "Riley and I have some unfinished business."

Cooper moved slightly to block his path. "You can take care of that later. Isn't it more important we make Len pay for his crimes? He's done so much wrong to you over the years. I'd think you'd want to make sure he spends the rest of his life in jail."

"I don't think…" Hollis started to say.

"It's okay," Cooper said, interrupting him. "Your wife is at the police station too. She sees the error of her ways. She tore up the prenuptial agreement Len made her sign. With him in prison, her trust will move to you. You've got big things waiting for you when you get back, Hollis."

Cooper was lying so convincingly that he nearly had me buying the story.

"You know about that?" Hollis asked, uncertainty in his voice.

"Yeah, she told us all about how her brother controlled the two of you." Cooper's voice had a hint of excitement as if he was glad Hollis was finally free. "Come on, buddy. You're the hero here. It's almost time to celebrate. Everyone is waiting for you."

"Riley though." Hollis stuttered over his words. He shifted his body to look past Cooper to look at me. "We didn't finish what we started."

I encouraged him to go with Cooper. "I'll be here waiting for you. Right, Cooper? You'll leave me here while you go back. I'm so tired anyway. I think I'll lie here and take a nap."

Cooper didn't even turn around to look at me. "She'll be right here waiting for you. You have big things waiting for you, Hollis. Lots of people are ready to congratulate you. You'll probably even be given a raise and a promotion at your law firm. I bet a lot of firms are going to be lining up to offer you a job." While Cooper was saying nice things, his patience was wearing thin.

Hollis started to argue again and Cooper couldn't take anymore. He lunged for the gun and knocked it out of Hollis's hands. It went skidding toward me on the ground. I wasn't able to move fast enough to get up and get it though. It didn't matter, Cooper was bigger and stronger. He had Hollis on his stomach with his hands behind his back before I even made it off the bed.

An explosion of activity followed as Luke and other officers rushed into the house.

As soon as Luke took Hollis into custody, Cooper rushed toward me and pulled me into his arms. "You scared us." He stepped back and looked me over. "Are you okay?"

I couldn't speak as the swell of emotion and the contents of my stomach bubbled up. I threw up right there on the floor near Cooper's shoes. As I dropped down to my knees and heaved, I considered that this wasn't my finest hour and maybe I wasn't cut out for all this danger stuff after all.

Epilogue

The heat finally broke two weeks after the incident with Hollis Hopkins. We were able to shut off the central air and open the windows, breathing new life into our days.

The case was still ongoing. Hollis was sitting in jail waiting for trial. After his arrest, he hadn't been able to find a lawyer in all of Little Rock to represent him. Even though he had initially gone to Adele, she told him there was no way she'd provide him a defense. The attack on the legal community had left her shaken and unwilling to help him. The rest of the defense attorneys in the city felt the same.

He finally had to bring in someone from Missouri who was also licensed in Arkansas. He admitted nothing during Luke's interrogation and insisted he had brought me to the house to protect me. While Hollis believed he hadn't left a lot of evidence behind, once the case started to come together, it was all there.

His wife cooperated with police and let Luke search their house in Little Rock. Shoved up in the attic was the hat and wig he'd worn along with the dark clothing witnesses had seen. The lab ran tests on the clothes and they came back positive for gunshot residue.

The weapons were found in the attic and the crawl space beneath the house. While the guns had no fingerprints, it would be next to impossible for Hollis to explain how guns used in the crimes had made it to his attic and crawl space.

He had more trouble than just the guns. His alibi fell apart when Luke was able to get the guard to confess to changing the record at the jail. Once Hollis was in custody and Luke figured out who his former client was in jail, Adele was able to connect the dots for her client, Buster, and he finally admitted who had given him the information about Clayton.

It turned out Hollis's client had deep ties to drug running and criminal activity. If he wanted Buster dead, he'd have made that happen. It was no surprise then why Buster wasn't going to rat anyone out. That was another piece of evidence that would be used at trial.

Most surprising was the connection to Clayton Dalton. Luke had returned and showed him a photo of Hollis and Clayton had confirmed he was the same man who had gone to his property thinking it was a range. The Lugar was found among the guns in the crawl space too. That's how Hollis knew Clayton might be the perfect setup guy. He hadn't considered that Luke would be sitting there with him during the Heights shooting. That's when he pivoted to his brother-in-law. Hollis had no choice but to insert himself into the investigation then.

I had already been notified by the prosecutor on the case that my testimony would be needed at trial. That had come as no surprise. Hollis had kidnapped me and admitted to the shootings and why. The motive seemed flimsy at best. We all suspected Hollis had a psychotic break and the psych evaluation had come back to confirm that. The judge had determined him sane enough to stand trial because he knew right from wrong and understood his actions.

The insanity defense wasn't going to work for him.

The biggest question for me after I had been rescued was how Cooper had figured out where Hollis had taken me. It turned out Len had given him the address. In the end, Hollis coming to us had gotten him caught.

I had been stunned to learn his connection to Grady. He had

uncovered the affair with Cat and then convinced Grady to confide in him. That's when Hollis sought out Cat at the coffee shop and slowly developed a friendly relationship with her in the hopes he might also have an affair with her. When he realized that Cat would only chat occasionally with him at the shop but didn't seem to want more, the rejection hit hard.

Luke thought that might have been his breaking point.

Nothing in his life was working – not his home life with his wife, not his failing legal career, and not getting the object of his desire. Hollis had alienated most people around him.

In the process of trying to get closer to Cat, Hollis had hacked into Grady's email, had seen some of the messages written, and overheard him ordering flowers for Cat. There was enough information that Hollis knew about Todd Hall too. When Hollis didn't win her over as himself, he invented Harvey. None of it worked.

Luke speculated that when Hollis decided to go on the shooting rampage he had unwittingly set up Grady. Because Hollis wasn't talking, Luke wasn't sure that Hollis was even aware he had done that. He had used Clayton and then his brother-in-law Len. Grady might have just been a happy accident for him and one that nearly cost me my life.

Grady went back to his wife who was still none-the-wiser about the affair. Luke made sure he would never contact Cat again.

We might never know why Hollis had designed such a convoluted web and carried out horrific crimes in the city. When it goes to trial, the prosecution will decide the best case motive and weave enough of a story that it would make sense to the jury. Whether it will be the absolute truth only Hollis will know. The investigation also showed that his upbringing was nothing like the one he had recorded for the podcast. I had never been able to find what juvenile facility he'd been in and nothing in his past indicated he'd ever spent time in one. We also weren't able to confirm any of the previous murders of the three women had ever happened. Another fabrication.

I was settling into the idea that I didn't have to do everything and that it was perfectly fine to hang around the house and rest while I was healing. The doctor said I hadn't done any more damage to my arm but that I needed to take time off work and heal.

Luke had been cooking dinner most nights or we were ordering out on nights he worked late. Cooper was taking the lion's share of investigations. After two weeks of staying still, I'd about had enough. I had one more week until the cast came off and I was ready to get back out there and live life.

Tonight, we were having Cooper and Adele over for dinner and I convinced Luke that I could make the salad and the vegetables while he cooked the steak on the grill. He and Cooper had been hunched over the grill, drinking beers, and talking about football.

I had finished the salad and was adding the roasted carrots to the bowl when the front door opened and Adele yelled a hello. She had worked late and hadn't arrived with Cooper. She came into the kitchen carrying a cheesecake.

"I didn't want to show up empty-handed," she said as she passed me at the stove and headed for the fridge. She opened the door and put it on the bottom shelf. Adele laughed as she turned to me. "Who am I kidding? I wanted cheesecake all day."

It was one of the reasons why I liked her so much. "Who doesn't want cheesecake?" I thanked her for bringing it and she asked about my arm. "I'm nearly healed and ready to get back to work."

Adele leaned against the counter and appraised me. "Are you feeling well enough to travel?"

"I'm fine to travel." I finished transferring the last of the carrots to the bowl and carried it over to the table. "Why?"

Adele gestured toward the chairs and we both sat. "I got a call this morning from an old colleague in Atlanta. She moved to Savannah around the same time I moved here to Little Rock. She was arrested this morning and accused of killing her husband. She wants me to represent her and I'm going to need a good investigator."

I had many questions. There was only one that was important. "Do you think she killed her husband?" I didn't mind a criminal defense case when I was sure there was at least a sliver of hope the defendant was innocent.

"I don't believe she killed him. I've known Amelia Keller for the past ten years and I can't imagine her hurting anyone. She loved her husband, and as far as I know, had a rock-solid marriage. I was a bridesmaid for them. I don't think she could have done it."

Adele's belief in her friend was good enough for me. I'd find out the circumstances of all of it later. "Do you think Cooper will mind if I go to Savannah after not helping him with cases here for the past few weeks?"

Adele's eyes lit up. "I spoke to him this morning and he said it was fine with him." She hitched her jaw toward the door. "He should be out there convincing Luke it's a good idea."

I turned, looked at them huddled together talking, and laughed. I focused back on Adele who had thought of everything. "Let me talk to Luke. If he's okay with me being gone again, I'm fine with it."

As if right on cue, Luke came in through the back door carrying the platter of cooked steaks. "I heard you're going to Savannah." He set the platter on the table and kissed me on the cheek before sitting down next to me. "I can manage around here without you for a little while. It might be good after everything that's happened for you to get out of Little Rock. You might enjoy the break."

I had felt some relief when Adele asked me to go that I hadn't wanted to acknowledge. It would be good to get out of the city after living in fear of the next shooting. We were all feeling it. That hyped-up adrenaline waiting for the next shoe to drop. I raised my eyes to Cooper. "You're good with me being gone?"

He shrugged. "I'll manage. In the last two weeks, we got a few surveillance cases and you don't like those anyway. We're covered with the new staff we hired."

It was decided then – I was going to Savannah to work on my next case. It would be good to have some time bonding with Adele too. We never got as much time together as we wanted.

I dug into my perfectly cooked steak happy that I had made such good friendships and had a wonderfully supportive husband. Life didn't always work out like I wanted and these moments were sometimes rare.

Tonight though, here in my kitchen with those I loved the most, I was grateful for what I had.

About the Author

Stacy M. Jones was born and raised in Troy, New York and currently lives in Little Rock, Arkansas. She is a full-time writer and holds masters' degrees in journalism and in forensic psychology. She currently has three series available for readers: the completed cozy paranormal Harper & Hattie Magical Mystery Series, the hard-boiled PI Riley Sullivan Mystery Series and the FBI Agent Kate Walsh Thriller Series. To access Stacy's Mystery Readers Club with three free novellas, one for each series, visit StacyMJones.com.

You can connect with me on:
- http://www.stacymjones.com
- https://www.facebook.com/StacyMJonesWriter
- https://www.bookbub.com/profile/stacy-m-jones
- https://www.goodreads.com/StacyMJonesWriter

Subscribe to my newsletter:

✉ http://www.stacymjones.com

Also by Stacy M. Jones

Watch for the next PI Riley Sullivan mystery in Spring 2024

Access the Free Mystery Readers' Club Starter Library
   PI Riley Sullivan Mystery Series novella "The 1922 Club Murder"
   FBI Agent Kate Walsh Thriller Series novella "The Curators"
   Harper & Hattie Mystery Series novella "Harper's Folly"

Sign up for the starter library along with launch-day pricing and special behind-the-scenes access. Hit subscribe at
   http://www.stacymjones.com/

Please leave a review for Fear City. Reviews help more readers find my books. Thank you!

Other books by Stacy M. Jones by series and order to date

FBI Agent Kate Walsh Thriller Series
   The Curators
   The Founders
   Miami Ripper
   Mad Jack
   The Fuse
   Dead Senate
   Close Killer

PI Riley Sullivan Mystery Series
   The 1922 Club Murder
   Deadly Sins

The Bone Harvest
Missing Time Murders
We Last Saw Jane
Boston Underground
The Night Game
Harbor Cove Murders
The Drowned Boys
What He Saw

Harper & Hattie Magical Mystery Series
Harper's Folly
Saints & Sinners Ball
Secrets to Tell
Rule of Three
The Forever Curse
The Witches Code
The Sinister Sisters
Scandal Knocks Twice
A Treasure Most Deadly